HER MURDERER

He could see that she was trying to focus. Her deep blue eyes seemed to be trying to separate him from her dreams. Was he real? She moaned and then yawned.

Dry lips parted. "You're my friend, Dr. Olson."

"Yes. Yes, I am, Cindy."

The tears came in spurts. She would cry and then she would put her hands to her eyes and rub. The confusion was a typical reaction to the drugs he'd given her. Confusion and an inability to act on feelings. Without the drugs she would have been shrieking at him, maybe even pounding on him with those little hands. Telling him what a creep he was, telling him that they would find her and kill him when they did.

"You're my doctor."

"Yes."

Muttered: "Trusted you." Then: "Those other two girls—you killed them, didn't you?"

"Yes."

Sobbing now. Despite the drugs she understood the implications of her words. He would kill her, too. "But you were my friend."

Just watching her now.

"Please let me go." A surge of energy. Clutching his arm. "Please let me go."

"I can't, Cindy. Even if I wanted to I couldn't. Not now…"

ED GORMAN

THE MIDNIGHT ROOM

LEISURE BOOKS 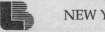 NEW YORK CITY

A LEISURE BOOK®

July 2009

Dorchester Publishing Co., Inc.
200 Madison Avenue
New York, NY 10016

ISBN 10: 0-8439-6108-2
ISBN 13: 978-0-8439-6108-9
E-ISBN: 978-1-4285-0700-5

The name "Leisure Books" and the stylized "L" with design are trademarks of Dorchester Publishing Co., Inc.

Printed in the United States of America.

10 9 8 7 6 5 4 3 2 1

Visit us on the web at www.dorchesterpub.com.

My own version of the Gold Medal novel in memory of old friends who were masters of the form:
Peter Rabe
Stephen Marlowe
William Campbell Gault
Robert Colby

Acknowledgments

To Don D'Auria for his patience; to Mark Johnson, Matthew Clemmens, Terry Butler and Diane Ceynar for their very helpful suggestions; and as always to Linda Siebels, whose sharp eye, excellent judgment and inventive humor are invaluable to me.

THE MIDNIGHT ROOM

PART ONE

CHAPTER ONE

November

Connie Nealon had dreaded this day and now it was here. Kelly's first birthday since her disappearance three months ago. Her seventeen-year-old daughter had been three days away from starting her senior year in high school before she vanished.

Any other birthday Connie would have been making the three-layer white cake Kelly had liked since she was tiny. And hiding presents in various parts of the house. Connie had known it was foolish to still play hide-and-seek games with a beautiful young woman who'd soon be going away to college, but despite the groans and fond smiles of her daughter and husband, Connie hid the presents like she always did.

But not today.

Ron was already off to work at the power company where he was an accountant. Connie had asked her sister to have lunch today but had backed out late last night. Trying to pretend this was just another ordinary day by going to a fancy restaurant would only make her feel worse. And make her sister worry even more about her. Eileen had once asked Ron if he thought Connie might be suicidal. Her question had shaken Ron so much that he not only told Connie about it, he went ahead and scheduled an appointment for her with a psychologist.

She supposed she wasn't helping herself by standing

in Kelly's room with its collection of dolls and stuffed animals, its posters of teen idols whose careers were as fleeting as the seasons, and the desk and computer where she so diligently did her homework. Three schools had already contacted her about scholarships. She'd decided on Northwestern, which had made Ron and Connie very happy. Their city of Skylar was ninety-six miles due west of Chicago, so Kelly wouldn't have any problem getting home several times a year.

She stood at the window. Gnarled black fingers screeched against the glass; ugly branches whipped in the wind. The backyard where Kelly had spent so much time in her early years looked forsaken now in cold November, the grass brown, the swing set empty, the chains clanging against the metal frame.

She knew she was indulging herself, as her counselor pointed out that she did too often. But her grief had become oddly comforting, as strange as that sounded.

The wind was so rough she wasn't sure if she'd heard the downstairs doorbell or not. She waited a moment to see if the sound came again. It did.

Lately their nice, respectable middle-class neighborhood had been assaulted by evangelicals trying to start the conversion process with pamphlets and requests to join them in prayer. Connie had always been religious but Kelly's disappearance had made her wonder if there really was any such thing as Divine Providence. If there was, why hadn't her prayers been answered? She'd been uncharacteristically rude with one of the evangelicals, a man who'd basically accused her of being a heathen. She'd slammed the door in his face.

The doorbell rang again.

She'd showered and changed into one of Kelly's sweaters and jeans earlier. The two had been wearing each other's clothes for the past three years. All she had to do was go down the stairs and answer the door. But even now leaving the perverse comfort of Kelly's room was difficult.

The fourth ring got her moving.

"Just a minute," she called as she hurried down the steps.

As she opened the door, she hoped she wouldn't see another pair of odd young men in white shirts and black ties toting Bible material. She was relieved to see a young woman in the familiar blue uniform of Swift Delivery Inc. standing there holding a square box for her.

"Good morning. I just need you to sign for this. Are you Mrs. Nealon?"

"Yes, I am."

Balancing the box with her left arm, she offered Connie a clipboard and a pen.

"I wonder who sent it to me."

"It's from Chicago."

Connie signed the form and then accepted the package. It was deeper and heavier than it had first looked. "Thank you."

She was glad to be inside with the door closed again. She'd never been much of a winter person. The sullen skies had always affected her moods. Seasonal Affective Disorder.

She had just set the box down on the dining room table when the phone rang. She stepped around the corner into the kitchen and picked up the receiver on the beige wall phone.

"How're you doing?" her sister Eileen said.

"I'm fine. Really."

"Really?"

She smiled. Irritating as Eileen's overprotectiveness was sometimes, she knew how much her sister loved her. And how much she loved her sister.

"I thought maybe you'd changed your mind. Do you good to get out of the house. Go have a very expensive meal at Pagliano's. You know how much you love Italian food."

As they talked, Connie leaned back so that she could see the box sitting on the table. Who would have sent it? What was in it? It couldn't have anything to do with this being Kelly's birthday, could it?

"Well, if you feel you want company, I'll be glad to run over."

"I appreciate that." But she was already distracted. The package. So odd to come on Kelly's birthday. Odd to her, anyway.

She had just hung up when she heard a knock at the back door. She walked to the window and looked out. There stood Heather Ryan from next door. Heather worked out of her home writing articles for health magazines. She was young, attractive. She was also a fine cook. She held a pan covered with aluminum foil.

Connie went down the three steps to the back entrance and opened the door.

"Baked you some brownies." Most of the time, as today, Heather wore track suits. This one, a dark green color, complemented her short, dishwater-blonde hair. She'd been to Kelly's last birthday party and obviously remembered the date.

Connie's eyes moistened. Sudden kindnesses sometimes made her emotional. Overemotional, really. She stepped out on the back steps and hugged Heather. "Oh, Lord, Heather, thank you so much." Heather had twin girls. She could easily imagine what Connie was going through.

"If there's anything you need, Connie, just call or stop over. Anytime. And I mean that."

The wind nearly ripped the door from its hinges. Connie grabbed it with one hand, taking the pan of brownies with the other. "Thank you so much." Her voice had tears in it.

Inside, she set the brownies on the counter, then tore a square of paper towel from the roll. Needed to dab her eyes and blow her nose. And then she remembered the package on the dining room table. She opened a counter drawer and searched for a pair of scissors. Armed and ready, she went straight to the package.

The address card was typed. The return read:

NEALON
NORTHWESTERN UNIVERSITY

Nealon? A relative? But did they have a relative at Northwestern? She couldn't think of any.

Brown wrapping paper was held in place with heavy white string. The scissors cut through both easily. The box itself was a dark purple, approximately a foot and a half long and three feet wide. The lid of the box was taped shut. The contents of the box had made no sound as she'd moved it around.

Newspaper was wrapped around whatever was inside. She lifted the thing out—a ball of some kind?—and set it down on the table. On closer inspection the newspaper was covered with clear tape. More work for the scissors.

Later on, in talking to a TV reporter, Heather Ryan would claim that even given the distance between her house and Connie's, even with the wind smothering most other sounds . . . Later on, Heather would claim that she was certain that she'd heard Connie scream when she realized what was wrapped in the newspaper.

The skull of her daughter.

Kelly had finally come home.

CHAPTER TWO

July

He hadn't counted on the black ski mask being so hot. Or was it his nerves that caused him to sweat so much as he crouched in the shadows of the detached three-stall garage?

This was his third burglary in four months. The first two had been simple and profitable. He'd been tense, of course. But not like this. The other two had taken place in houses where the owners were out for the night. This one involved forcing the owner at gunpoint to take him inside.

The car he was hunched down in front of was a classic red Bentley 1960 sedan. Even getting inside the garage had required skilled use of burglary tools.

The July heat stayed at seventy even though it was ten o'clock. He had checked the windows of the Tudor-style mansion for any sign of life. None. The owner lived here alone. A popular figure in the city of Skylar, he was being toasted on his forty-fourth birthday by his friends at the country club. He was known as an early riser and hard worker. He probably wouldn't be out late.

The car on the far side of the garage was a 1957 Corvette. The man had eclectic tastes in classic automobiles. The car he would arrive in tonight would be a black 1984 Ferrari Testarossa. He was apparently in a sporting mood this evening.

The mansion was on the northern edge of the city. The sounds came mostly from the interstate that was a quarter mile to the east. Trucks roaring through the night. The occasional hot rod and the steady drone of tires on pavement. Closer by, he heard stray dogs, night birds, the air-conditioning unit in back of the place.

And then came the swaggering sound of one of the finest sports cars ever made. Unmistakable. Sounding like a missile as it raced up the long driveway, headlights brilliant on a spot just above where he crouched.

A radio or CD: classical music.

Then the lumbering sound of the third segment of the garage door lifting. For a terrible moment he thought he might be sick. The gun made all the difference. Taking a man captive made all the difference. Very different from his first two burglaries. Very different indeed.

The Testarossa swept inside and the overhead lights in the garage came on. He crouched lower. The music died, the engine died. An unnerving silence in which every sound was exaggerated. The man coughing. The driver's door opening. The scrape of a shoe on cement.

He was in no position to see what the man was doing. He wanted to stand up but he first needed some sense of where the man was in relation to him. Was he facing him? Was he walking toward the door? No, not that. There were no sounds of walking.

Then a single word: "Damn."

Impossible to guess what the man was referring to. There was no choice but to ease upward and take the chance of being seen.

He almost smiled when he saw the man bending over the trunk of the car, cloth in hand, wiping away something that obviously gave him great displeasure. Classic car owners were probably offended even by a little road dust.

He had to move now. If he gave the man a chance to get out the door into the night, all the planning, all the fear would have been for nothing. The man knew his grounds. He could run and hide. The only choice left would be to kill him. He didn't want to think about that.

"Hands over your head. Move back against the wall."

He made his voice loud and harsh. But the snap of it was lessened by the clear sound of his nervousness.

The man looked up as if in disbelief. "This is insane. You're robbing me?" An outrage, an insult. Someone of his status having a gun pointed at him by someone who was no doubt a common thug? No fear. Just that cold contempt.

"You're going to take me inside."

"The hell I am."

He had to give it to the bastard. Not even a weapon could intimidate him. Or maybe he was just acting. Maybe he was frightened but was able to control his demeanor.

He moved out from behind the Bentley and walked the length of the Testarossa. "You heard what I said. You're going to take me inside." His surgical gloves were running with sweat.

This time the man said nothing. Just watched him. Apprehension, if not fear, shone in his eyes now.

"Let's go."

"Maybe you don't know who I am."

"Somebody important. Otherwise you wouldn't have said that." The sarcasm felt good. Relaxed him. "You're Dr. Peter Olson. So now that I've kissed your ass a little, you do me the favor of taking me into your house."

"What if I won't?"

"You know something? I don't know. I don't think I'd

kill you but I'd probably give you a brain concussion and maybe break some bones. Just because you're such an asshole."

Olson sighed. "I don't like this at all."

"I didn't figure you would. Now move."

Olson moved. He walked like a belligerent student who'd been sent to the principal's office. He took small steps and he kept glancing over his shoulder and swearing. Once he said, "You're going to pay for this."

Olson used a security card to get inside. As they walked the six steps from the back door to the kitchen, the physician turned abruptly. He'd obviously considered jumping the man with the gun. But then the man with the gun took the next step and pushed the gun in his face.

He wasn't good at identifying the things he saw. Everything looked expensive, almost oppressively so. For a moment he felt uneasy in the presence of all this wealth.

They stood on a parquet floor before an imposing, winding staircase.

"I have some cash in my den. I also have a little jewelry."

"The cash I'll take. The jewelry you can keep. Let's go."

Either the doctor had simply resigned himself to being robbed or he had some plan that had calmed him down. Maybe he had some kind of secret security alarm.

He followed Olson down a long hallway to the den.

The cherry hardwood floors gleamed in the light the doctor had turned on. He kept his distance. If Olson was going to do anything it had to be soon. He didn't want to be forced to kill him.

The den looked like a movie set. Wall-to-wall book-cases. A massive globe. An antique desk that would have looked even more antique if a small computer hadn't been sitting on it. A Tiffany lamp that lent the room gentle shadows. A large plasma TV screen was on the east wall. Beneath it was DVD equipment.

Olson walked behind the desk and reached down for a drawer.

The man in the ski mask clicked the safety off the gun. He was glad it made a noise. Olson heard it, too. "I don't know if you have a gun in there but even if you do, you wouldn't have time to get a shot off. I'm ready to go right now."

"No gun. Just five thousand dollars in cash."

"Let's see it. But very slowly."

He wasn't sure about Olson. Maybe he was so arrogant he thought he could grab a gun, throw himself to the floor and kill the intruder.

The money was banded. Green, green cash. Olson tossed it on the desk beside the computer. "Unless you want jewelry, that's the best you're going to do here tonight."

"That's a start."

"I suppose if you've got a van parked somewhere you can start hauling some of my art collection out of here. But then I doubt you'd know how to sell it anywhere."

"Probably not. I'm not a wizard like you."

"I didn't mean it that way."

"Sure you did. Now let's talk about the safe."

Olson had been good at keeping his face unreadable. The occasional flicker of fear was the only sign that he was being robbed. But at the mention of the safe his eyes widened and a faint gasping sound came from between his lips.

He didn't know what Olson had in the safe. But it sure was something he didn't want to part with. There were various ways doctors could accumulate large amounts of cash. The news frequently carried stories about doctors who dealt drugs. For only one example.

"I don't have a safe."

"Sure you don't."

Olson hesitated. "Well, that's technically not true, what I said, I mean. Yes, I have a wall safe but when I bought this place, the previous owner had died without giving the realtor the combination. So I've never used it."

"Show it to me."

"What's the point?"

"I'm just curious."

"It's a waste of time."

"Everything you're saying makes me think it isn't a waste of time at all."

Olson raised his arm. Pointed to the watch on his wrist. "This is a Patek Philippe. I paid twenty-seven thousand dollars for it three months ago in London."

"Very nice. I appreciate it. Take it off and lay it on the desk."

Olson forced a smile. "You've done very well for yourself this evening." He laid the watch next to the five thousand dollars.

"Now the safe."

Again Olson looked affronted. He was obviously one of those men who believed that given enough cunning, the world would always bend to his will. "I thought we made a bargain."

"No bargain. The safe."

He moved so swiftly he surprised himself. He was around the desk and putting the gun to Olson's temple before either of them quite knew what was happening.

"This could go off. I don't want it to."

This time panic shone in Olson's eyes. "Just be careful with that damned thing."

"The safe."

Olson was known as a good tennis player. His photo was in the paper sometimes. He had the lithe bearing of an athlete. Until now. He seemed to collapse inwardly. His breath came in anxious bursts.

All the man with the gun could think of was what could be in that safe. Olson was coming apart.

Olson led them into the shadows to stand before a framed portrait of a man who looked a good deal like himself. His old man, most likely.

He clipped on a small lamp on a nearby table.

"Probably need a little help to get it open."

"I told you I can't get it open."

"Please. We're past the point of that kind of bullshit, all right?"

Olson rallied. "I don't know who you are but I'm going to find out. And then I'm going to have you torn apart."

"Get going on the safe."

The setup was conventional. The portrait swung back to reveal a small wall safe. Olson put his hand up to it, then paused.

The armed man was tired of it now. He wanted the safe open, the contents revealed. And then he wanted out of here.

He brought the gun down against the back of Olson's head hard enough to drive him into the wall. A muffled cry escaped Olson and his knees began to buckle.

He grabbed Olson by the hair and slammed him into the wall again. "I'm done fucking around. Now open the safe."

He had defeated Olson. He had taught him a bitter

humility. In the light the blond hair showed dark red blood where the gun barrel had made contact.

Olson was beyond even threats. He said nothing. He just went to work.

"I'll give you all the money. I just want you out of here."

Olson's right hand vanished inside the safe. He started taking the bundles out one at a time.

"How much is in there?"

"I'm not sure. Maybe fifty thousand."

Olson handed him each bundle as he retrieved it from inside. They were placed on the small table next to the lamp. There were eight bundles in all.

"That's it." Olson started to swing the door of the safe closed.

He brought the gun up against the side of Olson's head. "Step back."

"What?"

"You heard me."

"That's everything."

"Maybe. Now step back."

Olson still hesitated. He was pushed away.

The open safe beckoned. The way Olson was acting, there was certainly something else in there. More money or some other kind of valuable. Holding the gun on Olson, he shoved his free arm into the safe and felt around.

At first he felt nothing. Just the dry metal of the interior. But when his fingers crawled to the back of the safe they touched two small plastic cases.

Made him curious. Olson had given away a good deal of money but it was these cases that he seemed most protective of.

He extracted them and looked at them. Two unmarked DVDs, one to each case.

"These are what exactly?"

Olson's gaze was fixed on the DVDs. "Family stuff. From my first marriage. That's why I didn't give them to you. They're just for me."

"Uh-huh. And that's why you kept them in the safe."

"They're valuable. They can't be replaced."

"You should see yourself."

"What?"

"You're scared."

"Of course I'm scared. You're holding a gun on me."

"Huh-uh. You didn't get this scared until I dragged these DVDs out of there." He remembered seeing a TV set and a DVD player in this great hall of a den. He was enjoying himself again. Watching the smugness flee that spoiled handsome face. "Let's take a look at these."

"I told you they're just family things. You'd just be wasting your time."

Whatever was on these DVDs must be pretty strange. His first thought was child porn. Be ironic if such a dashing figure as this doctor turned out to be a pedophile.

He handed the plastic cases to the doctor and said, "There's a machine over there. Go set it up so we can watch these."

Olson seemed to be paralyzed. He held the cases loosely in his fingers and stared at the open safe. He looked older now. Vulnerable.

"C'mon, Doc. This should be fun."

To make his point he raised the gun and pushed the barrel against the doctor's forehead. "Move. Now."

Olson's eyes fluttered shut and he inhaled deeply, as if he were summoning all the strength he had left. When he opened his eyes again his appearance was that of a man who had resigned himself to whatever fate lay just ahead. He didn't even look nervous now. Just forlorn.

In the gloom another small light went on. Olson

needed it to set the TV up. He worked efficiently. One time he paused and glanced back.

"Whatever you're thinking, Doc, forget it. We're going to have a look at this stuff and there's nothing you can do about it."

Olson went back to work. The screen bloomed with light. Olson inserted the first of the DVDs and stood back from the set.

The man with the gun walked over and stood next to the doctor. "Let's have a look."

Olson said nothing. The misery he was feeling filled the room. Images began to appear on the screen.

The man had seen more than his share of porno. He'd even seen a few videos of sadomasochism that got very rough. But right away this was different.

A room that is covered in the kind of plastic sheeting that could be rolled up and disposed of. A pretty dark-haired girl lying naked on a table also covered in the same plastic sheeting. The camera moves in tight on her face and then loses her as she struggles to get up. The man's sense is that she has been drugged and is just now coming awake.

Her face is wrenched back into frame and then it happens. The cunning, cutting blade; the pale, vulnerable throat; the lens splattered with blood. Grotesque expressions, silent screams.

Somebody's daughter, somebody's sister.

"You are one sick fuck," the man said, trying to sound much tougher than he felt. He clipped off the video, not wanting to see any more. "Now I know what happened to the two girls who've been missing. That was the one named Sharon Flynn."

Olson just watched him, warily. He was now a small animal suddenly confronted by a predator.

"Goddamn, man. Nobody would blame me if I cut

you up right here just like you cut up Sharon Flynn. You are a sick son of a bitch. By rights I should walk over to that phone and call the police."

"You don't need to do that. We can talk."

Tough as he sounded, outraged as he was at what this man had done to the two girls, he still enjoyed the wildness flaring in the doctor's eyes and voice. Desperation. Terror.

Then he smiled. "And what would we talk about, Doc?"

"I think you know. I'm a wealthy man."

"It's funny," he said, "that's just what I was thinking, you fucking sleazebag. How you're a wealthy man and all."

CHAPTER THREE

September

"You see juror number six?" Detective Kim Pierce said.

"The one with the heavy eye makeup?" Detective Michael Scanlon said.

"Yeah. She'll be the holdout. The maternal thing. I watched her watching him. I could read her mind. *Such a cute little boy, only nineteen and deserted when he was only fifteen, he couldn't have possibly stuck up a convenience store.*"

"You really think so?"

"Trust me. The kid'll walk. Hung jury for sure."

The two detectives had arrested Bryan Gaines at a bar where he was drinking underage the night of the robbery. He had nearly three hundred dollars cash on him and the same killer switchblade the terrified clerk had described to them. The one with the American eagle on the handle.

This morning, five months after the arrest, they testified at his trial. Afterward they went to a nearby café where they now ate scrambled eggs and toast.

Kim was one of those women whose looks you couldn't appreciate until she smiled. And dressed up a little. Today she wore a starched white blouse with a black pants suit. Her long blonde hair gave her the look of a very sexy schoolmarm.

Most detectives giving testimony tried to look their

best. Michael wore his only good blue suit, which was way too hot for the Indian summer heat. He was a tall, angular man with a sharp face mitigated by melancholy brown eyes.

Kim started to butter her toast, then glanced up and said, "Damn, look who's here."

Michael figured that with that tone of voice she could be talking about only four people, and three of them were in prison. That left only Lisa Hepburn as the person who was likely to invade their booth.

While the relationship between police and press was sometimes troubled, each usually relied on the other for a variety of favors. Only the dumbest reporter and the dumbest cop picked fights unless there was a serious reason to do so.

Lisa Hepburn, the lithe blonde whom plastic surgery had turned into a beauty, stood at one of the nearby tables chatting up two judges while giving them a closer look at her undeniably striking body, today sheathed in summery yellow.

"Remember, if she starts choking on something, you don't know anything about CPR."

Michael laughed. "You really hold grudges."

"It doesn't bother you? The way she's always running stories about us?"

"I just consider the source."

"God."

"What?"

"She's looking over here."

"So? Eat. Forget her."

"If she comes over here I'm getting under the table."

"That presents some very interesting possibilities."

"Remember, no CPR."

Lisa always sent her smiles ahead. They were her calling cards. Her perfume came close behind. It was erotic to the point of being deadly. On the wrong day it could put a man into a coma. Both smile and perfume were about to take their toll on the detectives.

Lisa and Kim had argued so often neither even bothered trying to be cordial to the other. "I've always thought you two should be a couple. You've both struck out so many times I'd think by now you'd see that you're the only two people who can stand each other."

"That's a *Seinfeld* line, Lisa," Kim said. "Jerry said it to Elaine and Puddy."

"Well, I'd be more up on my TV if I wasn't so busy all the time. Investigative reporters never have any time for themselves."

"Who said you were an investigative reporter?" Michael said.

"It won't be announced till tomorrow. But the station is creating an investigative team. Steve Call and I."

"Wow, all that brain power," Kim said.

"We wouldn't have to *have* an investigative team if the police were doing their jobs a little better, I suppose. For a small city of 150,000 we have an awful lot of crime."

"Lowest crime rate per capita in the Midwest," Michael said, starting to feel as irritable as Kim did.

"Tell that to the families of the two girls who got their daughters' skulls sent back to them." She angled her head to smile and dispatch another Hollywood wave to a young man with hungry blue eyes. "And now there may be a third."

Kim and Michael looked at each other. A local girl named Cindy Baines had not been seen in a day and a half. She was fifteen. Since there was no evidence yet that a crime was involved, no Amber Alert had been issued. But there had been plenty of TV and radio stories about her. "Skull," as the killer had become known in comic-book style, might be at work again. That possibility flooded official stomachs with enough acid to burn right through the lining.

"We'll have to wait and see. Hopefully she'll turn up safe."

"May I quote you on that, Detective Scanlon? I'm sure everybody with teenage girls will feel a lot more confident when they hear how aggressively you're trying to find her."

Michael was about to tell her that in fact he was going to see the girl's parents. But then he decided to hell with it. He didn't have to explain himself to this bitch.

There were reporters the police liked. They were critical of the officers when there was just cause but they didn't use the cops for ratings points.

It was free-fire with Lisa. The cops hated her but so did her fellow reporters. She was a camera hog, a dilettante (she had been a runway model in Chicago previous to becoming a "reporter") and a ruthless competitor. Nobody on either side blamed you for taking target practice on Lisa. The mystery of it all was that in two years she'd doubled her station's ratings. Her story was almost always the lead story. She'd been offered the anchor desk twice. Both times she'd given sappy speeches—well publicized, of course—about how she wanted to get the truth out to the people of Skylar and she could best serve that truth by staying on as a working reporter. It was whispered that more than half the teenage boys in the city had pictures of Lisa in a swimsuit pose to inspire them to self-abuse.

"We'd invite you to join us, Lisa, but I don't think I'd be able to eat if you were any closer to me."

Lisa smiled at Michael. "Pathetic, isn't she?"

"We're all pathetic, Lisa," Michael said. "It's just that people like you always think you're the exception."

A former running back and now criminal defense lawyer named Rod Ames came up behind Lisa and put outsize hands on her slender shoulders. "I'm sorry I'm late, Lisa. Let's have something to eat."

"I thought investigative reporters never rested," Kim said.

"What?" Ames said.

"Oh, nothing," Lisa said. "They just enjoy trying to belittle me because I'm not afraid to report the truth about the police. Good and bad."

"Mostly bad," Michael said.

"Well, maybe if you were a little more professional, Detective Scanlon, I wouldn't *have* so much bad news to report about you people."

"Hey," Ames laughed. "Is she a pistol or what?"

His large hands guided Lisa's slender shoulders toward his table.

Kim's cell sent a melody into the air. She listened and said, "We're both here now." She glanced at Michael. "All right. Twenty minutes." She clipped off.

"That was the chief. The mayor's hysterical. He wants Captain Myles to be in our conference room in twenty minutes. He wants you and I and Steve there, too."

"You know how Steve likes meetings," Michael said. Steve was Michael's older brother and also a detective.

"And Horan's going to be there, too," Kim said.

"The mayor's number-one boy. This is going to be a really shitty day," Michael said.

CHAPTER FOUR

One day three years ago the warden had called Leo Rice into his office and said, "Leo, I'm afraid I've got bad news for you."

What Rice was figuring was that his father had passed. The cancer. The last time his father had come to see him he was twenty pounds lighter and having a hard time breathing. Lung cancer was a shitty way to go. But the old man was in his sixties and, except for doing five years in Joliet as a young man, had managed to live his life pretty much as he'd wanted to. Leo had seen his father kill a man one night in the garage, hitting him across the head with a tire iron and then using his foot to kick him all the way dead. Leo and his brother Bobby helped their father wrap the man in a tarpaulin and then drive him sixty miles to a certain point in the river and dump the body in the midnight waters. They had been sixteen and fifteen respectively, Leo the oldest.

Neither of the boys would actually kill anybody for a few years. In the interim they contented themselves with breaking bones. They were both classified as dangerous sociopaths by the school psychologist who dealt with them. She issued her report on the same day that she recommended them being expelled from their high school. There was evidence that they had both raped a girl who was too afraid to testify against them. There was also evidence that they had cut the brake line on the car belonging to a teacher who had ordered Bobby out of his class for grabbing a girl's breast in front of everybody. The teacher had suffered a concussion when he couldn't stop his car from slamming into a tree. Evidence, yes, but not enough to satisfy the county attorney.

So his father was dead, the man who'd raised the boys after breaking the nose and arm of the wife he believed had cheated on him. The boys hadn't seen or heard from their mother since. She was afraid to contact them.

"Your brother Bobby was shot to death last night by a police officer in Skylar."

Rice could still remember the feeling. First time he'd ever experienced it. As if his body temperature had dropped fifteen degrees without warning. Had never felt that cold before. Or since.

His brother Bobby. His only true friend. The only other person he'd ever been able to talk to. His brother Bobby. And some cop had killed him?

"Are you all right?"

"Yeah."

"You want a glass of water?"

"Nah. No thanks."

"I'm sorry about this, Rice."

"Yeah." So stunned he was having a hard time breathing. Like the old man with his lung cancer.

On the day he was paroled—a parole angrily disputed by the parents of the girl he'd tossed off a second-floor balcony after she'd told him that he'd impregnated her; baby dead, girl with three broken ribs, attempted murder charges brought against him—on the day he was paroled he drove to Chicago, where he collected five thousand dollars he'd left with his aunt.

"What're you going to do?" she said. She'd spent a

few years in prison herself. She had been heavy into blackmail and counterfeiting for a time but it had caught up with her. She had also helped his father rob a bank once. That one the police didn't know about.

"Kill that cop."

"They'll just kill *you*, Leo. And it won't bring Bobby back."

"I don't care."

"So you kill him and then what?"

"I haven't thought that far ahead."

"I have some friends who can set you up in Mexico. But you got to think this thing through, Leo. Do it right and let me know in advance so I can get this Mexico thing set up."

"I'll do that, Aunt Sarah."

"You're not even listening to me, are you? In one ear and out the other."

"I just want to kill the son of a bitch. Then I'll worry about Mexico."

CHAPTER FIVE

Clay Horan said, "The mayor's very afraid that this missing girl—Cindy—that the man who killed the other two girls has taken her. Needless to say he's not happy that the man is still roaming around here somewhere."

"We're not happy about it, either, Clay," Detective Captain Bob Myles said. "I mean, in case you might be thinking otherwise."

Horan was a creature of gray Brooks Brothers suits, white button-down collars, club ties and great and abiding ambition. Michael had sat next to him one night at one of the mayor's interminable soirees and, over the course of several drinks, the very bright twenty-five-year-old had confided that his goal was not to seek office himself but to ultimately join one of the large Chicago firms that ran the careers of politicians. Consultants, they were called. The power behind the power.

"You know I didn't mean that, Bob," Horan said. They were on the second floor of the police department in the conference room, a large, sunny office. Kim, Michael Scanlon and Steve Scanlon were present, though Michael wondered if his older brother Steve was hearing any of what was being said. In addition to a few razor nicks and bloodshot eyes, Steve smelled of whiskey. The brothers sat together opposite the other three. Michael hoped that they couldn't pick up the scent.

"All the mayor wants is for me to tell the press that we've got an organized effort going to find this girl," Horan said.

"Way ahead of you, Clay. You're looking at our entire detective team. And we'll be hitting the streets right after this meeting."

Michael's gaze met Kim's. He knew they were thinking the same thing. This was all public relations. Certainly the mayor wanted the girl found, but even more important than that right now was giving the public the *appearance* that every effort possible was being made.

"But we have to be realistic," Myles said, turning his head to Horan as he spoke. Myles was a hefty man with a golf red face and bald pate. He still wore his high-school football ring and could get downright lethal when he started talking about his grandkids. Legend had it that some of his stories went on so long people actually fainted. Fortunately he could laugh at himself and consequently got kidded a lot. "We'll be interviewing people about the girl but this is a busy department. We've got to keep moving on other cases, too."

"I appreciate that," Horan said. "But that doesn't mean we have to mention it to the press. We need to make this sound urgent. As if it is the number one priority."

"Actually, it *is* the number one priority, Clay," Myles said. "We're just as afraid as everybody else. But right now there's a possibility—and I'm only saying a possibility—that we're dealing with an unhappy teen-ager who just wandered off somewhere. Doesn't want to see her folks or her friends. That's not unheard of, you know."

"We say that, the press will have us for lunch. That won't sound urgent enough."

"There's no sense panicking people," Michael said.

"We're not panicking them, Michael," Horan said cordially. "It's just that we need to sound serious. And if we say we think she might just have wandered off, it'll sound dismissive."

No wonder he wanted to be a political handler, Michael thought. Though he hated to admit it, the guy was good at spin. But his moment of begrudging admiration ended quickly. The odor of whiskey came strong again. And Steve made a small but unmistakable whimpering sound that Michael knew had nothing to do with this meeting.

Horan checked faces, seeking agreement. He got it. "This is what I'll tell the press, then. You'll all get copies of my statement and I'd appreciate it if you stick to the points I'm making." He was smiling, sure of the laugh he'd get. "After all, we've all got the same enemy, folks. Lisa Hepburn."

The meeting ended with handshakes at the door. Horan lingered, saying good-bye to Kim. Michael tried not to notice. He knew that Horan had asked Kim out a few times but she was seeing someone else. Unfortunately that someone else was no longer Michael Scanlon.

Steve Scanlon went into the men's bathroom. Michael followed him. Steve went immediately to the sink, where he palmed as much water as he could and splashed it on his face.

"You all right?"

"This going to be another speech?" Steve snapped.

Growing up they were frequently mistaken for twins. Same black Irish good looks. Same kind of temperament, too. Impulsive, reckless, hotheaded, very much like their father, who'd been a Skylar police officer all his life. Three years ago Michael had changed his life. He'd eased up on the drinking, the one-night stands and the easy cop anger. He liked to think that he was finally, at thirty-three, in the process of growing up. He wanted to help his brother do the same. But Steve had come to hate him for even trying.

"I'm worried about you. And so's Dad."

But there was no more time for talk. The door opened up and Myles walked in. "Well," he said, starting to unzip well before he reached the urinals, "Horan wasn't so bad today, was he?"

CHAPTER SIX

As Kim pulled up in the driveway of Ted Anderson, Cindy Baines' boyfriend, she watched a Scottie terrier jump around a green John Deere power mower being pushed by a tall, slim teenager in a blue T-shirt, denim shorts and running shoes with white socks. A nice suburban snapshot, the house ranch-style and well kept, as were all the houses on this block. Even when she climbed out of her unmarked car the boy she assumed was Ted had yet to notice her, thanks to headphones that apparently fixed his attention.

She liked the scent of fresh-cut grass. She'd cut the lawn many times growing up. Easy way to get a tan. Also easy way to watch all the neighborhood boys cruise by on their bikes.

The Scottie noticed her before Ted did. The cute, diminutive dog came trotting up to her. She bent and petted him several times. Ted was just starting to turn around at the end of his property line and come back in her direction. That was when he saw her. He glanced at the car. Police cars were police cars. They didn't have to have emergency lights on top to be recognized.

He whipped off the headphones, killed the motor, wiped sweat from his forehead with his forearm and then came walking toward her. He had a small bottle of water tucked into his back pocket. Before speaking he took two deep drinks.

"You're here about Cindy."

"Yes."

"It isn't bad news, is it?"

She wondered why she was surprised that he had soft brown eyes and short brown hair. She hadn't formed a psychological picture of Cindy. Had she expected a tougher kind of boy because of Cindy's home situation?

"No word yet."

His sigh of relief was audible. "Thank God. My whole family is really scared. They love her as much as I do."

Another surprise. How many teenage boys were that frank with their feelings? Or was it a ruse? A good disguise if he'd played some part in her disappearance.

"So everything was fine between you?"

"Sure." Then he paused. "Well, we had a few problems. One problem, really."

She put out her hand. They shook and then she showed him her ID.

"You were saying that you had one problem."

His eyes studied the ground. "It's pretty personal." The Scottie came up. He reached to pet it and then said, so he wouldn't have to look at her, "She wouldn't do it with me. I probably pushed it too hard. Now when she's missing—" He stood up and faced her. "I feel terrible about it."

"But other than that you were getting along."

"Well, right up until the past couple of weeks." He swiped a few blades of grass from his cheek.

"You were arguing?"

"No, not arguing. She was just acting kind of strange. Like she had a secret of some kind."

"And you didn't have any idea what the secret was?"

"What I was afraid of was that it was another boy."

"Why do you say that?"

"Well, I admit I get jealous sometimes. I mean, I don't yell at her or anything. She usually tells me I don't have anything to worry about and we get right back to where we were. But this time was different."

"In what way?"

"She told me not to pick her up a couple of nights at the ice cream place where she works. I always pick her up. She just said she had something she needed to do and that I just had to trust her."

"Did you argue with her?"

"Not argue. But I was mad. You'd be mad, wouldn't you?"

"Sure I'd be mad."

"And that's all she'd say. That's what I think happened to her. She was seeing somebody and he did something to her." Misery lent him the look of a little boy. "My mom and dad, they just assumed we'd get married someday. They really like her. I wasn't kidding about that. She comes over for dinner and watches TV a lot. We know about her home life—her parents don't care about her at all. I mean, I should feel sorry for her dad being in a wheelchair and all, but he's such a bastard I can't. Not the things he says to her."

She couldn't tell if it was sweat or tears in his eyes but she suspected the latter.

"When was the last time you saw her?"

"The afternoon before she disappeared. She walked me to my car after school. She knew how upset I was about not being able to see her that night. She wanted to try and make things right with us again. She kissed me good-bye and took off. She got a ride to the ice cream place with another girl who works there. Now that I think about it I was sort of a big baby, I guess." Then in a burst: "She isn't dead, is she?"

Kim knew for sure that the moisture in his eyes was tears. His voice shook with them.

"I'm pretty sure she's not," she lied. "A lot of times these things turn out all right."

"Seriously? You really mean that?"

What was one more lie? "Sure. This may be nothing more than all the stress getting to her and she just went off somewhere to be alone."

"God, I sure hope that's what happened."

Yes, Kim thought, I do, too.

CHAPTER SEVEN

"Sorry to keep you waiting. I'm Don Sullivan."

In a yellow short-sleeved shirt, a clip-on brown tie, brown trousers and sand-colored Hush Puppy loafers, the lanky Sullivan looked like a middle-aged man in a domestic sitcom circa 1965. The balding, friendly neighbor with the inexplicably sad brown eyes.

Except here at Roosevelt High School the sadness likely came from all the trouble the school had on a daily basis. When Michael had been in high school, Roosevelt had been a pretty tame place. Its working-class students, white, black, brown alike, had managed to coexist without trying to kill each other. No longer.

Sullivan was one of three guidance counselors here. His office was painted a strange purple, his desk was two inches deep with papers and his computer screen had a crack running straight down the center. On a shelf above his computer stood several framed photographs of his wife and children. And of his grandchildren. No doubt he prayed to these photographs every day. They were the gods of sanity in a school that had the reputation for being a cell block.

Sullivan sat down in his swivel desk chair, faced Michael, threw one thin leg over another and said, "After you called, I started to pull up all the information I had on Cindy but then I decided I didn't need it."

"Oh?"

"She's one of my favorites. One of the innocents, if you will."

"Innocent in what way?"

"In her case, I'm pretty sure she's innocent in every way. Not all our kids are, of course. You hear a lot of explanations for how they behave. It's genetic, it's environmental. Those kinds of things. I go to two conferences a year on the West Coast—good excuse for counselors all over the country to get away from the war zone for awhile—and there are always a few speakers who talk about that. What turns young people into predators. I used to worry about that but I don't anymore."

"Why not?"

Sullivan shrugged. "Because it doesn't matter. It's what people do that counts. You can lose your mind worrying about *why* people do certain things. All that matters is that they *do* them." He smiled. "I'm giving you a speech. What I'm trying to say is that poor little Cindy is the opposite of a predator. She's a victim. Capital V."

"Here at school?"

"Everywhere. Starting at home. She lives in the worst trailer park in the city. The health department's always out there. Cindy's come to school twice with rat bites. One of them got infected. They had to stick her in the hospital. Her dad's paralyzed from the waist down. He got into a fight and somebody pushed him off the back of a truck. They didn't kill him but I'm not sure they did him a favor. He's become a religious fanatic. He quotes the Bible all day long and watches TV ministers. Nobody gets inside the trailer except the wife, himself and Cindy."

"Why?"

"He says they'll bring 'sin' in, you know, contaminate the place."

"How about the wife?"

"Kind of fading party girl. I'm sort of old-fashioned, I guess. I don't think moms should have tattoos up and down their arms. She goes out a couple nights a week—I certainly can't blame her for that, the way life is in that trailer—but then the father screams at her for a few days afterward. All the usual. Slut and whore, things like that. He says the same things to Cindy, though I'm pretty sure he's wrong about her."

"How so?"

"I think we've become pretty good friends, Cindy and I. She stops in just to talk. She tells me about her life. She's still a virgin, unthinkable as that is. And that's a problem for her because her boyfriend keeps threatening to break up with her if she doesn't sleep with him. She was in just a few days ago. She sat right where you are and cried about it."

"Is she the kind of girl who'd just take off, go somewhere?"

"I don't think so. Something terrible may have happened with the boyfriend—his name is Ted Anderson and he's a junior here—or at the trailer. Maybe it was so bad that she just decided she couldn't take it anymore and went somewhere. But my impression is that she doesn't have much of an extended family. And she's never mentioned any friends outside of those who work at the ice cream store where she works."

As he talked so knowingly, so fondly about the girl, Michael began to wonder if this man had kidnapped her. The only photo Michael had seen of her certainly showed her to be a wan, attractive waiflike beauty. The type that men get protective about. And sometimes protectiveness becomes possessiveness. And sometimes possessiveness becomes psychosis. Not out of the question that this man might have abducted her.

"How do you think she felt about you?"

"Me?" Surprised.

"Saw you as a friend?"

"Why, of course. At least I hope so. She always said that I was her *only* friend when you came right down to it."

"Did she ever try to be *more* than a friend?"

One leg slid from the other. He put both feet on the floor and sat up straight. "I was going to say that I can't believe this but of course I can. I had a friendly relationship with Cindy and you want to know if it was ever romantic."

"Or sexual."

He laughed. "Detective Scanlon, quit being a cop for a minute and look at me. Take a good *hard* look. I grew up a nerd and I'm still a nerd. My wife and kids call me a nerd. Now do you think that a girl like Cindy, a very attractive girl, would ever look on me as anything except a father figure? And believe me, I've never looked on her as any more than a very decent girl who needed help."

"You mentioned that she was having trouble with her boyfriend."

"He wanted to sleep with her. You couldn't blame him. Most high-school kids sleep together these days. But there was something else, too. Lately, I mean."

"What was it?"

"I'm not sure. But the last few weeks she seemed distracted when she was here. And at peace with herself. Usually she's agitated, nervous."

"Did you ask her about it?"

He nodded. "Yes. But all she said was that she was beginning to see that maybe things would work out for her. And she started leaving early. We usually spent an hour together. The last time she only spent half an hour.

I could tell that I wasn't important to her anymore. Somebody had taken my place."

"Somebody or some*thing*?"

"No, somebody. I wondered about that, too. I thought maybe she'd taken up drugs but she has asthma very badly. She's always afraid she's going to have an attack and die. She hates people who take drugs. No, she's met somebody. But I don't have any idea who it is."

The hour bell rang. "Outside that door I've got a very troubled young man waiting to see me now. He's trying to keep from getting expelled. I think I'd better wrap this up and see him."

Michael crossed to where the counselor sat and shook his hand. "You've been a lot of help. I appreciate your time. Sorry I had to ask you a couple of those questions."

"No problem. The thing is to get her back. I just pray to God her skull doesn't show up in a box at her parents' trailer."

"Yeah," Michael said. "That's in the back of everybody's mind."

CHAPTER EIGHT

Detective Steve Scanlon hadn't been in church for over a year. He'd managed to concoct sudden illnesses for both Easter and Christmas, much to the displeasure of his wife and the disappointment of his children.

Following the meeting in the conference room he'd come straight to St. Matthew's, the church of his childhood and early married years. He sat in a back pew. There were only a few people in the church. The older ones were here from habit. The others were likely here because something had gone terribly wrong in their lives. Cancer, divorce, loss of their jobs.

He had hoped that sitting in the silence of the shadowy church, with the votive candles of red and blue and green so fervently bright in the darkened coves on either side of the altar, would help him. The Stations of the Cross with the dying Jesus, the nave with its paintings of the Virgin and the saints and the scent of incense had been able to comfort him at certain times in his life.

The Scanlon boys had reversed roles. Rather than Steve, the older brother, setting the example for Michael these days, it was Michael who'd cut back not only on drinking but hitting the clubs where cops were popular. But then Michael had never been the dedicated cocksman Steve was, something Steve had always taken pride in. Conventional wisdom in the extended Irish family was that Steve was too good-looking, too clever, too reckless for his own good. Numerous fights. A girl pregnant in high school. A DUI rap over the holidays in his junior year in college, a rap his detective father had managed to get dismissed. He'd never seen his father, a pretty straight cop, more ashamed of him. Or angrier. His early years on the force hadn't done his father proud, either. The old man wasn't much for citizens whining about police abuse but Steve had broken a man's arm while taking him into custody. Even though the charge was eventually dropped, the old man made it clear that he suspected Steve had let his sometimes frightening temper lead him to hurt a suspect unnecessarily.

The family had hopes when Steve got married to Wendy. It had been assumed that he would choose a woman who was not unlike him. He'd dated plenty of them, even lived with one briefly. They weren't bad women in the eyes of the family but they *were* frivolous. Aunt Maggie always told the story of how she'd spent an hour talking to one of these ladies once. Not only was the woman twice divorced, she had made surgically certain that she could never have children. The woman probably said a lot more but after those two confessions, Aunt Maggie probably wasn't listening.

The door leading from the rectory side of the altar opened and a familiar face appeared. Sister Mary Therese was one of the few nuns who'd been nice to him in high school. Most of the others had seen him only as the boy who'd gotten a girl in trouble. She had been a pretty woman in those days, even in her black-and-white habit. Now she wore a blue suit and white blouse. She had gray hair and had to be well into her sixties. But as she saw him and started toward him he realized that she was still pretty. Her smile said that she was glad to see him.

She stopped to speak to a few of the people in the pews closer to the altar, then worked her way back to him.

"It's always nice to see you, Steven."

"Nice to see you, too, Sister."

"I see your wife and children at Sunday Mass. I'm sure you must have police matters to take care of."

Just because she'd liked him—in his youthful arrogance he'd wondered sometimes if she might have a little nunly crush on him—that didn't stop her from preaching the gospel.

"Well, you know, I—" he stammered.

She put her hand on the shoulder closest to her. "That's all right. It's not my business, anyway. I'd just like to see you more often. How're you doing?"

He wanted to confess. You confessed to priests, not to nuns, but right here and right now he wanted to confess. He wanted to say I have two problems that could destroy me. He wanted her to listen to him and then give him the advice that would straighten out both problems. And with that advice he would walk out of here and right the things that had made concentration just about impossible.

"Oh, I'm doing all right."

She looked at him with the X-ray vision only Superman and nuns possessed. Gently she said, "You look tired."

"You know, the job."

"The crime rates, yes. I wish people would stop complaining about the police. The city council cut the budget for one thing, and for another that drug gang is still here."

"I wish there were more people like you. We're all putting in a lot of overtime."

A lie, of course. The state his mind was in he was

slacking off on most of his cases. Fortunately, most of them involved nonviolent crimes. Embezzlers generally didn't affect the public welfare the way killers did.

"I just hope that missing girl shows up soon. And that she's all right. We all said a rosary for her this morning."

His throat tightened. His words sounded forced. "We're hoping the same thing, Sister. And a lot of the time that's what happens." He tried not to picture Peter Olson. But it was impossible.

"Well, I'm saying a lot of prayers for her." She smiled. "And I'm saying a few prayers for you, too, that I start seeing you at Sunday Mass again."

He reached out and took her hand. He didn't want to let go of it.

"Thank you, Sister." His forlorn tone obviously stopped her for a moment.

"You know, you can always talk to Father O'Brien, Steven. He's only in his thirties and he understands the modern world much more than some of the older priests do."

"I'll think about that, Sister. I really will. Thanks again."

After she left, he had an odd thought. What did they call it? Sanctuary; yes, sanctuary. Maybe he could sit here for the rest of his life and not have to deal with the two demons clawing at his heart and soul.

Yes, sanctuary. Magical sanctuary.

CHAPTER NINE

The young man behind the counter was reading an Incredible Hulk comic book and wearing a 300 Spartans T-shirt. Kim remembered her youngest brother when he'd gone through the comic book phase. The memory felt good.

"Excuse me," she said.

Git 'n Go was one of the most cluttered convenience stores she'd ever been in. Good reason why. It was a small concrete block building crammed with enough food, beer, pop, pastries and gadgets to stock three stores of the same size. The smells were a mixture of bad microwave pizza and disinfectant.

His brown eyes rose slowly from his comic book. The heavy acne on the narrow face probably explained the damaged look in the gaze. "Yes, ma'am?"

She had her identification ready.

"I bet I know why you're here. Cindy."

"Yes. We're talking to everybody we can find who knew her. One of her friends called in and said that she spent some time here just about every day."

He seemed to be blushing. Kim wondered why he was embarrassed. Or afraid.

"I guess we were friends. Sort of, anyway. But you really want to talk to the woman who works the night shift."

A pretty black woman toting an even prettier baby girl came in and handed the young man money for her gas. Kim of course had to goo-goo the baby with her eyes. The woman smiled at her. The sweet-faced baby smiled. "That's a good sign," the woman said.

"What is?"

"She smiled at you. Usually she cries when she meets new people. Even after seven months she still cries when she sees my sister."

"Well, then, I'm very flattered."

The transaction finished, the woman and her baby walking through the door, Kim said, "What's your name, by the way?"

"Jason. Jason Lewis."

"You said that you are friends 'sort of.' I'm not sure what that means."

The flush was back beneath the acne. "Well, you know. She's a very pretty girl. And you know how it is with pretty girls." Then, as if realizing that he may have inadvertently insulted her, he said, "Well, you're pretty. You should know."

There was an endearing awkwardness about him that she liked. She was so used to street kids or drug-gone kids that she enjoyed his old-fashioned goofiness. The Incredible Hulk included.

"Well, thank you. But I still don't know what you mean."

"Pretty girls. They always have all kinds of boys hanging off them. She likes me okay but she likes a lot of the kids around here."

"Do you ever talk to her about her life?"

He shrugged. "Oh, yeah, sometimes. I'm a little older so I guess she thinks I know more about stuff."

"She ever talk to you about running away?"

"Not exactly. But her mom and dad—well, they're pretty hard on her."

"You have any idea where she might be right now?"

The gaze flickered. A millisecond. But she noted it. She couldn't decide if the flicker had been because of her question or because at the exact moment she'd spoken the door had opened and a teenage girl came in.

"I've been thinking about it. I don't know. But it kind of scares me."

The girl, ponytailed and too heavyset for the tight Toby Keith T-shirt and jeans she was wearing, pushed past Kim and said, "Pack of Winstons."

"Need to see some ID."

The girl needed a few acting lessons. Her indignation and scorn were pretty hokey. "You don't recognize me? I've been buying cigarettes in here for over a year."

"Not from me."

"Well, from everybody else."

"I'll still need to see an ID."

She glared first at Kim and then at Jason. "You're a creep, you know that?"

He just shrugged.

She hit the door with enough force to drive it off its hinges.

Jason turned back to Kim. "Like I said, you'll want to talk to Inez. She usually comes on at six, but she's got a sick sister in Chicago. She's there now. The boss may have to pull in somebody else for the night shift."

Kim was about to ask him more questions but the door was flung open and three teenage boys, pushing and shoving, surged through the door like an invasion.

She took one of her cards from her pocket and set it on the counter. The boys were giggling about something. She had to lean forward to make sure he heard her. "There's my number at the police station and there's my cell phone." She scanned his eyes. She remembered the way they'd suddenly flickered when she'd asked him if he had any idea where Cindy was right now. "If you think of anything—anything—that might be useful, call me. And I don't care what time it is."

He was about to say something but then he raised his head and yelled, "You break that, you pay for it."

She turned to see one boy tossing a quart of beer football style to another boy.

"Wow, I'm scared," the receiver laughed. "Zit-face is gonna beat us up."

"You be all right?" she said to Jason.

A frown was his answer. "It's my job."

She thought about flashing her badge and hassling the teenagers but then she realized that they would only come back later and make things even worse for him.

She left.

CHAPTER TEN

This is Cindy's dream—

Her mother shrieking at her father and her father shrieking back at her beginning to make her cry, to curl in upon herself under the tiny desk where she does her homework. She repeats the magic words she used to hear on a Saturday morning cartoon show from when she was six and seven.

The stars of the show are running down a midnight road with this week's monster after them—the pitch of the monster's voice identical to those of her parents' combined—when one of the kids remembers the words that will let them escape their Nightmare World.

The magic words always work, always send them back to where they live—a land called Haven—in this gleaming cottage in a meadow resplendent with blue sky, green grass, golden butterfly, crystal lake. And it is here they will laugh and sing and be safe from monsters until the following week.

"Send us to Haven. Send us quick."

How desperately she wants to be in that meadow with those three kids.

When she wakes now she only half wakes. She is in a room she doesn't quite recognize at the moment. A veil seems to be drawn across her eyes and her muscles seem to be pushing up against an incredible weight. Lingering images of the meadow are quickly fading as she mutters "Haven."

The pain causes her to jerk upward. Between her legs she feels as if she's on fire. She's never known pain of this severity. And certainly not in her vagina this way.

Then she realizes why the veil is over her eyes. Three years ago she had her tonsils out. And when she woke up after the operation the same kind of veil was over her eyes in the hospital room. Drugged. She's been drugged.

She forces herself to sit up, push her legs off the cot, to pull up the long sleepshirt someone gave her and to examine herself. The misery is even worse now as she lifts the sleepshirt and looks down at herself. Starting just above her pubic hair is a deep bruise that is more black than blue. It can be seen continuing under her blonde hair.

As she continues to tenderly check herself, she realizes that she is no longer a virgin. She also realizes that if she had not been drugged she would probably be sobbing. But everything she feels is dulled except for stabs of fear. She had wanted to save herself until she was absolutely certain that she had found the right boy. Probably that boy would have been Ted.

But now, through the murk of the drugs, she realizes how futile saving herself had been. Saving herself for the absolutely right boy and then this happens.

This.

What exactly *is* this?

She knows that she knows.

It is a question of reaching into a small dark space and pulling it out into the light.

Reaching in and—

Dr. Olson.

Meeting him, but him getting afraid that people might misunderstand their relationship and accuse him of terrible things that would cost him his right to be a doctor.

There.

Dr. Olson.

He had never once tried to kiss her or even hug her. But in the course of six sessions with him for dealing with her asthma she knew she'd made a father-friend even wiser than Mr. Sullivan at school. And he was so handsome. She'd had dreams of giving herself to him more than once.

The first nights sliding into his car where he waited in the mall parking lot. Just driving around and talking. Her talking, mostly. Telling him all about her home life and how someday she hoped to go on to college and become a schoolteacher. And about Mr. Sullivan. And him warning her about Mr. Sullivan. Saying that a very pretty young girl like her had to be careful of older men. And her giggling that maybe she should be careful about *him*, too. And both of them laughing about it.

She can't believe the pain. It's obvious that he put some kind of ointment on her but whatever it is it isn't working very well. And where is he and why is she in this atticlike room with the winds slapping the exterior walls and the entire interior covered in plastic sheeting?

At first the drugs kept her from strong feelings. She felt sedated for these first few minutes. But now her emotions are strong, vivid.

Fear.

As she begins to think about the two girls who vanished over the last year or so. High school girls like herself. The only trace of them to be found in the skulls delivered to their parents.

Skulls.

Oh, shit. What is going on here?

Mr. Sullivan, please help me.

Please. Wherever you are. Please help me.

PART TWO

CHAPTER ELEVEN

Michael Scanlon found his father Jack sitting in what the Gentle Hands nursing home called the sunroom. He was alone in the long, narrow section that overlooked a steep hill and a wide creek. As usual he sat in a wheelchair with a blanket over his lap and a paperback book in his hand. Jack Scanlon read Western novels the way crack addicts took crack. He started this up in the seventies—before his boys were born—because the Western had pretty much vanished from both the tube and the screen. The bureau in his room was stacked high with Westerns.

Michael paused in the doorway, scanning the chairs and loungers that were arranged the way they would be on the deck of a ship. The tinted ceiling was glass, too, so the room was warm. The air smelled of various kinds of medicines. He always had a shock when he saw the old man, though he saw him at least three times a week. It was as if there was a fixed picture of the red-haired, burly police detective of Michael's youth and this other man, this imposter, violated that picture.

Following his second stroke, Jack Scanlon had lost thirty pounds. His flesh had turned gray; his body had become permanently stooped. The once blazing blue eyes had faded and the voice was often without much power. He had startled Michael a few times by bursting into tears when he talked about his wife and how lonely he was for her. The idea of the gruff, proud old man crying in front of him had been unthinkable. He'd only seen his father cry once before, when Michael's mother died five years ago.

If his father heard him coming, he didn't let on. He continued to read his Western by a man named Robert J. Randisi. He looked up only when Michael touched his shoulder. He wore a blue chambray work shirt that was at least one size too big for his diminished body.

"You bring Steve with you?" The yearning was in both his eyes and words, the rutted wrinkles of his shrunken face seeming to draw even deeper with the mention of his older boy. Steve had always been his favorite. First-born male, made sense. Occasionally this had bothered Michael while he was growing up. But he loved his old man too much to let it damage their relationship.

Michael pulled up a footstool and sat on it, facing his father. "He's pretty busy, Dad."

"Haven't seen him in two weeks."

And for two weeks every conversation he had with his younger son started this same way. *Where is Steve? Not even a phone call. What the hell is wrong with that guy, Michael? Wendy calls me a couple times a week, Michael, and lets me know how the kids are doing. She's quite a gal. Steve don't appreciate what he's got there. And you can tell him that for me.*

And now, as always: "The last time I saw him he didn't look so good. Real agitated. There something wrong with him and you won't tell me? I asked Wendy the same thing and she got all quiet and changed the subject. She's a sweetie."

"We've just got a lot of work to do," Michael said. "We've got two people on vacation and Steve is picking up a lot of the slack."

The old man's voice cracked with anger. This was the old man he'd grown up with. If the subject had been something other than Steve, he would have enjoyed seeing the old man fired up. "He's so busy he can't pick up a phone?"

"I'll make sure he calls you, Dad."

"He isn't in any kind of trouble, is he?"

"No; no trouble. Just busy, like I said."

Jack Scanlon's head lolled back and his eyes closed momentarily. Between rheumatoid arthritis, stroke and age, his body was a dartboard of pain and discomfort. He sighed deeply. He was like a fighter who had to rest between rounds. In a minute or two the eyes would open again, the head would return to a conversational position and they would continue talking.

A nurse appeared in the doorway. She was apparently checking to see where some of her patients were. She recognized Michael, smiled, waved. Michael waved back.

"I hear from my old buddies at the station more often than I hear from Steve. Down there my name still means something." His pride was his history as a police officer. Second generation, he'd been. And now both his boys were detectives.

"I'll talk to him, Dad."

"And how about you? You asked Kim to marry you yet?"

Michael laughed, though he felt pain as he did so. They'd gone out for a year. Several trips together. Lots of expectations on Michael's part. But somehow it had never happened. Whenever he brought up marriage she had turned elusive. There were reasons to wait; why spoil things when they were having so much fun? But he became adamant and that was when she carefully, thoughtfully, gently eased out of his love life. This was before she'd met the wonderful Dr. Olson. She hadn't dumped him for anybody else. She'd simply decided that theirs wouldn't be the marriage she wanted. His first wife had left because an office romance became a second marriage for her. In ways that was easier to accept than to be turned away for no real reason. It was easier seeing her every day now but no matter how many nights separated them, no matter how many dates or even sleepovers he had, she was still in his mind.

"My old man the matchmaker. She's seeing somebody else."

"Well, she shouldn't be."

"I'll tell her you said that."

"You need a woman like your mother."

"A good woman, you mean."

"Kim is a good woman."

"Dad, she's in love with somebody else."

"Buy her some flowers."

God, he loved this crazy old bastard. He'd always been like this but was even more so following the stroke. If you just acted on a problem you could resolve it. That was the old man's belief. The amazing thing was that Jack Scanlon in his prime had often been able to do just that. But fixing broken romances was beyond even his old man's reach.

"How about this missing girl?" Jack Scanlon often reverted to type. A conversation frequently consisted of him firing questions at you as if he were interrogating you. And you'd better keep your answers snappy.

"Don't know much yet."

"Sounds bad."

"She's had a troubled home life. Could be she just ran off."

"I hate to see the chief and all you people get picked

on by those damned reporters. They never give up mentioning about those skulls. I don't blame 'em, though. That's pretty gory stuff and that's what the public likes."

"I'm working on it and so is Steve." He knew instantly that he'd said the wrong thing.

The old man fixed him with the evil Scanlon eye. "You've talked to him today?"

Didn't want to say it but he had to. "We had a meeting with Myles and Horan this morning."

"Horan? That kid from the mayor's office?"

"Yes."

"I see him on TV all the time. Pretty slick. You can tell he likes the spotlight."

"Not as much as the mayor."

But the old man returned to what ailed him. "You had a meeting and you found time to come out and see me but Steve couldn't?"

"He had other things to do. He really is busy."

"That's a crock. He knows I'll ask him questions. That sweet little wife of his is too loyal to say anything but I can tell they're having some problems. She can't keep that out of her voice."

"Like I said, Dad, I'll talk to him."

A deep, ragged sigh. Another round had ended. A skeletal bruised hand lay trembling on the arm of his wheelchair, the bruises from where IV needles had been inserted. The head fell back again, the eyes closed. But this time he began snoring.

Michael rose and leaned over his father and kissed him on the forehead. *I sure love you, old man.* He didn't know how long his father could hold out. He'd already hung on much longer than his doctors had thought he would. The prospect of the old man dying sometimes turned Michael into a scared little boy. He'd been the same when his mother had taken sick. He saw death frequently in his role as police officer, often terrible, violent, sickening death. But nothing matched the fear of losing one of your own.

He gazed down at the old man and smiled. Then he left.

CHAPTER TWELVE

Kim always wondered how many of his nurses Dr. Peter Olson had slept with.

It couldn't be coincidence that all of them were attractive, slender women in their thirties. None were great beauties. That would have been gauche in a medical office. But they were certainly appealing. And they also just happened to be bright, friendly and efficient.

"Good afternoon, Kim," Marjorie, the brunette at the registration desk, said as Kim approached. "He's actually running ahead of schedule so you shouldn't have long to wait."

"Isn't that against the doctors' code?"

Marjorie smiled. "I'm pretty sure it is. But we'll keep it to ourselves."

The waiting room was painted in warm browns and golds, with framed paintings to complement the walls and the nubby furnishings also done in browns and golds. There were four other patients waiting, two women, two men. Kim was leery of waiting rooms. She selected a recent *Time* magazine and went immediately to entertainment news.

She used to watch the faces of other patients in waiting rooms, but one time—different doctor—a woman sitting alone staring straight ahead began sobbing so violently that Kim rushed to her to hold her. The woman put her tear-soaked face to Kim's and cried, "I'm dying! I'm thirty-six and I'm dying!" A nurse hurried to take her back to one of the examination rooms, leaving Kim to feel powerless and hopeless. She'd wanted to comfort the woman in some way. Big deal she was a cop with a gun and badge. She was just as helpless as anybody else. She'd felt guilty about it for years after.

She'd only had time to read about two stays in rehab, a divorce and a sitcom cancellation before the nurse named Willow came out from the door leading to the examination rooms and said, "Kim. We're ready."

Willow was three inches taller than Kim's five-eight. Though her body suggested frailty her manner was always energetic and happy. As she led Kim down the hall to examination room D she said, "You're sure looking good, Kim."

"Thank you. So are you."

Willow laughed. "Mutual admiration society."

Room D contained an examination table, sink, four-shelf medicine cabinet and pale blue wall phone that matched the pale blue walls.

Kim took her place on the examination table.

"He won't be long. Nice to see you."

"Same here, Willow."

Like a motel room, room D was haunted by the ghosts of good news and the silent screams of bad. Kim was here for her continuing migraine headaches. Frustrating, sometimes quite painful, but a long way from some of the diagnoses that had been given in this room.

In his white coat Dr. Olson looked more handsome than most of the hunks who played docs on TV. The blond hair only increased his good looks. He moved with the grace of an athlete, that lithe, continuous motion that seems streamlined.

"Afternoon, Doctor."

He closed the door behind him and started walking to her, slipping the stethoscope from around his neck. "I'm assuming since you made another appointment that you're still having migraines."

"Unfortunately, yes."

And then he was kissing her, raising her up from the table as her arms wrapped around his shoulders and she gave herself to him despite her plans.

"I've missed you," he said as they separated.

"Oh, no. That's not your line. That's mine. Three unreturned phone calls and not a word from you in a week."

He put his hands on her shoulders, helped her back up on the table. "I could give you some legitimate reasons but I'm not sure you'd listen to them."

"You were 'busy.' "

"See. That's what I mean. No matter what I say you'll be angry."

Deep sigh. "God, Peter, I deserve better than that."

"You certainly do. And to prove it we're going out tonight."

"It's humiliating having to make an appointment just to see you."

"So the migraines—"

"—better."

"The meds—"

"—worked."

"I was thinking of the club."

"I was thinking of ending it."

She hated the whine in her voice. Even more she hated living at the mercy of anybody. But Peter in particular. She'd never been quite sure why he'd asked her out. She'd been to enough city government dances and dinners to know that he never appeared anywhere without a stunning woman on his arm. A stunning woman who existed in the rarefied atmosphere of what passed for high society in a city this size. She knew she was attractive, but just that. Not even pretty, exactly. Appealing, she supposed, in a clean-cut kid sister way. Nothing a wealthy and popular doctor would be interested in.

"It just pisses me off." There. She liked the sound of that better. Vulnerable still but at least not whiny. "I'm tired of trying to build my life around our surprise dates."

"Hey," he said, dropping his hands from her shoulders. "Now that's not fair. I've seen you two or three times a week for—what is it now—ten months? I'd consider that being a pretty major part of your life. Especially since I'm not seeing anybody else."

"You say that but I'm even beginning to wonder if that's the truth."

"You're really angry."

"You're damned right I am."

And then he took her in his arms again and this time the kiss lingered and despite herself, she felt the urgency of her need for him. Lust and love. Tidal relationships that she could not deny or escape.

"Oh, shit," she said after they parted for a second time.

"You're always so romantic."

She couldn't help it. She laughed. "I came here to tell you not to call me."

"You came here," he said, "to vent. And you did. And I had it coming. And if I didn't love you so much I wouldn't feel like hell right now. For not calling you back last night."

"Two calls last night and one this morning."

"I'd kiss you right now but then I'd never get out of here. We'd probably knock down walls once we got going."

That sounded nice, knocking down walls, but she didn't want to give him the satisfaction of saying it.

He kissed her forehead. "That'll have to do us until tonight. When I promise you we'll make up for it. And I imagine you're pretty busy, too."

She stepped down from the examination table and straightened her blouse and jacket. "Right now I'm trying to find a witness to a mugging that took place at Campbell Mall two days ago. And trying to help the county attorney get enough evidence to put this drug dealer away for good."

Peter straightened his medical jacket, fixed the knot of his tie. "And didn't I hear something about a young girl missing?"

"Oh, God. I don't even want to think about that. We're hoping that she just ran away. Everybody's afraid it's the same guy again. The one who sent the skulls back."

He took her hand and led her to the door. "Well, let's hope for the best. Sometimes these things actually do turn out all right."

She squeezed his arm. "I'd just like to get my hands on the bastard. He'd never forget it."

"No," Dr. Peter Olson said, "I don't imagine he would."

CHAPTER THIRTEEN

The real estate office again.

Rice had no problem following Steve Scanlon. Scanlon had never seen him before. Leo Rice had been in prison when Steve Scanlon shot and killed his brother.

He had been following the detective since coming to town a day and a half ago. And this was the fifth time in the last thirty-six hours that the detective had swung by the imposing white two-story real estate office with all the expensive foreign cars in the lot.

But then when Steve Scanlon started following the bronze Mercedes that had been in the lot, Rice was able to figure out that the detective was having some problems with the sexy if somewhat cold woman who drove it. The way he was following her told him that. Rice had seen this before. Guy gets obsessed with a woman and lets his whole life get fucked up over her. Even so-called "family men" with a wife and two kids stashed at home. Rice had googled the name Steven Moore Scanlon many times before coming to Skylar, a town where his brother had been working as a chauffeur for an airport service.

And now they were taking another pass at the real estate office again, two thirty in the afternoon. Didn't this cop have anything better to do than keep circling the place where the dark-haired woman worked?

Apparently not.

The detective slowed down as he passed in front of the office. He did this every time. Then he gaped at the two glass front doors as if he expected her to magically appear. And then he roared off. Pissed or embarrassed or sick of himself for being such a pussy? Hard to know and Rice didn't give a shit anyway. He just wanted to figure out the best time and place to waste this bastard.

This time Steve Scanlon led him to a small bar called The Illini Inn out near the highway, where an industrial park sprawled over a flat plain that had otherwise been left to ragged grasses.

First thing Rice wondered was if the detective ever came here at night. He tried to picture the gravel parking lot when it was dark. This was a possible place to shoot him. There couldn't be any witnesses, which was problematic, of course, with a parking lot where people were coming and going.

Watching Steve Scanlon exit his unmarked police vehicle and head inside, Rice decided it would be amusing to go inside and have a beer with the prick. The Rice boys had never looked like brothers. Bobby had the fair, almost delicate looks of their British mother, where Leo got the blunt, shanty Irish looks of the father. And given the beard Bobby had favored, Rice felt he would be safe.

He parked his aunt's blue Dodge sedan next to the unmarked police car and went inside.

The place was decorated like a frat house located on the U of Illinois campus. Jerseys, football helmets, bronzed footballs and basketballs, framed photographs of past greats, even a plasma TV streaming video of highlights of past football and basketball teams. There had been men in prison who were big sports fans. A few of them cut each other up over arguments about games and teams, in fact. Leo Rice liked boxing and nothing else. He enjoyed the elemental battle, especially if the coon got his lunch handed to him. When there were two coons fighting he didn't have a favorite. He just enjoyed the sight of them wasting each other. All other sports bored him.

Light streamed in the front window, revealing a wide, clean place with booths lining one wall and a long bar on the opposite wall. There was a clear area in back where some people probably danced when they were drunk enough. This place would be like Mardi Gras after a football or basketball game. Probably could barely get into the place. And all those crazy sports fans pounding on each other and hoisting drinks if they'd won and bitching and maybe even picking fights if they'd lost. Wives would get pissed at husbands for flirting with other gals and husbands would get pissed at wives who let somebody grab a feel here and there. Rice and Bobby had spent some time in after-game places like this, plundering cars in the lot. Some of the people were so wasted from all the drinking at the game that they left valuable items lying on the seats of their cars. Rice and Bobby had found a lot of things to take to fences.

Steve Scanlon was already seated at the bar when Rice walked in. Except for a man and woman in a booth, Rice was the only other customer on this drowsy, hot afternoon.

Rice sat several stools away from the detective and ordered a beer from the man wearing a short-sleeved button-down shirt in the official blue and gold colors of his team. While he was fixing Rice up the bartender kept talking to the detective.

"How you been, Steve? Ain't seen you in awhile."

"Hanging in there." Sullen.

The bartender raised his head, apparently surprised by the tone. "Everything all right?"

"Busy, I guess."

"I imagine. That poor girl missing. They catch that fucking creep, I'd just cut his balls off and then set him on fire. ACLU'd go nuts but fuck 'em. Mostly Jews and faggots anyway."

"No shortage of faggots."

"Had a pair of them in the other night. The regulars weren't too happy about it."

"Flamers, huh?"

The bartender laughed. "About burned the place down they were so flaming." He set a bottle of Bud and a glass in front of Rice, though he was still talking to Steve Scanlon. "A few blacks, no problem. Not a lot of them, then there'd be a problem. But a few. No sweat. Fags and Mexes are different." He picked up Rice's two singles and carried them down to the register across from where the detective sat. "Had a few Mexes in awhile back and of course somebody at the bar starts talking about illegal immigration. I tried to head it off but then *everybody* starts talking about it. So the Mexes get pissed and start arguing back. I finally had to ask them to leave. First of all I'm not for all these illegals, anyway."

"You think they were illegals?"

"Nah. One of them's worked at the Midas Muffler down the street for years. But the thing is these days you see a Mex of any kind and you immediately start thinking about illegals. This is a neighborhood place. White guys. I gotta think of my business."

"Hit me again." Scanlon. He angled left on his stool and took in Rice. Gave him one of those long hard cop stares that shake up most private citizens.

Rice met his eyes and smiled. "Cop?"

"Yeah." Suspicious. "How'd you know?"

"Used to be one myself."

"Yeah?" Still suspicious.

"Chicago."

"Detective?"

"Yeah."

"What district?"

"The fifth."

"What unit?"

"Organized crime." He smiled. "I pass the test?"

"Guess so. You looking for a job?"

"Vacation. Have some relatives in Rock Island. Just working my way back home."

"We've got a nice town here."

"Looks like it." He picked up his glass. He had two swallows left. He feigned a toast and took a deep swallow. "Need to be hitting the road. Like to get home before dark."

He eased himself off the stool. Left three quarters on the bar.

"Nice to meet you. My name's Bill Noles, by the way."

"Steve Scanlon."

The men nodded at each other. Rice walked out. He wondered what they'd say about him as soon as the front door closed. He was pretty sure the detective had bought his story.

Exhilarating, that encounter. Arrogant prick thought he ran the universe, knew everything like most cops. Pretty funny to have your killer sitting a few barstools away from you and not know it. Throw a lot of questions at him trying to put him on the defensive and then end up buying his bullshit story.

He got in his car and drove down to a building supply store parking lot. Had a good view of the bar so he could start following Steve Scanlon again.

The temptation was to kill him close up, he thought as he sat there waiting. Beat him badly before shooting him. But that would be foolish. Too many chances of being seen. Of leaving DNA. Of leaving some kind of evidence behind without realizing it.

A quick clean kill with the gun. Tell him why he was dying and then make him die.

Steve Scanlon walked out into the bright harsh sunlight fifteen minutes later, wincing in the blinding rays, stalking to his car with the same kind of stride you'd expect from a cop.

Rice didn't know the name of the woman who was driving the detective crazy but he sure wanted to thank her. You got crazy about a woman who didn't want you and you died a hundred deaths a day.

He definitely wanted to thank her.

CHAPTER FOURTEEN

Michael had called the Baineses before he went out there. Three minutes on the phone made him think that the girl might well have run away. Natalie, the mother, sounded half-drunk, while in the background, fighting for dominance over a TV evangelist shouting about saving your soul, an angry male voice kept bellowing, "I don't want no cop out here!"

The trailers were small, rusty, battered. There was no paving, just narrow dirt trails as streets. Little kids in grubby clothes and even a few wearing nothing but dirty diapers stood on their ragged patches of grass, watching him pass in his unmarked blue Ford police car. Doomed already, some of them, doomed as their parents had likely been.

Natalie Baines must have heard him approaching because now she stood holding the torn screen door open. "It's not going to be any better than it was on the phone. Now he's saying that she's probably dead and that it's God's will. This motherfucker is gonna be dead if he keeps it up, I can tell you that."

"You wanna talk, you talk out there. I don't want him in here. Dragging his filth into my home!"

"You heard him." She focused her anger on Michael. "You think it's any wonder I go out at night? How'd you like to live with that 24/7?"

Ten years ago she'd probably been a pert little blonde with merry blue eyes. But now, in her black Big & Rich T-shirt and tight jeans, she was a small, weary woman with a tic under her left eye and long angel tattoos on both her arms. She smelled of perfume, beer, sweat, cigarette smoke. These scents were joined by the smells from inside, the odors of food, liquor, dog shit and the claustrophobic living space that badly needed to be aired out.

"Out here is fine," Michael said.

Before she could answer, Giff Baines shouted, "He just doesn't want to hear the truth. He's like you. She's a little slut and it's all your fault!"

Then, even more shocking than his words, Baines started sobbing.

She closed the door and came down the concrete block steps. "He wasn't always like this, I hafta say that for him. He was a good man till he got in that accident. And he got into it because of me. We were all drunk in the back of the pickup and Neely, the man he was fightin' with, Neely called me a whore. That's how it happened. Giff stood up to defend me and Neely shoved him. Shoved him right off the back of the truck and we were moving a good thirty miles an hour."

Michael decided he didn't need to be inside the trailer to feel oppressed. This was one of those stories that were so ridiculously dark they were perversely funny. He remembered a line from one of his college English courses. "Right at the point where tragedy becomes absurdity." Some poet. But poets only wrote about it. Cops lived it every day.

"So all he does now is sit in front of the TV and drink beer and listen to all those ministers on the tube. You couldn't drag him into a church before but now he's got a Bible on his lap most of the time and he even makes me send those bastards money. I've got a pretty good job and with Social Security we're doing all right. But I hate sending those con artists even a dime. I've got an aunt the same way. She sends this one fifty dollars a month if you can believe it."

She was making a point of not talking about her daughter. All her fear, all her anger, all her remorse was being poured into this biography of her husband. She was probably afraid that she would be as crazy as Giff if she couldn't take her mind off it for at least a short while.

Michael had to force her back to reality. "You said you'd make a list of friends for me. School friends and where she worked at the ice cream place."

"You think he's right?"

"Right?"

"About being dead?"

"I hope not, Mrs. Baines."

The saddest looking mutt he'd ever seen approached him. It was missing a good part of its left ear and some kind of wound was still healing on its right side. The dark eyes contrasted sharply with the light brown coat. Eyes that should have reflected anger given all the scrapped cars, broken bottles, smashed windows and piles of garbage showed only innocent affection. Michael leaned down and patted the dog. The dog brushed up against him, pleased with the gesture of friendship.

This was when he went on autopilot. For the next few minutes he said all the supposedly right words of reassurance that he'd accumulated over many years on the force. She clearly made an effort to believe him. Inside, Giff had turned up the volume on James Dobson. Michael wasn't religious but he understood what people got from being in a church. The sense of community, the security of having like-minded friends who would help you if you needed it. But he could never understand why you would send money to a media loudmouth who cynically built empires on the backs of hardworking honest people.

She finally dug in the back pocket of her jeans and withdrew a white number-ten envelope folded in half. She almost fell over with the effort. She was drunker than he'd thought. "I put some names down there. School three and work three. You shouldn't have no trouble finding any of them. Channel 3 called me, by the way. They want to put me on the news. They said they'd be out to do an interview."

Inside, Baines was sobbing again.

"He goes back and forth. He screams at her for being a little whore and then he starts feeling guilty and starts crying. It's just crazy." Then her own eyes grew moist and her chin began to tremble. "You don't really think she's dead, do you?" Grasping his wrist, holding tight. "You don't, do you?"

"I need your help, Mrs. Baines. I need you to really think back about the last couple of weeks."

"I can do that."

"What was her mood like?"

"Well, she's moody, if that's what you mean. Feels sorry for herself a lot."

He almost laughed out loud. *She felt sorry for herself living in all this human waste? Gee, how insensitive Cindy must be. Who wouldn't appreciate this fine home with a pair of loving parents?*

"Specifically."

"Specifically?"

"Yes, did she get into an argument with anyone?"

"Well, she wouldn't tell me if she did. A social worker come out here a couple months ago because somebody at that goddamned school called and said we weren't good parents. Probably that faggot Sullivan. He's a real

creep. He's been talking against us for a long time now."
She started to tilt to the right. Michael put out his hand
and steadied her. "She won't tell us nothing after that
social worker bitch was here. All she says is that as
soon as she's eighteen she's movin' out and never wants
to see us again."

Imagine that.

And more reason to think that poor Cindy might just
have had enough and decided to be eighteen earlier
than the calendar allowed.

He stared at the list written on the back of a mustard-
stained envelope that had come from the telephone
company. He'd learned all he could here. He was leery
of hearing the tortured man inside start to sob again.

"All right, Mrs. Baines. I'll be back to you as soon as
I have some more information. If you think of anything
please call the police station. They'll get hold of me right
away."

"If she just ran away we're gonna be really pissed.
She's worryin' us to death with all this."

Even though he hurried to get back to the car, he
heard, when she opened the trailer door, "You whore!
You showin' off for that cop out there?"

Michael was just walking to his car when his cell phone
chimed. He recognized the voice and smiled. "My favorite sister-in-law."

"My favorite brother-in-law."

Wendy had been saddled with the chore of helping
Michael's older brother Steve stumble toward something
resembling maturity. Michael himself was still stum-
bling along that same road—and far from the finish
line according to his former wife Linda—but at least he
was trying.

He knew Wendy well enough to understand that her

amused voice was a trick. She was a high school teacher who worked on a lot of student plays. She knew how to fake a good mood.

"I just wondered if you'd like to stop by the house around supper time, Michael. I'm making sloppy joes and iced tea."

"Now that sounds good."

"But in order to eat your sloppy joes you have to eat your broccoli first. I want the kids to see that even big strong policemen like their vegetables."

"Umm, broccoli. Can't wait."

"Steve said he'll be busy tonight so I thought it'd be nice to have a man at the dinner table."

"I appreciate the invite. I'll be there."

He'd learned that Wendy never divulged over the phone why she wanted him to stop by. She always waited until he was there and when Beth and Nick were out of the room to talk to him. The subject never changed, though. It was always Steve and the fragility of her eight-year marriage to him.

"Around five thirty all right?" he said, thinking that he could stop at the ice cream store on the way out.

"That'd be great. I just got home from school and need some time, anyway."

"See you then."

Her only hint that something was wrong was when she said, "I really appreciate this, Michael."

The sadness was unmistakable. This time she didn't even try to disguise it.

CHAPTER FIFTEEN

Michael had never conducted an interview with an ice cream cone in his hand before. A single dip of extra-creamy vanilla forced upon him—though he didn't put up all that much of a struggle—while speaking to the third of the three high school students who worked at Creamy Cone in the Northland mall. They were taking classes in retail and worked two hours a day as part of their studies.

Mandy Beaumont was a small girl with vivid blue contacts and an active ponytail and a yellow uniform with the logo of ice cream cones on her collar, cuffs and the jaunty horizontal cone-shaped paper hat she wore. The long narrow place smelled of milk, air-conditioning and malt. They sat at a tiny table in back on chairs designed to resemble those in old-fashioned ice cream parlors. That they were plastic instead of metal hadn't bothered the designer, it seemed.

"Cindy has a boyfriend, right?"

"Yes, and then there's this sort of mystery man." She was licking her cone with a catlike tongue, pausing only to answer his questions.

"Mystery man?"

"I called him that. Two nights in a row she left ten minutes early. I work extra hours for the money. Right before closing time, I mean. I watched her both nights.

She walked down a row of cars and disappeared. But then I saw taillights—you know how they do, kind of flare up?—and I figured that was her. That she'd gotten in a car with somebody."

"Did you see the car?"

"Huh-uh."

It would be ungallant to mention that she had peppermint ice cream on her little bunny nose. "Did you ask her about it?"

"Yes. But all she said was that she just walked over to the bus stop and waited for the bus."

"And you didn't believe her?"

"She wouldn't take a bus. Nobody takes a bus. And anyway, buses don't run out to that trailer park where she lives." She became aware of the ice cream on her nose and swiped it off with a quick finger. "She was seeing somebody she didn't want anybody else to know about."

"The other two here didn't mention anything about a mystery man."

"They didn't see her meet him. I was the only one. I mean we all talked about it but we couldn't figure it out. Then when her mom called and asked if we'd seen her I started thinking about her meeting somebody way out there in the parking lot."

If Mandy's surmise was correct, she was meeting somebody she wanted to keep secret for a serious reason. Probably not somebody she could easily explain. If it was a boy from school or a boy she'd met at a club, he probably wouldn't have any reason not to pick her up at work like any other date. Without any good leads a story like this one tended to fix the mind. The mystery man became an intriguing figure.

"Could you show me the lane she walked down?"

"You mean leave work here?"

"Just for a few minutes."

"They're really strict about that. Jenny—you talked to her first—between us, when we do anything she doesn't like she tells Mr. Dodge."

"He's the owner?"

"Uh-huh."

"Well, I'm sure he'd want you to help find Cindy."

She stopped licking her cone and leaned forward. "What if she just ran away?"

"We can't rule that out yet. But we have to keep looking for her, anyway."

"I keep thinking of the mystery man. You know, sort of sweeping her off her feet. Have you ever met her folks?"

"Yes."

"Well, I'd sure run away if they were *my* folks."

"Let's go. I want you to show me about where you saw the taillights those nights."

She devoured the rest of her cone in a crushing last bite. She wiped away her ice cream mustache and then said, "All right if I go to the bathroom first?"

"Fine."

Mall traffic was heavy because of various sidewalk sales. At first she wasn't sure which area was the right one. They walked around long enough to get their faces nice and shiny with sweat. Then she said, "Here."

They were near an exit.

"What makes you think this is the right place?"

"The sign." She meant the back of a large sign that identified the mall and used an arrow to direct shoppers to the entrance. "I remember the sign. That was where she always disappeared. I could see the red of the taillights in the sign."

"That's very good detective work."

She glanced at him with that dopey girl face of hers and smiled. "Really?"

"Really."

"Wait till I tell Ricky. He's my boyfriend. He always tells me how stupid I am."

"Well, you can tell Ricky for me that I think you'll make a good detective someday."

"Everybody says I should be a model. Or a rock singer. But a detective sounds cool."

Model or rock star. All those TV shows that pandered to the fantasies of young people had long been taking their toll. He had a friend on the force whose thirty-seven-year-old son had been in Nashville since he was eighteen hoping to get a record contract. He'd met the son a few years ago and liked him. There was something inspirational about such determination. But also something sad.

"I might have to call you again, Mandy."

"That'd be great. I really do want to find her. All the trouble she's had with her folks. I really feel sorry for her. You should see her hands. She kind of twitches sometimes. All the way up her arms. Nerves. And then she looks embarrassed. I read this article online about how some young girls try to find boys who remind them of their fathers. I told her about it and she laughed and said, 'Well, you don't have to worry about me. I'm not looking for anybody like my father.' So maybe this mystery man is real nice to her. Maybe that's why she wanted to keep it a secret. So it wouldn't get spoiled or anything. Sometimes it's bad luck when other people know about your love life."

After a few more minutes of her chatter, he slipped away and went to the business office of the mall.

A middle-aged woman in a security uniform asked if she could help him.

After she'd checked his ID and paused in her demolition of a stick of gum, she said, "I'm sure this is about the missing girl. She was a cutie. I saw her a lot when I'd go for ice cream."

"What I'm interested in are the security camera tapes for the section of parking lot in front of the ice cream parlor."

"That'd be Rod."

"Is he here?"

"He had to take some of the equipment downtown for repair. He'll probably be gone for awhile."

"I'd appreciate it if you'd tell Rod what I'm looking for. If you'll give me his cell phone number I'll call him in awhile and then run back out here and look at the video. All right?"

She was already scribbling numbers on the back of a business card she'd plucked from a stack of them on the counter. "Here you go. We all want to find her. Good luck."

CHAPTER SIXTEEN

Steve Scanlon stood at the entrance to the condo complex swimming pool and watched Nicole McKenna lying facedown on a folding lounge chair. She always tried to take Wednesday afternoons off. Some kind of status thing.

Needless to say, Nicole had undone her bikini top. Sitting in the lounge chair next to her was her boss Bob Gargan.

Steve had studied psychology in night school before taking his exam for detective. He knew how dangerous jealousy was for people, men in particular. Gay men were no exception. Gay murders were sometimes massacres. There was something in the male body that turned men psychotic when they felt sexually betrayed. And no matter what Nicole told him, there was no doubt she was sleeping with Bob Gargan. No doubt at all.

The sun was pitiless. The pool lay between the two buildings of the upscale condos. Red and yellow lounge furnishings stood empty. The area would be full in a few hours or so when all the thirty-something lawyers and doctors and advertising people who lived here would come wheeling their sleek new cars into the parking lot.

They were Nicole's kind of people, not his. He knew he wasn't as slick and knowledgeable as they were and they knew it, too. The few times she'd introduced him he saw a certain pleasure in their eyes. A cop with a wedding ring had come under the spell of the resident goddess of Terrace Heights. They might have felt sorry for him if he was more their kind. But for all his good looks and gym-sleek body—and even despite the fact that he was allowed to carry a badge and a gun—there was something a bit foolish about him. He didn't belong here, their eyes said. He should have been home with his wife and kids and his mortgage and his back-yard barbeques.

He unclenched his fists. He took several deep breaths. And when he started walking down the length of the pool to where Nicole and Gargan were he managed to look jaunty. He smiled at the only two other people around the pool at this time, two slightly overweight but sumptuous-looking women in string bikinis. They were just lifting themselves from the pool, dripping silver water. They returned his smile.

Gargan was a hairy bastard. The hair he lacked on his head was all over his arms. He was in his forties. He had a wife and kids, too, but as the co-owner of the city's most successful real estate business, he also had access to his employees the way nobody else quite did. Steve had checked him out. Boozer, chaser, leading citizen. He and Steve had recognized each other instantly as mortal enemies. Gargan had one particular advantage over Steve. He could call the mayor and complain that a police detective was bothering one of his Realtors and that he was getting tired of it. Steve had to be careful.

"Well, look who's here," Gargan said, lifting a hand in Steve's direction. He had a rugged face and a boyish smile. He was one of those indisputably masculine men who just naturally dominated most rooms he walked into. He hadn't yet figured out how to dominate Steve. But then Steve hadn't figured out how to dominate him, either.

Nicole angled her chic face so that she could see him out of one exotically blue eye. "I thought we sort of had a deal, Steve."

"Well—" Then: "Yeah, I guess we did."

She'd told him to stay away, that if he came near her again she'd tell Gargan to call somebody important.

Gargan's smile held steady. He knew what was going on here. He was a Roman senator watching a gladiator who was about to die.

Steve was surprised he was able to speak. The words scalded his tongue and mind. This was complete humiliation and he alone was responsible for it. "I was wondering if I could talk to you for a few minutes."

"Aw, Steve, that doesn't sound like a very good idea. I think it's all been said." This, of course, was Gargan speaking. "I know it's none of my business but Nicole's my best employee and a very good friend. I look out for her." Then he stood up. He wore a white short-sleeved shirt and white ducks and deck shoes. He was apparently under the impression that he was on a yacht.

Nicole's long fingers were quickly and nimbly tying the strings of her top together. Even her delicate wrists had always fascinated him, their feminine perfection.

"In fact, Nicole and I need to discuss a little bit of business," Gargan said. He smiled. "The kind of business a detective would probably find pretty boring, actually. Though a guy like you could do all right for himself in real estate, especially with the ladies."

Nicole swung her long legs off the lounger. She held out her hand. Gargan took it and gently helped her to her feet. The full effect of Nicole shocked Steve into remembering how complicated his feelings were for her. Sex as he'd never known it before, but also a need that teetered on madness.

"So if you'll excuse us," Gargan was saying.

"I want to talk to Nicole. Alone."

Gargan assessed him with cold green eyes. "Steve, I'm trying to be civil about this. But you're making it difficult for us and for yourself. If I'm not mistaken, you're on duty right now. And that means that you're not only taking care of personal business when you shouldn't be, you're also wasting a hell of a lot of the taxpayers' money. Not everybody would be real happy to hear about that."

Steve's hands were fists again. He felt a gathering pressure in his head and chest. The kind of pressure that had usually preceded swinging on an opponent. He was of the old school. The first punch often decided the battle.

He felt Nicole's gaze on him. She knew him well, knew what was about to happen. She eased her slender, perfect body between the two men and said, "Bob, why don't you wait for me upstairs? I won't be long. Fix us drinks, in fact."

"You be all right?"

"Of course."

Gargan hitched his white ducks up and said, "I'm trying to be decent about this, Scanlon. For Nicole's sake. She's tried to make you do the right thing by her but you won't. You don't seem to believe that she doesn't feel real good about you having a wife and two kids at home. People get the wrong idea about her because she's so beautiful. But she's a decent woman whether they think so or not."

Gargan's words and tone confused Steve. Nicole had insisted all along that she and Gargan were nothing more than friends. And the way Gargan spoke now sounded as if it were true. Simply being friends with a woman, especially a beautiful woman, was not in Steve's experience.

"Thank you, Bob. I'll be upstairs in a few minutes."

Gargan nodded to her, then looked at Steve and smiled. "You take good care of this little lady. You hear me?"

They watched him walk to the far end of the pool and then disappear into the stairwell that would take him to the second floor.

"I thought we had an agreement," she said. "You made your decision and I made mine."

He'd hoped that there would be the chance for a sentimental moment or two before plunging back into their long-standing contentiousness. But she was still angry, still hurt.

"We need to talk."

"In case you hadn't noticed, Steve, we're talking."

"Not here."

"Oh, God. You mean go to some little dive where nobody will see us and start arguing again? That's how we spent the last month. And I'm exhausted from it. It's starting to affect my work. That's why Bob's here. He's trying to help me get my focus back."

"Yeah. I bet."

"You never believed me when we were seeing each other. I guess I shouldn't expect you to believe me now."

He hated hearing her refer to them in the past tense. She seemed so accepting of it. As if she'd meant it when she said it was over. "It doesn't have to be over."

She shook her head and smiled sadly. "You really like torture. I don't. It isn't easy to stay away from you but it's even harder being around you. You think I'm this terrible woman because I want a career and the kind of life that I enjoy. I'm not promiscuous. But I like a little adventure in my life. Before we started seeing each other I went to Europe once a year, I went to Vail several times, I even spent a week in LA with a girlfriend of mine who's working as a writer on a sitcom. It isn't all that glamorous but it's what I want, Steve. What I need. You're married and you have a family. You love your job. Even if you divorced your wife and we got married, I'd be unhappy and we'd have a terrible time. It wouldn't be right for either of us. I care about you, Steve. I wouldn't want to see you destroy yourself that way."

The sorrow that always took him when she talked this way enraged him, made him swing away from her, try to find words. She touched his arm and he turned back to her. "There are management jobs in security. I could get one of those."

But he knew how foolish that sounded. Not even a management job in a good security company would give them the kind of life she wanted. She had made a great deal of money and with Gargan's help invested it well. She wasn't rich by any means but she was certainly secure.

He wanted to bite back his bitterness but he couldn't. "Travel around with Gargan is what you mean. That's what you're really saying."

She shook her head. "You'll never believe me, will you? He really is like my brother. All the men hitting on me all the time. All the women talking about me behind my back. He's the only friend I've got in the whole company."

"I still say he's trying to get you into bed with him."

"If he is, he's sure taking his time about it." She startled him by taking his hand, sliding hers into it. "I'm sorry for you, I'm sorry for your wife and kids and I'm sorry for me. We never should have gotten involved. I have an old college friend who says she has a sign on her bathroom mirror that says 'I don't do married men.' I should have had that sign on my mirror, too, I think. It just never works out." She squeezed his hand. "You can help us both by making it a clean break, Steve. You coming over here isn't going to be good for either of us."

What he said next was so strange that he wondered at first if he had even said it. "What if we made a real clean break? We said good-bye to everybody and moved away. Maybe to California. Or Arizona. There's a lot of money out there."

She slipped her hand away. Surprise filled her voice. "You could walk away from your children just like that?"

"I'd see them three or four times a year. Lots of fathers see their kids that way. And I'd call them every week." He knew how desperate he sounded. He didn't care.

"You think you could do that when it came right down to it? Walk away like that?"

He searched her face. He wanted to see some evidence of hope, some sign that she was taking his words seriously.

"For you, I could."

She ducked her head and put her fingers to her forehead. "Oh, God, here we go again. You're dragging us right back into it, Steve. I've said what I want to. This is wrong and it could never work. We're just very different people. It's over, Steve. I can't do this anymore. I don't think I even *want* to do it anymore. We've done it all and said it all. And now it's time to just go our separate ways."

She turned and started walking quickly to the end of the pool and the inner stairwell. He went after her but just then, two young women in string bikinis appeared and spoke to her. She nodded and hurried on. The two women approached him, towels over their shoulders. He'd seen them before. He was sure they knew who he was. He and Nicole had had many noisy battles in and around her condo.

Were they smiling at him or smirking?

He walked back to the front gate before they could get any closer. Before he could get a good look at their amusement and scorn. People loved to feel superior. And by now he was probably legendary in these condos as the married cop who wouldn't leave the beautiful real estate agent alone, even when she pleaded with him to do so.

He had no energy left. It had all been spent in the few minutes he'd been with Nicole. And she wasn't his only problem.

There was a teenage girl missing and he had a pretty good idea who'd taken her. A man he should have turned in a couple months ago. But now he couldn't turn him in. Not without turning himself in and facing a very long prison sentence.

Leo Rice was back in his car several minutes before Steve Scanlon left the pool area and walked, shoulders slumped, to his own. Rice had followed him here and then risked going to the swimming pool entrance to see whom he was visiting. The woman, whoever she was, was a no-doubt beauty.

He hadn't yet been able to figure out who the older guy with the woman was. But he didn't have any trouble reading the pantomime between Steve and the woman. She had been alternately angry, melancholy and angry again, though less so than the first time.

The breaking-up syndrome. Rice had never experienced it himself. Women were pussy. The only real female friend he'd ever had was his aunt. But he'd heard plenty of breakup stories in Joliet. Even some of the deadliest cons in there had breakup stories. And no matter how they tried to cover it with anger it was all too easy to hear the hurt in their voices. Bitches really fucked them up.

So Leo Rice had lucked out. A man this crazed over a woman, a man so miserable, would be fun to watch for a brief while before killing him.

He gave the cop half a block head start and then began following him again.

CHAPTER SEVENTEEN

The temperature was cooling and dusk was upon them. There seemed to be as many fireflies as stars. Five-year-old Beth sat next to her Uncle Michael. To reach the table she needed three hardcover books for support. She wore a Miley Cyrus T-shirt and a pair of jeans. Her brother wore an Iron Man T-shirt and a pair of jeans.

Wendy also wore a T-shirt, a white one unadorned with pop culture references. Light from the small battery-run lantern illuminated the bowls of sloppy joes, potato salad and kid-dreaded carrots and broccoli. It also burnished Wendy's face with a soft golden glow. Wendy was one of those women people always called attractive. Beautiful didn't describe her, nor did cute, nor did even pretty, exactly. But there was something appealing in that small cheerful face that had always made Michael happy. She was the kid sister except for the slender body. The body was definitely for mature adults, though given her penchant for loose blouses and pants it was almost a state secret. She'd told him once that she dressed modestly because of the junior and senior boys she taught. They were bold enough without any added encouragement.

"You finish that sandwich, honey, then I'm going to take you and Nick up for your baths and tuck you in bed."

"I want Uncle Michael to pitch me the ball." Beth was a Wiffle-ball fanatic.

"A little dark for that, sweetie," Michael said, lifting her up and setting her on his lap. "I'll come earlier next time."

"I hit a good one yesterday. I wanted to show you."

"Well, you'll be even better the next time-you show me." One of those ridiculous things grown-ups say to kids.

"There's beer in the fridge," Wendy said to Michael. "Why don't you grab one and watch a little TV? I should be done in twenty minutes or so. If you don't mind."

"I need to make a few calls, anyway. That missing girl still hasn't turned up."

"I'm afraid to let these two out of the house anymore." She leaned down and kissed little Nick on the head. "I remember how people said it was so bad when I was growing up. Those look like the good old days now."

He found a pilsner glass and filled it with a can of generic beer. He smiled at that. She'd come from a poor neighborhood and was frugal to the point of pain because of it. This was one of the many clashes she'd had with Steve over the years. He had never been able to hang on to money because of his gambling.

Bad enough before that goddamned casino docked up on the river. In the three years that it had been destroying families and promoting crime, Wendy's frugality was the only thing that had kept them afloat. Steve had taken to spending a good share of the paycheck before bringing it home. The way drunkards did. But addictions were addictions. Wendy had talked to him, Michael had talked to him and the old man had talked to him. It broke the old man's heart.

Doris Scanlon had died five years ago of a heart attack. No medical history of it. The old man had been sixty-three years old. He had been a detective for thirty years and a uniformed man before that. But he lost interest in his work and retired. One week into retirement he had a stroke.

Once Michael was sitting in the living room he used his cell to call the security man at the mall. He'd talked to him just before five o'clock.

"You plannin' on stopping out yet tonight?"

"Maybe in an hour or so."

"Well, we're ready for you. We've got the tape from that part of the lot. We're going through it now. Maybe we'll have something for you by then."

"Thanks."

His second call was to the precinct to see if there was anything new on the bank robber they'd been looking for or on Cindy. Nothing on either one.

He was just putting the cell back into his suit coat pocket when his pilsner glass was magically lifted from the end table and filled with golden brew again.

"Sorry I'm so cheap. I probably should have stopped and bought you some Budweiser. But I'm always in a hurry to get home and get the kids from the daycare center."

He hoisted his glass like some dumb shit in a commercial. "This may be the best beer a man ever had."

She had a little-girl laugh that he'd always enjoyed hearing. "Yes, to a man who's too polite to tell you it tastes awful."

She went over to the couch and sat down. The living room was small but appealing, with a fireplace and built-in bookcases on either side of it. The three framed paintings were colorful and modern but comprehensible. And the well-kept hardwood floors and Persian rug gave the room a real sense of style.

"I want you to know that I found these by accident.

As often as I've been tempted to go through Steve's things, I've always resisted. And not because I'm such a highly moral person, either. It's because I'm afraid of what I'll find."

Whatever she'd found he already knew was going to be bad.

She plucked an envelope from the arm of the couch. He watched as she withdrew what appeared to be some kind of credit statement. She unfolded it. Visa.

"Steve left this in his gym bag. He's always been forgetful but lately he's worse than ever. Anyway, I always take his gym clothes and throw them in the wash. That's how I found this. It's for an account I didn't know he had. It's set up in the name of J. T. Scanlon. He's been running up to five thousand dollars a month for the past two months on this account. Pays it off promptly."

Where the hell was Steve getting five thousand dollars a month?

"And here are some of the items he charged this past month. Lingerie. Perfume. Jewelry. A weekend in Chicago—the one where he told me he was going to a law enforcement conference. And a new suit for himself. A suit I've never seen."

His instinct was to say that maybe there was some rational explanation for this. That somehow it couldn't possibly be what it seemed. She'd been aware of some of his one-night stands in the past. At last count they'd been to three different marriage counselors. She fought relentlessly to hold the marriage together. She'd had a child's faith in the notion that he would change someday. That this would all be worth it.

But now she knew better. And so did Michael.

She dropped the credit statement in her lap and laid her head back and closed her eyes. They sat in the terrible silence.

"I always knew one of his little flings would get serious. You don't spend all this time and all this money on just anybody."

"I'm sorry, Wendy."

She sat up straight. "You're sorry and I'm sorry. I'm sorry for me, to be honest. But mostly I'm sorry for the kids."

"Me, too."

"I don't even care where he's getting all this money. Cops have ways."

"Sure. And you don't find many cops who don't take a little on the side once in awhile. Do somebody a favor and get yourself five or six hundred. But not this kind of money. This is serious money."

"You think he's in trouble?"

"I don't know but I'm going to find out."

"He'll resent you for getting involved. You two have had a pretty delicate relationship ever since you took my side a few years ago."

"I just don't want our father to hear about this. It'd kill him."

She closed her eyes again. Sighed. "He's such a sweetie. The kids love him so much. And so do I."

"He feels the same about you. He's always happy to see me or Steve. But nobody makes him as happy as you do. You remind him of our mother, I think."

The phone rang. The way she stared at it sitting there in its plum-colored plastic casing, she seemed not to understand what it was. Or how it worked. Or how she was supposed to respond to the ringing. Then she was on her feet. She swiped the receiver up and put it to her ear.

"Hello." Pause. Irritation. "You people aren't supposed to be able to call us." She slammed the phone down and flung herself with great exasperation toward the couch. "Assholes." Then: "Telemarketers. You can tell how upset I am. I'm careful never to use dirty words because if I use them at school, then they'll likely come out at home. The kids will pick them up soon enough without me helping them."

"Has he been coming home every night?" Michael asked as she seated herself again.

"Oh, he comes home. Late. Usually drunk. A lot of the time he grabs a blanket and sleeps on the couch. It can't be very good for him. But he gets up and goes to work."

"Do you ever sit down and talk?"

"I try. I'm always up before he is so I make breakfast for him. But he always says he's too groggy to talk in the morning so we'll talk at night. Which obviously never happens, either. He's having an affair, Michael. This isn't just one of his little girlfriends. All my friends hated me for putting up with them. They thought I should have left him a long time ago. But the girlfriends never affected our marriage, oddly enough."

"You never told me any of this before."

"I was ashamed. Ashamed of myself, I guess. And ashamed of Steve. I didn't want it to get back to your father. I didn't want him to know. The way he's always idolized Steve—"

"You're sure this is a woman. Not gambling."

"I thought of that. But I could always tell when he was gambling. He had to use his paycheck. It was pretty easy keeping track of him. But now he brings his paycheck home and it's all there. He used to cash it before bringing it home when he was gambling." She paused. "But I have wondered about his clothes."

"His clothes?"

"Two new suits. And some shirts. I keep looking to see them on one of our charge accounts but they never show up. And I know they're expensive."

"How is he around the kids?"

"Oh, he loves them. That's obvious. But lately he treats them like he treats me. Doesn't pay a lot of attention to them. And it gets to them, especially Beth. The other night I found her crying and she said she didn't think her daddy loved her anymore."

As he listened, Michael felt alternately angry at and sorry for his brother. Much of the trouble Steve had gotten in over the years involved women who'd proved elusive. Despite his looks and success with most women, he always gravitated to women who were unattainable. That was one reason family and friends were surprised when he married a sensible woman like Wendy. But even there Michael had always felt Steve had done so in reaction to a demeaning relationship he'd had with a powerful female attorney from Chicago. Steve had still been a patrol cop then and he'd gotten in trouble for driving back and forth to the big city so often in a month's time. He'd come to work on a few hours' sleep. He'd become irascible with his fellow officers. And one time he'd had something like a meltdown in the locker room following a phone call from the lawyer telling him that she wanted to break things off. None of this tallied with Steve's exterior self—the macho, handsome, reckless lover boy that so many women in the local clubs still wanted in their beds.

"I need to talk to him."

"He'll resent it."

"I don't give a damn if he resents it. I don't want any of this to get back to Dad. That's one thing. And the other is what he's doing to you and the kids."

"I still love him as much as I ever have. I almost wish I didn't."

He wanted to stay here. One of the things he missed about his first marriage was the sense of home it had given him. A nice apartment. Nights spent eating late and watching TV and making love before going to sleep. A mate in the morning and a weekend of thinking of new things to do. A home like this one. A wife like this one.

"I'm sorry I dragged you into this."

"It's time I got involved. I can't order him to do anything but I can talk to him. Reason with him. Or try to, anyway."

"Maybe he's really in love this time. Maybe he can't help himself."

"You think you could handle that?"

"What choice would I have?"

There wasn't much he could say to that.

At the door he held her. She clung to him like a child to a parent. She was such a damned good woman.

"I'll do what I can," he whispered and kissed her on the forehead.

CHAPTER EIGHTEEN

Other than the fact that she didn't feel as well-dressed, attractive, intelligent or witty as the other women in the candle-flickering shadows of the country club dining room, Kim was enjoying herself. Having come from a working-class family, she had naturally believed that wealthy people weren't as warm and compassionate as the folks she'd grown up with in her old neighborhood.

This prejudice had quickly been put to rest when she began wearing her first police officer's uniform. Bad people came from every walk of life. And surprise of surprises, some of the wealthy people she'd met had been decent and helpful and honest.

Leaving her, tonight, unable to blame anybody else for her discomfort. She just didn't belong here.

But she did enjoy the sights. The dining room offered views of the tennis courts, the swimming pool, the first three holes of the golf course. And against the brilliant stars she could see the lights of aircraft large and small.

She wished she could relax, let the wine (who knew from wine? The good doctor had ordered it) have its intended effect.

"You look lovely in that dress."

"Oh, yes, downright beautiful."

"And the fact that you can't take a compliment makes you all the more lovely to me. I'm surrounded by egomaniacs and narcissists." And then that glorious patrician smile. "Myself included, of course." The smile was replaced by a frown. "I'm sorry I've neglected you. Is this helping any?"

"If I keep drinking it'll probably help a lot." Not wanting to admit the way she felt out of place here or the confusion she felt about him. She would always live at his mercy, she knew that. She didn't like to think of herself that way.

"Then I'll order a gallon the next time the waiter comes by."

A gray-haired waiter in a white jacket was there. Asking if the meal had been satisfactory.

"Excellent for me. Kim?"

"Me, too," she said. The middle-aged waiter smiled and gave a half bow. "The lobster risotto is becoming one of our most popular dishes. Is there anything else?"

Kim shook her head.

"I guess not, Ken. Thank you."

"Thank you, Doctor." He nodded at Kim and left.

"I don't remember seeing him at McDonalds," Kim said, joking to make herself feel better.

Olson laughed. "You mean they don't have waiters there?"

"Oh, that's right, you've probably never been there. I don't think they let Testarossas in the parking lot." The ride over here had been an event in itself. The power of the engine. The sleek, unerring, missilelike way it held the road. "I guess we live pretty different lives."

"I think we went through that on our first date, remember? That's a bit melodramatic in my case. Most of the time I'm only dealing with everyday illnesses."

"Me, too."

"But you're a detective. You deal with violence. Are you as busy as usual?"

"I've got open cases involving a car theft ring and an embezzler. The worst is trying to locate this drug gang member who's afraid to testify against his friend. His friend happened to accidentally shoot a six-year-old in the leg. He was trying to kill another gang member but he missed."

"I'm afraid I'd be judge and executioner if I had to deal with people like that."

"We talked about that, too, on our first date."

"That was a great first date, Kim. Best I've ever had. I just wish you didn't have to work so hard. And then you've got this girl who's missing now on top of everything."

Kim took a long sip of wine. She needed it when she thought of the skulls that had been delivered to the parents of the two girls. "We're hoping nobody kidnapped her."

"I have a special interest in this. Cindy's been my patient for a couple of years."

"I didn't know that. What's your impression of her?"

"Nice kid. Bright. Decent. But her parents are hopeless." He quickly sketched in Cindy's home life.

"Then she could be a candidate for running away."

"Possibly."

"We look for patterns. The other two girls came from very solid middle-class homes. We knew right away that it was unlikely that they'd just taken off."

"But no leads on Cindy at all?"

"I wish there were."

"If there's any way I can help—"

He paused. On a small bandstand opposite the dining area a four-piece combo—piano, upright bass, drums and trumpet—began to play.

Kim recognized the song within four bars. " 'Laura.' "

"You must like the standards. So do I."

"I didn't have much choice where 'Laura' is concerned. It's my grandmother's favorite song. Whenever she babysat me she played this old Sinatra album. She always sang along with 'Laura.' And I have to admit it's pretty romantic."

"Romantic enough to dance to?"

Dance? Kim thought. I have been known to get out there and pretend that I know what I'm doing. After a few drinks, especially. But dancing as in endangering my partner's feet? This could be where I completely disillusion the poor doctor. He'll find out what a klutz I am.

But while she was thinking about it he pushed back from the table and stepped to her chair. He reached down and took her hand. She couldn't refuse him. And a few minutes later she was in his arms on the polished hardwood dance floor, feeling the power of his strong body as he gently guided her through the steps.

She wanted to break it off—leave his arms, tell him it was over. But she knew she wouldn't. She was doomed to loving him.

The next song was "Stella by Starlight," another Sinatra song her grandmother had frequently played. Because the combo went into it immediately after ending their first number, the dance partners never separated. There were several couples on the floor now and they all seemed to be as intimately happy as Kim and Peter.

"You're really a good dancer."

"Flatterer."

They danced on. And the longer they did the more comfortable she felt with him.

But finally the spell was broken. She needed to visit the ladies'. It was impossible to sustain romance when your bladder was revolting.

"If I mysteriously disappeared for a few minutes would you be here when I got back?"

"Unless I happen to meet somebody else and get married."

"I guess I'll have to risk that."

Just as she was turning to go, he said, "Let's make sure we have a great weekend together."

She turned back to him and kissed him full on the mouth.

"I'd let that lady arrest me any time she wanted to."

A hand on Olson's shoulder. The voice could have been any middle-aged male member of the country club. They were all fascinated with his choice of dates. A lady cop, especially an attractive one, intrigued men with over-lacquered, over-pampered wives.

"I'm lucky, that's for sure," Olson said, not looking up to see who'd actually spoken. Then he drifted away.

Tonight he wanted to find out if there was any information on Cindy. He'd originally started seeing Kim because he liked the irony of it. Killer and cop. And cop without a clue. By now he'd even come to like her in certain ways, though one night when she'd stayed over he'd had to stop himself from stabbing her in her sleep. He'd ended up in the first-floor bathroom masturbating and drenching his face in cold water. He would never get away with killing her. The urge passed and he went back upstairs and slept the rest of the night with her.

Kim sat down. She smelled of fresh lipstick and perfume. "Thanks for not getting married while I was gone."

"Well, I came close but I decided I'd better wait." The copyrighted Peter Olson smile. "See what the future holds."

"It's fun to think about, isn't it? The future?"

"Indeed it is," he said, "indeed it is."

Little Cindy waiting for him in the carriage house.

CHAPTER NINETEEN

As he stood inside the front door of The Golden Cage watching all the young female customers parade themselves around in the upscale bar as if they were in some kind of nookie contest, Rice decided that when it was all over and Steve Scanlon was dead, the only two things he was going to do for a full week were drink whiskey and fuck eighteen-year-old chicks. He'd be in Mexico and while he wasn't too keen on the prospect of Mex chicks, what the hell. He'd clean them up real good and then ream them out of their empty minds. In prison there were men who pined for wives and girlfriends. Rice had always had the looks to make any kind of commitment unnecessary. Couple weeks, maybe a month was the longest he could stand to be with the same woman.

The Golden Cage was noisy, shadowy, crowded. From what he could tell, the ages here ran around thirty for men and maybe six, seven years younger for women. The men wore subdued sports shirts and dark slacks. Their hair was cut as carefully as the women's. They radiated the kind of arrogance that made Rice want to kill them. Take a couple of them outside and cut them up and then set them on fire. Maybe do likewise with the chick who was just now looking him over, pleased with the handsome face and muscular body but leery of the karma. She probably had a few thousand stashed in her twat. He'd dated a rich bitch once. She was lucky to be alive. This rich bitch smiled anxiously and then hurried away.

A long bar, a wide but shallow dance floor, speakers that threatened to separate the place from its foundation. Strobe lights creating a visual excitement that made everybody dancing look a lot better than they would in normal light. Though smoking wasn't allowed, the aroma of pot drifted through the place. The restrooms were probably drug dens.

The men who watched him walk the length of the bar knew immediately that he wasn't one of them. The face compelling but somehow crude. The rage in the eyes unsettling. No doubt the chocolate-and-vanilla duo that guarded the front door would come trailing him inside in a few minutes. Checking him out. Seeing if he'd caused any trouble.

The bartender looked gay. Very thin, pretty blond boy. Lot of men in prison would have liked him. A lot. He smiled like a girl.

Rice had to shout. "Budweiser."

"You bet." The bartender shouted right back.

As he drank his beer he wondered if the pickup would be as easy as Nolan had promised him it would be. *Hey, she's my wife and she runs this place for me. How's she gonna say no? Last time she visited I told her about you getting out and that she might have to help you a little. How's she gonna turn you down, man?* Just luck, coincidence that Rice had known somebody in stir who was connected to Skylar.

He could have picked up a gun from his aunt but an ex-con traveling with a gun was a stupid idea. Anything could happen when you traveled. Could be something you didn't have anything to do with and then some cop gets some kind of dog sense about you (cops could catch a criminal scent the way hunting dogs could scent quail) and he'd be back in Joliet.

So the connection had to be made here, tonight.

When he was ready to ask where he could find Polly, a female bartender stood in front of him asking him if he wanted a refill. Not much in the face but the way her store-boughts pressed against her summery yellow blouse reminded him of how much he wanted and needed a woman. But he had decided to wait until after Steve Scanlon was dead. He needed to focus. Women were a nuisance.

"How do I see Polly?"

More shouting.

"Polly the owner?"

He nodded.

"Any special reason you want to see her?"

"None of your business."

"Hey, nice talk."

"How do I see her?"

"Brenda!" another bartender hollered from midway down the bar.

She, apparently, was Brenda. She glanced down the bar where four waitresses had collected. Looking impatient. "You have to talk to the two men at the front door," she told Rice.

She hurried away.

The black monster had only one earring. The white monster had two. They both wore red muscle shirts so they could show off their steroid consumption. They were flirting with a pair of girls in miniskirts and sequined tops.

Neither man appreciated being interrupted by Rice.

"You want somethin', man?" the black bouncer snapped.

"I need to see Polly."

"Nobody sees Polly."

"Who's Polly?" one of the girls said to the other.

"That's not my understanding."

The white bouncer grinned. "What the fuck is that supposed to mean?"

"It means I was told by her husband to ask for her when I got in town and that she's going to be very pissed off if you two clowns stop me from seeing her."

He didn't have a chance against them physically but he knew that once he dropped Nolan's name they didn't risk moving on him.

"Nolan ain't here, in case you haven't heard." White.

"I know. He's in Joliet. So was I till about a month ago."

"Joliet? Isn't that where the prison is?" one of the girls said to the other.

"How do we know that's true?" Black.

"You don't. You call Polly and you tell her that Rice is here and that Nolan said to tell her that I brought a gift for Sarah Jane."

By this time the girls had stepped back a foot. Convicts were people you saw on true-crime shows and what they did to women you didn't want to even *think* about.

"Wait here." Black. He stepped away and used his cell. Spent less than a minute and then said, "This dude and me are gonna see Polly."

To the girls he said, "You go in and have yourselves some fun."

The girls giggled. One of them looked at Rice and said, "He's kind of scary."

They sucked themselves up so they wouldn't have to brush against Rice as they went inside.

"Guess they don't like you." Even the grin was steroid big.

Rice just watched the traffic on the street outside. Big firefly headlights in the muggy darkness. Smells of chink food from the place next door. Odor of rain.

"Follow me." Black.

The men at the bar, trying to look cool and sly, forgot nookie long enough to wonder where the big bouncer was leading the angry-looking dude. Neither man paid them any attention. And when he came to knots of people the black man skillfully parted them without getting rough or hurting feelings. And they continued straight on back to a metal door that had no handle.

The bouncer used his cell phone. He said a few words. Rice didn't catch any of them. A sharp buzzing sound and the door opened. The bouncer pulled it wide and said, "It's the office directly back from here. She's waiting for you. Hurry up. I got to get back to the door."

Then Rice found himself standing in a long narrow hallway lighted with widely spaced wall sconces. Drywall painted a deep red lent the constricted confines a hellish cast. In the middle of the hall was a conventional door with a conventional knob. No security gizmos.

From the door a woman of forty or so emerged. Her years as a competitive swimmer had kept her as lithe as a much younger woman. Even from here Rice could see the impish, sensual quality of the finely made face. He'd seen many photographs of her. Nolan had bragged on her. And with good reason. In her pink, belted dress, her dark hair cut fashionably short, she had a strange impact on Rice. Like one of those corny movies where a man dreams of a sexy woman and that sexy woman somehow comes to life.

Polly Nolan came forward like a politician working

a room, with her hand outstretched and a smile shining in her dark eyes. "It's so nice to finally meet you. You're one of the few reasons Ron is able to stay sane in that place. I'm worried about him now that you're out."

The touch of her hand in his made him wonder if he didn't need a woman after all. And not wait until Steve Scanlon was dead. He'd have to look into a hooker when he got back to his motel tonight.

"C'mon back and let's have a drink."

The office was short on personality and long on efficiency. Two mahogany desks complete with computers, four filing cabinets in a row, a security screen that let her see what was going on in the bar. On one desk was a large framed color photograph of Nolan and herself taken probably ten years ago. She hadn't lost much of her beauty. The same couldn't be said for Nolan. In the photo he was a robust, handsome, confident-looking man. These days he'd lost thirty pounds and his skin was almost as gray as his hair.

A small dark blue couch flecked with traces of gold was jammed up against the west wall.

"We're redecorating my office in the middle of the hall so everything got pushed into here. I miss having all my usual things around me."

She said this as she brought him the scotch straight up he'd asked for. She'd taken the same. She kept the liquor in one of the drawers in the filing cabinet. "Nice dry bar," she smiled. "And I don't know if Ron told you but 'Sarah Jane' was the name of my collie when I was a little girl. I still have dreams about her."

She perched herself on one end of the small couch and handed him his drink. "How's he doing in there? I still remember that night. We'd had a fight and he got in the new Lexus right after we closed up for the night and took off. Very, very drunk. He hit that car with the two teenagers in it about an hour later. It was probably my fault as much as his. I was in my 'bitch' phase back then. I'm sure he wouldn't have been in that accident if I hadn't been on his case."

She talked too much, which he didn't like. But the translucent skin, the gleaming dark eyes and the erotically full mouth he liked a lot.

"He's doing all right."

"He hasn't turned queer, has he?"

The jokey way she said it surprised him. Kidding on the square. "Not Ron."

"How about you?"

"Not me, either, Mrs. Nolan. But I'm not here to socialize. I've got things I need to do. I'm hoping you've got the gun Ron arranged for me."

She leaned back against the couch. Made a face. "I shouldn't have said that. About Ron. I was just having a little fun. That's what I meant about my 'bitch' phase. I think I'm being funny but people take me seriously."

She was starting to sound like she was on *Oprah*. She didn't seem to have any reality outside herself. He wished he didn't want to rip her clothes off as badly as he did. He killed his drink, stood up. "I really need to get going."

Then she was on her feet and standing within inches of him. "I knew you'd be here sooner or later. So I got the rifle you need. A .270 caliber Remington Model 700. And with a very expensive scope. But I also couldn't stop thinking about how much I miss Ron. Sleeping with him, I mean. He's a great lover." The dark eyes grew dreamy. She was some actress. Knew how to handle every moment. "I get so lonely. I know it's not easy for Ron. But it's not easy for me, either."

With a single blunt finger shoved into her chest, he pushed her away from him. "He'd know, Mrs. Nolan."

"And how would he know if we never told him?"

"He'd know the next time you visited him."

"Well, I haven't been completely chaste, you know. I'm not proud of it but I have to go on with my life. And he doesn't know about any of them."

"He'd know if *I* was one of your little boyfriends. The first time one of you mentioned me he'd see it on your face and I'd never want to do that to him."

"A man of honor." Her bitch phase. She hadn't been kidding. She walked over to a sliding closet door, pushed it back, reached up on tiptoes. He watched the play of the muscles in her calves. She had good legs. She brought down a long rifle case.

"I was hoping we could be friends."

"Not that kind of friends, Mrs. Nolan."

"Maybe you weren't being honest about Ronnie. Or yourself. Maybe you and he got a lot closer in there than you care to admit." Then: "My bitch phase. I'm just pissed that you want me but you won't do anything about it."

She was some piece of ass. Treacherous as hell. Nolan was probably safer in prison. How long had Rice been in here anyway? A few minutes. And they were down to this already? "You don't want to make me mad, Mrs. Nolan. You wouldn't like me when I'm like that."

He walked over to her and yanked the rifle from her hand. He grabbed the two boxes of shells from the desk. And then without warning he slapped her hard enough to draw blood on the corner of her mouth.

"He loves you, Mrs. Nolan. Personally I'd cut your throat. But he loves you. And so I'll never tell him about this for his sake."

"You bastard," she said.

He didn't feel good about anything until he was in his car with the windows rolled down and the night air killing her scent.

CHAPTER TWENTY

The carriage house was over a hundred years old and had been refurbished four times down the decades. It had gone from housing buggies and carriages to being home to Model T's and the Stutz-Bearcats then Packards and in later years became a museum of sorts, Peter Olson having had craftsmen fill the ground level with artifacts from every historical era. The rear door had been taken out five years ago and was now a wall. The windows were curtained and entrance was possible only with an electronic security card. The front door had been reinforced.

Upstairs in the atticlike room was where he killed them. The lime pit was where he destroyed them, three hundred feet into the woods behind the structure, the most impenetrable part of the rolling estate. The room required the same security card as the front door.

The plastic sheeting that enveloped the cot where they slept, the table where they were killed and the tripod where he set his camera had the smell—at least to him—of surgical gloves.

He went over and stood above her much as he would with a patient in the hospital. He eased the covers down. Her breasts shaped the top of her sleepshirt. Very sweet breasts. She'd kept trying to cover them as he'd raped her. Irrational that she should protect her breasts while he was violating her but women's motives had always eluded him. Creatures unto themselves.

He could see that she was trying to focus. Her deep blue eyes seemed to be trying to separate him from her dreams. Was he real? She moaned and then yawned. Her breath was foul and he leaned back away from it.

Dry lips parted. "You're my friend, Dr. Olson."

"Yes. Yes, I am, Cindy."

The tears came in spurts. She would cry and then she would put her hands to her eyes and rub. The confusion was a typical reaction to the drugs he'd given her. Confusion and an inability to act on feelings. Without the drugs she would have been shrieking at him, maybe even pounding on him with those little hands. Telling him what a creep he was, telling him that they would find her and kill him when they did.

"You're my doctor."

"Yes."

Mumbled: "So sore."

"You'll be fine. The pain should be gone by tomorrow."

Muttered: "Trusted you." Then: "Those other two girls—you killed them, didn't you?"

"Yes."

Sobbing now. Despite the drugs she understood the implications of her words. He would kill her, too. "But you were my friend."

Just watching her now.

"Please let me go." A surge of energy. Clutching his arm. "Please let me go."

"I can't, Cindy. Even if I wanted to I couldn't. Not now."

"But to just kill somebody—"

She tried to sit up. She had no strength left. Spider webs of spittle connected her lips. Her eyes still hadn't focused properly. She fell back against her pillow.

"Please," she said, "please." She was slipping back into sleep.

"Go to sleep, Cindy. You're tired. And it's better for you when you sleep."

He stood up, eager to be away from the stench of her. He could see that she was trying to rally for one last plea. But it was too late for her and in moments she was snoring.

He flipped off the light, stepped outside the room and used the card to lock the door.

CHAPTER TWENTY-ONE

He was two drinks and four phone calls down, Steve Scanlon was.

He'd chosen the bar at random. Over by the stadium. On the route he frequently took to Nicole's place.

"Another one?"

Scanlon nodded to the bleached-blonde Amazon behind the bar. She wore a pink tank top that was pleading for mercy. When she set a new scotch and water in front of him, she said, "Can't get through, huh?"

"What?"

"Your cell phone. I see you keep punching in a call."

The place was small and empty. He was the only customer at the bar. There were three couples at tables somewhere behind him.

"When my boyfriend and I break up, he always cuts me off on the phone. I keep calling and calling him but the prick won't answer. And it's been that way for five years. We always have the same old arguments and he always does the same old thing with the phone. Really frustrates me. Really pisses me off."

Hearing her talk this way settled him down a bit. Reality. He was so angry and frantic that he felt hermetically sealed. There had been no other reality until she'd started talking.

"Sort of the same situation for me."

"Bad one. Must've been, huh?"

"Very bad. The worst."

"It'll probably be all right. You think it's over but somehow it never is."

He thought of Gargan. He still didn't believe Nicole. Maybe he hadn't slept with her yet but that was clearly his objective. And even Gargan wouldn't be enough for her. He supposed that she was right. Just because she wanted more than simply getting married and raising kids didn't make her a bad woman. Nor did wanting money that would allow her to sustain that lifestyle. That was rational thinking, he knew. But he couldn't be rational for more than a few minutes. He had a murderous, animal need for her. Nothing else mattered.

The Amazon must have seen that he'd slipped back into crazy mode. She put a long, silken hand on his and said, "It'll be all right. Really. Sometimes I think you men take this worse than women do. I saw a TV shrink once who said that's because men aren't used to dealing with their feelings. It freaks them out."

A frigging TV shrink. That was all he needed.

The front door opened and two laughing couples came in. The drunker of the two men shouted, "Hey, Regina, we're gonna liven this place up!"

Regina grinned and waved at them. She moved swiftly to the end of the bar, joining in their merriment.

Steve went back to his cell phone. Punching in the numbers. He knew he would get the "leave a message" robot.

He was stunned when the call went through.

"You never give up, do you, Scanlon?" Gargan. "Now leave Nicole alone or I'll be calling the commissioner. And I mean that." He clicked off.

Not even a pep talk from Regina could help him now.

CHAPTER TWENTY-TWO

The uniformed man who ran the security tape for him was watching professional wrestling when Michael arrived. The shadowed room with the TV set and the videotape machine was small and bare. Two stacks of tapes stretched a few feet up along either wall. The monitors for the live cameras would be out in the front office.

"You're a little early." The thin, red-bearded man could not rip his eyes away from the screen even as he spoke to Michael.

"I didn't realize there was a set time."

"I usually take my break about now." Eyes at least flicking in Michael's direction once, twice.

"Were you able to find the tapes we need to look at?"

"Yeah, sure."

The crowd was going psychotic as a guy dressed as a matador picked up an SS soldier and hurled him out of the ring. If only WWII had been that easy.

As the man watched this, willing Michael out of existence, his hands dug into his front pocket and he withdrew a pack of generic cigarettes. He tamped one out, put it in his mouth, dug out a red plastic lighter, and lighted his cigarette all without once looking away from the screen.

The Nazi was now back in the ring and by the look of things he was mighty pissed off. He charged the matador head down, like a bull, but the steroid-swollen red-garbed figure whipped his cape from around his shoulders and held it out as if he were in the traditional ring of his countrymen. He fanned his cape out. The Nazi made a pass at it but the matador whipped it away at the last minute, and the Nazi went sprawling into the ropes to the delight of the crowd. Now the Nazi regrouped and set himself to charge again while the matador played to the crowd by doing fancy tricks with his cape.

The Nazi, head down, was about to charge again when—

"I guess you didn't read the rule book."

"Huh?" the security man said, forcing himself to pay attention to the detective.

"No smoking in here. And there probably should be a rule about watching wrestling, too."

"Well, shit—" the security man started to protest.

"I'm not trying to be a hardass. Just take your smoke outside."

The security guard stood up and said, "I'll finish this and be right back."

"Good," Michael said, knowing he'd smell like a cigarette by the time he left here, "then we'll get to work."

At the door the guard said, "Thanks for not giving me the speech about not smoking. I got a ten-year-old and she's on my ass 24/7."

CHAPTER TWENTY-THREE

"Norman Rockwell," Olson said as he pulled the Testarossa up to the curb of Kim's small house.

"Pardon?" She'd been looking out the window at the cozy homes on both sides of her street.

"That's what this neighborhood looks like. Norman Rockwell. There are even a few picket fences. I'll bet there are nice old granddads who sit out on those swings every day and dispense wisdom to all the kids in the neighborhood."

"You almost sound sentimental. I can't believe it."

"Well, I don't want to get carried away. But believe it or not, even I think about settling down someday."

"But you'd like to settle in a big house like the one you have. You're not exactly the picket fence type."

But then what did she know about his type?

After he had killed his first girl while attending a medical conference in Denver he began studying psychology to see what had made him do it. Completely impulsive. Seeing a young woman sitting on a bus stop bench several blocks from his hotel. Nobody around. Him sitting down. Her afraid of him at first but then charmed by his good looks and sleek manner. And then slowly, carefully convincing her to go have a drink with him. His car just around the corner. All the while searching for onlookers.

He hadn't even been able to control himself long enough to get her in the car. On the dark side street he slammed her head so hard against a tree that she began bleeding from the ears. Then he proceeded to beat and stomp her to death, ultimately dragging her body into the alley and sliding it under a rusted-out car that was up on blocks.

For the next few months he studied serial killers. He hoped to find some explanation for his behavior. He didn't regret it; he in fact looked forward to killing more women. But he was curious about himself. He had never treated animals cruelly as a boy, he had never suffered from bedwetting, he had never felt unloved by his parents, he had never felt sexually inadequate, he had never indulged in arson or any other type of criminal aberration. His only conclusion was that there was no conclusion to be drawn, no real explanation. He realized that all this profiling the FBI did was little more than a way of calming nerves. If you could identify cause then maybe it wasn't so terrifying. But Olson knew better. He was death waiting to light on someone.

Over the course of eleven murders he developed a procedure that he now followed carefully. Except for this time. This time, the only time, he had succumbed to kidnapping somebody he knew. One of his own patients. Reckless for sure. But it was the recklessness that made it so exciting. Even the sexual thrills had waned the last few times he'd killed. There was pleasure but there wasn't that staggering, dizzying feeling—the grand cosmic orgasm that lasted for days—that was his reward for his risk and trouble. He'd only put the bodies into lime and sent out the skulls to increase the thrill.

The experts would say that he took this kind of chance only because he wanted to be stopped. Caught. Put away. Maybe even executed.

But what better way to guard against being caught than by sleeping with one of the detectives who kept him informed of everything that was going on with the investigation?

She leaned her head on his shoulder. Sometimes tenderness repelled him. As now. "It's a nice thought, though."

"What is?"

"You and picket fences."

"It just might happen."

She yawned. "So much for romance."

He yawned. "Autonomic reaction."

She sat up and said, "I really am tired but I don't want to go in, I guess."

"Well, I'm really tired, too. And I've got to get some sleep. My patients don't appreciate it when I fall asleep while I'm looking down their throats."

"I could see where that could be a problem." Then: "Before I get tempted to start making out, I'll say good night." She gave him a quick kiss on the lips and opened the door. Just before she closed the door, "I really enjoyed tonight. I didn't think I would. But—I did."

"Me, too, Kim. But I think you know that. And please keep me posted on Cindy. I'm just afraid for her."

"I wish her parents cared about her half as much as you do, Peter."

"I just always felt so damned sorry for her," he said, "and now look at what's happened."

CHAPTER TWENTY-FOUR

The parking lot. Night. Grainy lighting.

Cindy walking toward the security camera. A five-year-old Dodge sedan. Forest green. Difficult to see the man inside. He wears a wide-brimmed hat of some kind, probably a fedora. The real problem is the license plate. Because of a shadow, reading the numerals and letters of the plate is impossible. The only thing that can be determined is the state the plates are from. Missouri.

Cindy was meeting somebody from Missouri? Michael wonders.

Internet, maybe. Lonely, desperate girl meets some creep online and begins telling him about herself. He no doubt sounds a lot more attractive and alluring than poor old nerdy Mr. Sullivan. Creep probably pretends he's not too much older than she is. And who knows, maybe he isn't.

He comes to town and she starts seeing him nights after work. The sex is probably inevitable. Sex is what *he's* after. The sex itself won't mean that much to her. But the sex means acceptance, intimacy. She's finally met somebody she knows she can trust with the gift of her virginity. In return for giving it she will be bound up in his love and understanding and protection.

Michael has seen this scenario played out too many times. Usually it ends in an older man having sex with an underage girl. But every once in a while there are catastrophic consequences.

He recalls all too clearly the look of the skulls delivered to the parents of the missing girls. And the dental record confirmations that follow.

"You think this is the guy you're looking for?" the security man asks.

"Don't know yet. But you've got her meeting him in the parking lot twice. They probably met other places, too."

Michael gets on his cell and calls the detective bureau. "How's it going, Jim?"

"Usual bullshit. How about you?"

"The missing girl, I'm looking at videotape from the mall where she worked. They've got two nights of her meeting somebody in the parking lot. Five-year-old Dodge four-door sedan. Forest green. Good condition."

"Any luck with the plates?"

"The first night I can see that the plates are from Missouri. But that's all. The second night he's parked too close to the camera to see anything except the car itself."

"I'll check with the boss and see if he wants to give this to the media."

"Thanks."

"You see the six o'clock news?"

"No, and from the way you said that I can tell I'm *glad* I didn't see it."

"They tore into us. Another missing girl. The guy who sent the skulls. No doubt in their minds. One of them's going to interview the mother."

"The mother's a drunk and probably a druggie. I'm sure Hepburn'll turn her into a saint."

"That's their specialty. Turning people who don't deserve it into saints."

"But right now I'm more worried about the Dodge than anything else."

"Right. I'll get on it."

After thumbing off the cell phone, Michael turns to the security man and says, "Who patrols that area at night?"

"I do, generally. I have a Jeep. I cover all sides of the mall."

"Did you ever see this green Dodge?"

"No. But then I don't start patrolling until around closing time. Making sure there aren't any teenagers getting drunk and smashing bottles everywhere. I've also got jumper cables in case somebody can't get their car started. Winters are a bitch out here. A zoo."

"Then I guess this is all we've got so far."

"Sorry I can't help you more."

"Appreciate what you've done."

He's glad to be in the night air, even if it is still too warm for his liking. He goes to his car and leans against it. Rumble of trucks, screech of fast cars getting off the mark, the night-hush of the whole vast Midwest rolling across the farm fields and forested areas.

The first call he makes is to Wendy. "Just wondered if Steve was home yet?"

"Not yet. Is something wrong?"

"No. I wanted to check in before I went looking for him."

"You don't have to go looking for him, Michael. He'll be home. And you need to get some sleep."

"I'll be fine."

"I just worry that he's hurt somewhere."

"He'll be fine, Wendy. I'll talk to you soon."

In his car, he opened up his phone book and started punching in the numbers of places his brother might be. There were two bars where cops hung out. There were an additional two bars where civilians drank that Steve also frequented. This was like dragging your old man out of a bar, the way some of his friends had had to do when they were young. He didn't like it, especially not facing Steve's temper. On a few occasions he'd had to haul Steve off somebody when they were fighting. On one occasion he'd watched as Steve picked up a wine bottle and smashed in the windshield of a kid who'd made fun of him. As much as Michael loved and admired him, he'd grown up fearing his brother, dreading the time when Steve suddenly became unrecognizable, became as dangerous and out of control as some of the men they would later arrest.

No luck in any of them.

The Visa bills. All that extra money. Steve had always been a luckless gambler. But had his luck turned? Was he on one of those streaks you read about occasionally?

The Golden Girl riverboat casino was where Steve used to *lose* all his money. Maybe now that was where he was *winning* it.

He thought about calling to see if Steve was there but the drive was less than twenty minutes.

The heat was cooling rapidly. He left the driver's window down. A stretch of interstate was the shortest way there. When he topped the first hill he saw the glistening black sprawl of the river tinted a dozen bright colors by the three-story riverboat. Shimmering green, gold, bloodred.

The parking lot was crowded, with cars gray and grim, with cars boastful and beautiful. It would be the same inside—the gray working class and the beautiful rich. There were something like seven hundred and fifty slots and video machines for the less adventurous and blackjack, craps, roulette and three- and four-card poker for those of a more suicidal nature.

Michael hadn't wanted the riverboat. He knew all the arguments—jobs, money for education, better entertainment on nights out. The jobs he agreed with. The downside, and always scoffed at, was that the mob always came up the river with the riverboats. Not the bent-nose boys or any of Tony Soprano's friends but the mob nonetheless. They were just better dressed, more articulate and only resorted to violence when necessary. And they were the ones who decided when "necessary" was.

He found a spot near the back row and walked to the riverboat. Gambling was apparently good for the libido. He counted three couples making out on his way inside. He assumed they were winners. Or maybe not. Maybe they were going to have solace sex. A good hard grind that would let them forget for a time how much money they'd lost.

He stepped from reality into life inside a pinball machine. He'd always thought of it that way. All the electronic noise from the gambling machines, all the lights, the laughter, the music from the second-floor lounge. Sealed tight.

He recognized a patrolman named Bill Eggers. The man was in uniform. He smiled when he saw Michael. There were always two armed off-duty police officers on the riverboat. In four years there had been only one incident, when a deranged man tried to stab a dealer he claimed was cheating him.

Michael was about to ask the burly but amiable officer if he'd seen Steve but Eggers said, "This must be family night, huh?"

So Steve was on the boat.

"Yeah. I thought I'd stop out and lose a few paychecks."

"Still don't like this place, huh?"

"I'm old-fashioned. Give people a chance to screw up and they'll do it. They don't need any help."

"You sound like a preacher."

Aware of how angry he'd sounded, Michael smiled. "That's my part-time job."

He passed row after row of machines. Women and men of all ages sat on stools in front of them. The machines tainted their faces with various hues and gurgled a variety of computer insults at them when they lost. Many of the people looked to be in a trance. If nothing else they were enhancing their arm strength.

Judging by the way the players were dressed, blackjack and craps were the chic games. Good-looking women in clingy dresses and men in expensive sports shirts and trousers hovered over the tables. A few less fortunate citizens also played but the eye went to the women in their glittery attire and slender, sexual bodies. Steve had probably slept with a few of them. He'd gone through a period when he cheated on Wendy only with married women of the upper classes. Something else neither Wendy nor Michael had ever told the old man.

There were four bars in the casino. To find Steve he had to go up to the second floor. A dark, horseshoe-shaped bar with two very pretty young women bartending. The only real light came from behind the mirror, an ethereal glow that lent a certain elegance to the setting. Floor-to-ceiling windows on either side looked over the river and the dim lights of upscale condos on the opposite shore.

When Steve saw him he frowned. Michael wondered if he'd called home and Wendy had told him about her conversation with Michael.

The redheaded bartender caught Steve's look and

turned to see what had made him unhappy. She had one of those perfect small-featured faces that are worth just sitting down and studying for the pure aesthetic pleasure. She said something to Steve and then left to take care of a customer.

"Room for me?" Michael asked Steve.

"Sure. Why not?"

The redhead glanced down the bar. Did Michael want a drink? He shook his head.

"You're not drinking?"

"Saving it for home. A good strong one. And then I hope six or seven hours' sleep."

For all the intensity his brother radiated there was still a distracted air about him. If he'd talked to Wendy he would have said so by now. The Visa. All the jewelry. All the lingerie.

The woman. That was Steve's problem.

Michael changed his mind. He signaled for the bartender.

"God, I didn't notice before." The perfect little face was perfectly delighted. "This is your brother."

"The Scanlon boys," Steve said. "Pride of the police force."

She offered her hand. She and Michael shook. "This one's on the house."

"I appreciate that. How about a beer? Bud is fine."

"Bud it is." Still delighted, she took her perfect little body and went in search of a Bud.

"Nice looking."

"Not much in the sack."

"Sorry to hear that."

Steve turned to face him. "Long time ago. Before I quit cheating on Wendy."

No point in even answering that kind of bullshit. "I talked to Wendy tonight."

Like an animal that senses mortal danger, Steve
froze, his mind trying to figure out the best response.
"She likes to bitch a lot lately."

"She loves you. She's worried is all."

"She's worried, I'm worried, you're worried, everybody's worried."

Michael said nothing. You had to wait Steve out. He
calmed himself down. If anybody else tried it he simply
got angrier.

The redhead put a bottle and a pilsner glass in front
of Michael. He smiled at her. Steve had his head down.
She shrugged and left.

"Something's going on, Steve. I'd like to help you if
I can."

"The good Samaritan."

"You're my brother."

Another silence. Michael drank his beer. Then:
"Would it help to talk about it?"

"No." Deep sigh. Staring down the bar at the redhead.

"I've never seen you like this before, Steve. It
scares me."

"You have no right to talk to my wife." The anger
again.

"She thinks you're in love with somebody else."

"And if I am, that's *my* business. Not yours."

Michael had foolishly been hoping for a denial. Foolishly.

"She sounds expensive."

"I don't want to talk about her."

"Maybe it's time you talked to Wendy."

"Maybe. But I'm sure as hell not going to do it because
she goes behind my back and calls my little brother so
he can start poking his nose in where it doesn't belong."
His voice was rising again. A glance from the redhead

brought a sigh from him. "I'm going through a bad time is all."

"So is your wife. And so is Dad. And so is the department."

"The department?"

"Cindy Baines? The missing girl? There's a good chance she didn't just run away. I've spent some time on it now. She was seeing somebody after work. Somebody she didn't want anybody else to know about. Or more likely somebody *he* didn't want anybody else to know about."

"What the hell are you talking about?" Half-angry, half-baffled, as if Michael had told him something impossible. "There's a lead on the guy?"

"Yes. Why is that so surprising? It's called police work. If you'd been paying attention you probably could have found this out for yourself."

"What's the description of the car?"

Michael told him about seeing the car on video. And also about the plates. The car could be from out of state or the plates could be stolen to confuse the police.

Steve's antagonism had ebbed over the past few minutes. "I'm sorry, Michael. You're right. I should've spent a lot more time on this today. I got distracted."

"Maybe you could make a little time to see Dad."

"I know. I start to go over there and something always happens."

But that was how Steve had always handled things. The promises. Yada yada yada. Passive-aggressive was the term.

"He misses you."

Blue eyes flashing. "I suppose Wendy's been telling him what a bastard I am."

"Wendy loves our old man. She keeps up a good front for his sake. Not for yours. He doesn't know anything about whoever this new woman is. He wouldn't have known about the others if you hadn't told him yourself when you thought you and Wendy might be splitting up. And you told him so you could pass it off as a few one-night stands instead of running around all the time."

"My brother the altar boy."

"You were an altar boy, too."

"Yeah, but I never bought into all that shit. You did."

"The point is you have to resolve this, Steve. If you want out of the marriage then tell Wendy that. She deserves the truth. It'll hurt her but it's better than you sneaking around. And look at today. You couldn't work on the job because this other thing is making you crazy."

Steve's sigh indicated resignation. "You're right. I've got to get on top of this." More promises. He pushed his hand out and let it rest on his brother's shoulder. "I'm sorry I'm always kidding you about what a saint you are."

"Nobody's ever going to confuse me with a saint, Steve. And you know that. And if it was just you, I wouldn't be so worried. You're responsible for what you do. But this is dragging Wendy and your kids down and eventually the old man's going to hear about it. He doesn't have long to live. You're his favorite son. This would crush him."

Steve's smile was sardonic. "Sometimes I wish you were the one he idolized."

"Pretty hard to do since you were born before I was."

"I know. The firstborn and all that bullshit. But you never gave him the grief I did and he still seemed to favor me. I used to feel sorry for you sometimes. Would've been easier for him and for you if you'd been his favorite." Then he was the familiar Steve, the swashbuckler that

Michael knew best. "And a lot easier for me, too, little brother."

"For you?"

"Sure. Then I could've run around all I wanted and he wouldn't have cared so much."

"There's some twisted logic there, I guess."

Steve laughed. "You've got to lighten up, little brother. I'm the one with all the problems, not you. Right now you and Kim should be in bed planning your wedding."

"I don't think I'm her type."

"You're her type exactly. She just doesn't know it yet. That faggot doctor—" He slid off the stool and stood up. "Now I'm going to try my luck with a little blackjack before I go home."

Now that Michael was standing, Steve did something he rarely did. He hugged him. "Baby brother, I need to be a little more like you and you need to be a little more like me."

Michael wondered why Steve was trembling.

The goddamned sweat. Same as it was prison nights when the heat stayed in the eighties. But here on this hill overlooking the parking lot of the Golden Girl riverboat casino there are mosquitoes to contend with, too. At least the cells didn't have mosquitoes.

Leo Rice is hidden behind a stand of birch trees. The scope on his rifle is fixed on the steps leading from the casino to the parking lot. He has followed Steve Scanlon here and has been waiting for over two hours for the man who murdered his brother to reappear.

Two shots, three shots at most.

At the base of the hill behind him, in another copse of trees, this time pines, he has stashed his rental car. He will run to it only after seeing the man fall to the asphalt. He wants to make sure.

The irritation from the heat makes his mind wander. Different thoughts. Kid brother who'd always needed protecting. The first bank job they'd ever pulled. So smooth it should be in a book somewhere. And neither of them even twenty years old yet. Their old man and the time they started working on a plan to kill him. But somehow he'd figured out what they were doing and mocked them with it. Dared them with it. But they were very young when all this was going down and they backed off.

And then thoughts of Polly Nolan earlier tonight.

Man, there was some bitch all right. But the rod filling his pants back there in her office had made him crazy for half an hour following. Should've fucked her like she wanted and then beaten her up for making him betray his friend Nolan. Maybe he'd get back to the bitch and do just that. He knew a whore once who could only get off if he slapped her around hard for awhile. She was a damned good lay. He'd dreamed of her a lot when he was in Joliet.

They come out in little groups for some reason, all boozy laughter and playing grab-ass and weaving their way to their cars. He's always been jealous of people like these—normal square bullshit people—but he's never been able to understand why. He certainly doesn't want to be like them. They don't have anything he wants aside from money or maybe nookie from their wives. But somehow they make him jealous. And make him feel an odd isolation and loneliness.

He should just open up on all of them now. To hell with waiting for Steve Scanlon. Just open up and cut them down and watch them scream and try to run. Watch them die.

Moonlight tints everything silver on the hill. A stray dirty white mutt walks in front of the trees he's crouched behind. It stops. Swings its mutt head around and looks at him. Sad baffled mutt expression on its face.

He's tempted to waste the mutt, too.

But these are crazy thoughts—he means to do his killing and escape—and he blames it on the heat.

How the hell can a cop spend so much time in a casino? Cops don't make that kind of money. Not even ones who are on the pad. And there is no way this douche bag is winning. One of Leo Rice's most dearly held beliefs is that all games of chance are rigged. And he has always been amazed that people don't understand that. You win, you lose it back soon enough anyway. So why bother getting conned?

And then there he is.

Coming down the stairs from the casino.

No other people in the parking lot now. Just the rock music from the lounge on the second deck and the clamor of the slots on the floor below.

Coming down the stairs and stepping now on to the asphalt.

And Leo Rice firing once, twice. The crack of the shots lost in the bad imitation of the Bruce Springsteen song.

And then the beautiful wonderful miracle moment itself, the way his brother's killer falls to the ground. Just straight down dead. No doubt about it. Just straight down dead.

Quickly collecting the spent cartridges and starting back down the narrow trail between the small spread of trees and undergrowth.

Throwing himself in the car. Ripping through the bumpy grassy ground leading to the street.

Hitting the air-conditioning. High as she'll go.

Oh, man; so good.

And then forcing himself to act like the nice normal

guy he'll never be. Obeying the speed limit. Maybe working late and heading home to the wife and kids. Kind of guy everybody likes. Trusts.

It won't be long now before there will be sirens. And more sirens once it's known that the dead man happens to be a cop.

He starts thinking about Polly Nolan again.

He should have screwed her, no doubt about it.

CHAPTER TWENTY-FIVE

At one point in the aftermath of the shooting a reporter noted that while most of the people in the riverboat casino poured out into the muggy night to see what all the sirens, lights and press trucks were all about, a fair share stayed inside and continued to gamble. Presumably these were the folks who would sooner or later be calling the Gamblers Anonymous hotline begging for help.

Within eighteen minutes of the gunshots, a group of fourteen uniformed officers kept the curious far away from the shooting site while the men and women who worked the crime scene began arriving.

A familiar-looking man leaned against his car. His name was Michael Scanlon. As the press would report later, his life had been saved by one of those stupid little accidents that happen to millions of people every day. Two or three seconds before the rifle had been fired, Michael had dropped his car keys. He had been in the process of bending over to pick them up. When he heard the crack of the gunshots, he flattened himself against the asphalt. Pure cop instinct. The shooter was probably under the impression that he had killed his man.

The man Michael was talking to was his brother Steve, who was saying, "But who the hell would want to kill you?"

"Nobody I can think of."

"Maybe he thought you were somebody else."

Michael had been thinking this himself but wasn't sure how to bring it up without igniting his brother's temper again. He was saved for the moment by the arrival of a big-ass dark blue Chrysler that contained not only the chief of police but also the mayor.

As the two men emerged from the vehicle, the gathering press strained against the restrictions the uniformed officers had put on them. These were the people they most wanted to get statements from. Except for Michael Scanlon himself, of course. But they knew better than to expect him to say anything.

While the gleaming casino set against the backdrop of a full lazy moon offered romance and excitement, the dour red and blue emergency lights and the military-like stream of official vehicles offered something more compelling for the moment. The prospect of a man who had nearly been murdered.

Mayor Tom Elmore was the grandson of Bryce Elmore, the only man who had ever run anything like a political machine in the city. Fifty-three-year-old Tom was the last of the family line. Neither of his children had gone into politics. He looked slim standing next to silver-haired, overweight Chief of Police Bill Hoover.

"I'm just glad you're alive and everything's fine, Michael," Elmore said before he'd quite reached the brothers. In his short-sleeved yellow shirt and tan slacks, he looked ready for a barbeque.

Then the men were shaking hands. Chief Hoover stood off to the side. He was rarely upstaged. But he knew that Elmore was even more rarely upstaged.

"The one question, Michael, the only one that matters right now—any idea who might have done this? Have you been getting any threats lately? Any particularly rough arrests?"

"No. Nothing."

"Thank God you're all right. I don't mind telling you, when Bill called me I was asleep and before my feet hit the floor I was scared as hell. This wasn't some robbery where some cop gets shot by a punk with a gun. This was premeditated murder."

"Well," Hoover said, coming over to be included in the discussion. "That's what it looks like but there are other possibilities."

"That's what I was thinking," Michael said. "What if it was somebody who wanted to get back at the casino for some reason? So he starts killing people who come here to gamble. Make it hard for the casino to stay open."

"I doubt it," Elmore said. He didn't elaborate. But then he never did. When he said something it was obvious he just assumed it was being hammered into stone tablets somewhere. "This is a case of a man with a vendetta against one of our detectives. And a damned fine one at that."

This was the first draft of the speech Elmore would give to the press before the night was over. The rumor was that sometimes he sat in his office watching videos of himself pontificating at various functions. Easy to imagine.

"This on top of the missing Baines girl," the mayor said, "this city is going to look like shit on the news."

"Here *and* Chicago," the chief said.

Up on the hill the various members of the crime scene team were at work with large lights and small. The people working on the trail and behind trees flashed their ghostly beams while the larger lights gave everything the look of eerie day.

Now that the promise of blood had been broken, the gamblers who'd rushed out of the casino started drifting back inside. If they'd had to buy tickets for this nonevent they would probably be demanding their money back.

"You sure you're all right?" the chief asked Michael.

"Yes."

The chief glanced at Steve. "Take care of him, Steve. Babysit him if you have to. We don't know what the hell's going on here yet." This was the kind of TV dialogue the chief always spoke when the mayor was around. He had learned *how* to speak it from the mayor himself.

Steve smiled at his brother. They sometimes laughed about the chief and his snappy patter. They liked the man but as with most public officials he had a clown side, too. But hell, as Michael often pointed out, so did they.

"You sure you don't need to go to the ER?" the mayor said.

"I'm fine."

"Damned lucky is what you are. Some bastard with a rifle. Think about those two killers who worked DC several years ago. A sniper can bring a city to a standstill."

"I'd better go check on how everything's going," the chief said.

"Good idea. I'll go with you."

Just what we need, Michael thought. The mayor kibitzing on a crime scene investigation. He was one of those men who always had to give an opinion to show that he was seriously involved in whatever was going on. That his opinion was frequently useless didn't seem to bother him.

"You really all right?" Steve said when they were alone and walking to their cars.

"Bruised knee's about all. Like the mayor said, I'm damned lucky."

"It doesn't make sense. You don't have those kinds of enemies."

Michael knew he would have to say it. He also knew that Steve would find his anger within thirty seconds.

"You're going to be pissed, Steve. But maybe he got us confused."

"What the hell're you talking about?" Already an edge on his voice.

"I don't have those kinds of enemies, but you do."

"Bullshit."

"All the married women you've slept with. All the fights you've had."

"Don't try and put this shit on me. We don't even know that he knew who he was shooting at. Maybe he was just shooting to kill anybody he could pull into range."

"Maybe. But it's something we have to consider."

They were at Michael's car. "Something *you* have to consider. Not me, man. I've got problems enough of my own."

The real anger never came, surprising Michael. Whatever his brother was going through seemed to have captured his mind completely. No room left for any other shocks.

"You all right?" Michael said.

Steve's smile was cold. "You're the one who was shot at and you're asking me if *I'm* all right?"

"Yeah, because I'm worried about you."

"Well, I'm worried about you, too, so that makes us even. And that means you should knock this crap off. I don't need you hovering over me."

This was the Steve he'd been expecting. Not anywhere near rage but irritable, pissy.

"You take care of you, I'll take care of me. All right?"

"Fine by me."

"You know I care about you, brother. It's just sometimes you're real hard to be around. You sound too much like Wendy."

"Yeah, who'd want to sound like Wendy? She's a terrible woman all right."

"Fuck you."

"Well fuck you, too."

And then Steve started walking back to his car, which was parked near the front of the lot.

Scanlon family reunion, Michael thought. I almost get killed and my brother and I have one of our usual arguments over it.

He needed a drink. He needed several drinks.

CHAPTER TWENTY-SIX

Wendy was sitting in the kitchen with a small glass of the inexpensive red wine she drank once daily. She spent half an hour a day online scanning medical websites. Her first priority was the kids. The best way to keep them healthy was to know what to watch for. Symptoms of trouble. When to go to the doctor. What questions to ask. Then she checked on adult health sites for Steve and herself.

She knew that she would have more than one glass of wine tonight. She wondered if confiding in Michael had been the right thing to do. Maybe she had only made things worse. She knew how angry Steve would be when he finally came home tonight. His temper was ugly, frightening. She tried to keep the kids from seeing it but it wasn't always possible. They cowered when they saw it or heard it. How could this be the father they loved? She felt the same way. How could this be the man she loved? She'd threatened to leave him twice. Both times they'd seen counselors. Both times he'd promised to learn how to control his rage. And to be faithful.

This time there would be no counselor, she was sure of it. He had fallen in love with somebody. She thought of how jealous he'd been when they'd first started going out. And had first been married. That was a long time ago. For years now she'd been little more than the woman he came home to. The sex was still good sometimes. He was a wonderful lover. She doubted she'd ever find that particular pleasure with another man.

What a mess it all was.

Car in the driveway. Rumble of garage door going up. Then footsteps and key in the back door.

Her stomach tightened. She wasn't sure she could handle his anger tonight. She'd collected all these words to hurl at him but she felt too numb now to speak them.

"Up sort of late, huh?"

"Yeah."

She didn't look at him. Stared at her glass of wine as he went to the refrigerator and grabbed a beer.

He came over and sat across from her at the table. He did this sometimes, knowing that the tension was a way of punishing her. He'd be quiet for a time as she waited for the explosion. And then it would come and she would cringe in the face of it.

"Talked to Michael tonight," he said.

"I thought you might." Still looking only at her glass.

"If I didn't know better I'd think he had a crush on you. He really likes you."

"He's a good man."

"You ever going to look at me?"

"No."

"Why not?"

"Because I can't stand seeing your face when you start yelling at me."

"Who says I'm going to yell at you?"

She said nothing.

"Everything all right with the kids?"

"Fine."

A long sigh. "I want you to know I'm sorry about all this."

Her head rose slowly and she met his gaze.

"I mean I've really been thinking about what Michael said and he's right. About the way I've treated you and all."

"Who's the woman?"

"I really don't want to talk about that right now."

"Oh. Right. Of course. It's none of my business."

"It's just I'm not ready."

"Ready for what?"

"To talk about it."

"Actually, neither am I." She leaned back in her chair and said, "I had it all planned for when you came home tonight. If you came home tonight. I was going to attack you. Really. Me. I was going to rip into you physically. Just to have the satisfaction."

"Oh Christ, Wendy, I hate to hear you talk like this."

"And then I was going to pack up the kids and drive over to my sister's and move in with her for awhile. But you know what?"

"You're pissed and I don't blame you. But I hate to see you like this. You look—crazy."

"Really? I wonder what would've made me crazy, Steve? It's been such a good marriage." But before he could speak, she said, "You get to live here one more night. You sleep on the couch and then you get up and go to work and then later in the morning when the kids are at daycare you come back here and get everything you need and you move out. You understand?"

"You really want it this way?"

"Yes."

"Wendy, I—"

"Don't say anything, Michael. Just go use the downstairs bathroom and get ready for bed. Then get the blankets out of the closet for the couch."

"Wendy—" But that was all he managed to say.

Then he was gone.

His words didn't matter. She sat there wondering what it would be like for the children and for herself and for their gray future. She would join the ranks of so many single working mothers. All the groups of them who couldn't find decent men to go out with, let alone marry. All the groups of them who were so busy with work and family that they wondered if they were doing an adequate job with either. All the groups of them who networked their frustrations and hopes over endless cups of coffee in the teachers' lounge and at various school functions.

But as bleak as she felt she knew that she would not try for a reconciliation. Did not *want* a reconciliation, even if he later changed his mind. She'd been weak far too long.

And then she smiled. Started snuffling up her tears and smiled.

She was done with him. After all the years of loneliness and humiliation, she was finally finally done with him.

Luck of the draw. Leo Rice drew the black bouncer.

Just after two a.m. Perfect silver moon. Back door of Polly Nolan's bar. Leo sitting on the hood of his rental waiting for her to appear and walk to her black four-door Beemer. Had to be her. The car Nolan bragged on, joking his wife had gone "yuppie" on him.

Drunker than he liked to be but functioning well anyway. Took more drinks than he'd imagined to calm down after killing Steve Scanlon. And in the process he'd started thinking of Polly. That was what he really needed. An hour with her. She'd wanted him. Well now she was going to get him.

Closing time. People shouting, laughing, car engines erupting, headlights exposing the littered parking lot, burst of exhaust fumes, the swaying people who shouldn't be getting behind the wheel, the last-minute make-out artists bold as hell dry-humping right in the middle of the asphalt so that cars had to swerve to get around them. Couldn't even wait to get back to their apartments to stick it in and Leo Rice wasn't about to blame them for that.

And then came the black bouncer.

Way he appeared was sort of officious. Almost comical. Throwing back the door, scanning the back lot like the Secret Service scoping out turf for the president.

All for some cheating little snatch like Polly.

When he saw Rice he fixed on him, then swelled himself up on his steroid ego and began the gunfighter swagger over to the rental.

"You got a good reason for bein' here, dude?"

"Better reason than you do."

"Yeah?"

"Yeah."

Bouncer was already glistening even though the heat had backed off. "I don't want you here, man. And neither does Polly."

"You ever fuck her?"

The hand reached his throat with snakelike stealth. Despite the share of brawls he'd had in his life, nothing had prepared Rice for the absolute merciless grip of the bouncer's enormous hands on him. The man not only cut off his oxygen supply instantly, he also cracked something in the back of Rice's neck. Sending a searing sensation all the way down his back.

Not entirely aware of what was going on, Rice felt himself being picked up and then hurled to the ground. He forced his eyes open just as the bouncer was about to bring down a long wide boot on his face.

"That's enough! Stop it!"

Things were said, things happened in the next two or

three minutes that Rice had a difficult time following as he pushed himself to his feet and tried to judge the damage the bouncer had put on him.

"You go inside. I'll handle this."

"I don't want you alone with him. You can't trust him."

"You heard me. Now back inside. I said I'll handle it and I will."

Rice was leaning against his rental. His lungs were starting to function normally again and the heat in the back of his neck was beginning to recede. He was shaken more than anything. But despite his injuries he took a long and fond look at Polly as she buzzed open her Beemer and went over there and brought back some kind of kit. She also carried a small bottle of Perrier.

"Emergency kit," she explained as she set the things down on the car hood. "How're you feeling?"

He wanted to say *I killed the bastard and now I'm going to get into your pants so how bad could it be, night like this?* But all he said was, "I'll survive."

"Both my bouncers are crazy. You have to watch out for them."

As she spoke, she opened the kit, took out a piece of cloth and began soaking it with the Perrier. She started to clean up his face. As she did so she pressed tight against him. Store-boughts or not, the feel of her breasts rubbing on his chest gave him an erection that was almost painful in its intensity. Then she pressed her hips against him to finish the job. By now lust had quelled any residual pain. His hands found her hips and pulled her even tighter.

"I thought I'd come back and we could spend some time together."

She continued to clean his face. "What about my husband?"

He laughed, though it hurt his throat. "Like you said, he won't ever find out."

She leaned out of his grasp, setting the rag down on the hood of the car. Then she came to him, her mouth on his, her tongue exciting him to blindness. This was going to be one of the great lays of his life. He knew it.

Later he would remember this pain as being even greater than the pain her bouncer had inflicted. He was standing there, his right hand moving up over the great wonderful swell of her breast when something like a heat-seeking missile exploded between his legs. There was a second when he couldn't explain to himself what had happened. Even though it was obvious.

And then he was sinking to the ground. And almost crying he was in such misery.

And then she was standing over him with her hands on her hips like a frigging dominatrix. "Men don't usually turn me down, dirtball. And when they do they sure as hell aren't dumb enough to come back again."

The point of her high-heeled shoe caught him on the side of the nose. Spray of blood, his entire body spasming in throbbing misery.

"And another thing, fuckwad. In case you didn't know it, you shot at the wrong cop tonight. And you didn't even manage to hit him once."

This time the toe went to his rib cage. But, with his entire body aggrieved, he barely felt it.

CHAPTER TWENTY-SEVEN

"Are you all right?" asked a reporter.

"I'm fine."

"Any leads on who might have tried to kill you?"

"Nope. And we're not even sure he was after me in particular. Could have been a sniper who just wanted to kill anybody who came along."

All this was before Michael had even managed to transfer his body from his own Volvo to the trusty black Ford the department provided. All three TV stations, two radio stations and the local newspaper had joined together to keep him inside his car, presumably because he would then have nothing else to do but answer questions.

"Do you know how many calls our station has gotten since yesterday noon about that poor missing girl?"

"Gosh, Lisa," Michael said, "from the way you say it I'll bet it's a lot."

"And that doesn't count the e-mails."

"Lots of them, too, no doubt."

Quick change of subject. Obviously no news on the would-be cop killer so on to the next headline.

At 7:37 a.m. the temperature was already seventy-four. The humidity was seventy-three. And the blue sky was cloudless. The police parking lot was adjacent to the west side of the building. It was open so nobody had any special difficulty getting to officers as they came and went. The joke was that this made it easier for pissed-off citizens to shoot at them.

This was Lisa Hepburn's Salute to Pink day. The pink suit, the pink blouse, the strappy pink sandals. She was a sexual confection and ultimately about as substantial as pink ice cream. She got the best ratings of any reporter in the TV market. The joke was you didn't know how empty her eyes were because the camera was always doting lovingly on her surgically enhanced bosom.

The serious questions would come later, from others. All Lisa wanted was for Michael to say something that she could use for her bitchy little remarks at the end of her report. True information didn't interest her.

"So there's not even a meeting scheduled about this lost girl yet?"

Michael pushed out on the door, forcing three of the reporters back so that he could stand up and start the slow march to the inside of the station. "Of course there's a meeting, Lisa. The three detectives assigned to the case will confer and talk about what we all learned yesterday."

As soon as he said it, he knew how she was going to nail his ass to the wall. Pretty stupid to say "three detectives."

"I'm surprised that the entire police force isn't helping."

And there you had it. Her report. He could write it for her. "Three detectives. Three detectives with plenty of other cases they're busy with. Three detectives spending just a few hours on a case that may already have seen yet another murder of a teenage girl in our city. Three detectives when a good share of the one hundred sixty-seven people in the police department should be out looking for her."

He was rougher than he planned to be. He pushed right into the crowd of reporters, shoving them back. If he wasn't mistaken, he even trod on one of Lisa's pink sandals. He was finished talking. They trailed after him like hungry dogs. A pair of uniformed officers stood next to the rear entrance, smiling. Much as they hated the press they were always happy to see one of the big bad detectives get reminded that they weren't such hot shit after all.

He was within ten feet of the steps when one of them said, "What if another skull gets delivered in a few weeks? Do you think the chief should resign?"

Michael stopped walking. Faced them. Held his hands up in a halting motion. "Will you please do this city a favor and stop trying to scare everybody? We're very concerned about Cindy Baines. Very concerned. Yes, there'll be a meeting. And it'll take place in about twenty minutes. And yes, we'll begin to get other officers involved. But right now we can't say for sure that she's been abducted. There is the possibility that she ran away. I'm not saying it's a good possibility but it's one that we have to consider. So I wish all of you would help us out by reporting any tips you get to us and asking the community to do the same. There is somebody out there who knows something that will help us. That, we're sure of. So let's please all calm down and try to help find this girl. Every one of us has an obligation to do all we can."

Even the uniformed men looked impressed. Hell, *Michael* was impressed.

Then he turned back toward the stairs and hurried up them.

He was just going through the door when he heard Lisa whine: "That prick stepped on my new shoes!"

The day had begun inside. Fresh coffee, fresh clothes, phones, faxes, computers, smiles among the staffers, whispers among the lawyers and their clients about to be interviewed or interrogated.

The first thing Michael noticed when he reached the detective bureau was that Kim was in place but not his brother. He wondered how bad it had been when Steve finally got home. Had she confronted him with the extra credit card account? The lingerie and jewelry? The possibility that he really had fallen in love with somebody else? Or had Steve not gone home at all? Had he spent the night with this other woman?

Kim was finishing a croissant and a cardboard container of coffee. When she saw Michael, she left her desk and hurried to him.

He knew people were watching so he felt awkward when she slid her arms around him and held him close in a way that was both sexual and maternal. "I'm so worried about you."

Rush of memories. All the ways they'd held each other in the months they'd been lovers. Texture of flesh, scent of hair, pattern of muscle and bone. He didn't want to let her go but he felt pretty stupid holding her like this.

"I'm fine." Easing her away.

"I called you all night."

"I unplugged the phone."

"So many people were worried."

He laughed. "That's why I unplugged the phone."

"You hear the boys on the radio this morning?" Kim said.

"I probably don't want to know."

"The boys" could only mean two local shock jocks known as Kenny and The Whale. Michael was of the belief that it should be legal to drown, shoot, hang, burn or disembowel—take your choice—all shock jocks. The sixth-grade humor, the nerdy machismo, the obvious terror of women . . . and, in this city anyway, the constant pandering to people who had grudges against people in local government. Lots of innuendo about corruption and sexual affairs. Serious criticism would have been fine. But mocking the mayor's waistline, the county attorney's huge nose, the parks commissioner's daughter's second arrest and incarceration in a psychiatric hospital . . . A lot of meanness in the world. It didn't need any more.

"I was only kidding. I just like to see your jaw muscles bunch up whenever I mention them. I'll just give you a synopsis."

He walked over to the desk that was next to hers and sat down. She wore a white silk blouse and a light blue skirt. She looked rested and happy. The eyes were merry and so was the voice. She was adding to her to-do list. She was obsessive about lists.

As he sat down and faced his computer, adjusting his chair to the left so that the sunlight angling through the window didn't reflect directly on his face, he heard Detective Captain Bob Myles walk through the door behind him. "You hear those assholes?"

"And good morning to you, Bob," Kim said.

"If you mean those jerks on the radio," Michael said, not looking up from his blossoming computer screen, "Kim tried to tell me but I don't want to hear it. Don't need the grief."

"They were making one of their stupid jokes about how the police department was too busy checking out YouPorn to be bothered with checking out this missing girl."

"Thanks for not telling me."

"And that's not all they said, either."

He carried a Wendy's sack that was stained on the bottom from coffee. His desk sat at the front of the room and faced the others. As if he were the teacher and they were the students. He was presently the best detective on the force. His mentor had been Jack Scanlon. He was near retirement and spent a good deal of his time talking wistfully about this small cabin he and his wife planned to retire to in Upper Michigan.

He got seated, opened his bag and began to devour a formidable breakfast sandwich of some kind. He was a large, square man who wore heavy suits even in July and August. He was a Knight of Columbus and got red-faced and irritable whenever anybody made jokes about Catholic priests. Around a large bite of sandwich, he said, "We need to find her. Or at least find out what happened to her."

Kim and Michael nodded.

"We've got plenty else to do, I know. But this is the one that's going to haunt us. And by the way, where the hell's Steve?"

"He must be a little late," Michael said, not realizing until it was too late what a stupid thing he'd just said.

"I know he's a little late, Michael. That's obvious. I meant where the hell is he since he's not here?"

"I'm not sure."

They stared at each other. Kim cleared her throat. Myles had never cared for Steve. Thought him too reckless, too sloppy, too much the charmer and the rogue. Only his affection for Jack kept him from easing Steve out.

Myles frowned. "You're aware that somebody put up five thousand dollars as a reward?"

They nodded.

"You're also aware that her classmates are going to hold a vigil for her tonight?"

"All this was on the radio this morning," Kim said. "Kenny and The Whale said that private citizens were doing more than the police force."

"I don't know why you listen to that shit," Myles growled.

"I guess it doesn't bother me as much as it does you two."

Myles whipped through some papers. "You know Ken Miller, the profiler we're paying all that money? Here's his latest piece of wisdom. He tells me to keep in mind that we're obviously dealing with a sexual sociopath who enjoys keeping the whole city all stirred up. Thinks he's superior, hates women, will keep on killing until he's caught." He slammed the letter back on his desk. "The kind of money the department pays this guy for part-time work is pretty damned steep for a letter like this. Hell, watch any true-crime show about serial killers on TV and you can learn all the same crap in twenty minutes. And now the chief wants to bring in a profiler."

Kim and Michael smiled at each other. There were several subjects that caused Myles to begin ranting. Profilers were one of his favorite targets. According to Myles, and to an increasing number of detectives around the country, profiling was more of a public relations stunt than a legitimate tool for law enforcement officers. Sounded good on TV, created a mythology that was useful in sustaining the idea that the FBI was the august institution it tirelessly proclaimed itself to be. And made the average citizen think that they were safer now that all these wizards were lending a hand to all these plain old dumb detectives.

Michael always agreed with about 50 percent of what Myles ranted about.

Myles' phone rang. Michael always knew when the chief had summoned Myles. The voice became almost courtly.

"No problem, Bill. I'll be in your office in about five minutes. And yes, that's exactly what we're talking about. And I don't blame you for being pissed about what those morons said on the radio. If I'd have heard it myself I'd probably have driven over to the station and broken some bones. And you can quote me on that."

What few writers about police departments ever got right was the amount of politics involved in the job. The hierarchy insisted on having its ass kissed at least three times a day even if you were running a fever and had lips so parched they were bleeding.

"His daughter called and told him what they said about him on the air this morning," Myles said after hanging up. "He wants to know what we're doing about the case."

"Well, I don't know about you two," Kim said, "but I'm taking the day off."

"Me, too," Michael said. "Thought I'd catch a movie and then get drunk out of my mind."

"Very funny."

He pushed back from his desk, stood up and began tugging his clothes away from his body. "Even in air-conditioning I sweat. I took a shower about an hour and a half ago and already I need another one." He straightened his tie. "I read your reports from yesterday. Just keep interviewing people. Somebody knows something. The way you describe her mother I wouldn't be surprised if she killed the girl and stashed the body somewhere."

"I thought about that myself," Michael said. "But she's so wobbly from booze and probably drugs that I don't think she could pull it off. Her daughter could have defended herself."

"Well, just keep going," Myles said as he hurried to the door and the stairs leading to the chief's office.

Michael told Kim what he'd be doing for most of the morning. He wanted to talk to Cindy's mother again, for one thing. He didn't believe that she had anything to do with her daughter's disappearance but he wasn't sure she'd helped him much, either. She'd had way too much to drink and her sad crazed husband's shouting had distracted her.

Kim planned to go back to the Git 'n Go to interview the night clerk and maybe talk to the geeky kid again.

Michael's phone rang. He lifted the receiver and heard Myles' voice say, "Turn on the TV quick. That crazy bitch is being interviewed live."

"What crazy bitch?"

"The girl's mother."

"Oh, shit," Michael said as he hung up. He strode to the nineteen-inch set that sat on top of a three-shelf bookcase and flipped it on. He hadn't needed to ask which channel would be interviewing the woman. This could only be Lisa Hepburn and Channel 3. Hepburn had convinced the Baines woman to come to the parking lot of the police department. Nice backdrop for a weeping woman with a daughter missing. Those insensitive, incompetent cops.

"Who's the crazy bitch you were talking about?" Kim said to his back.

Scanlon nodded to the TV set and said, "Both of them."

And just as he spoke, there she was in all her comely pink glory, shoving her phalluslike microphone into the face of Mrs. Natalie Baines.

Dressed in an attractive long-sleeved beige dress, her hair washed and combed, her makeup carefully applied, Natalie Baines looked like all the other tragic mothers who appeared on TV screens around the world pleading with people to find their daughters. She wasn't wobbling, either. She must have managed to keep away from the bottle. It was early yet.

As for her clothes, Channel 3 was notorious for helping

to clean up, dress and make up the people they wanted to use as witnesses in their ongoing battle with city government, a battle that kept them solidly number one in the ratings. In less than an hour Channel 3 could have every drug dealer in the city looking like a Harvard grad. The problem came when these people opened their mouths. But Channel 3 had a partial solution even to that. The reporter loaded the questions so that the person being interviewed had little more to do than nod or say "yes" or "no."

As Lisa was doing right now. "You said that when Detective Michael Scanlon came to visit you yesterday he was rude and didn't seem much interested in finding your daughter. More like a courtesy visit than a real attempt to find out anything about her?"

"That's right, Lisa. He couldn't wait to get out of there." Hard to know if her sudden tears were real or camera inspired.

"And that isn't your only problem, is it, Mrs. Baines? Isn't your husband permanently disabled?"

"Paralyzed from the waist down. For life."

More tears. Real ones. Much as all this TV was bullshit, the sober Natalie Baines had finally had to confront the reality. Her daughter was gone. Lisa could turn it into tabloid trash but Natalie's sorrow remained honest. "I just want everybody who's listening to know how much we love our daughter and the wonderful life we have together. I'm asking anybody who knows anything to call the police with any information they have."

She began sobbing and slumped against Lisa. Lisa put her arm around her, no doubt worrying if anything on this low-rent woman would rub off on her pink suit, and said to the lens, "Or you can call Channel 3. There was a lot of criticism about the other two murdered girls, that citizens had a tough time getting the police department to take any of their tips seriously. At Channel 3 we'll listen and then we'll call the police. We'll make darned sure that they listen to us."

The shot widened out to show the maternal arm around the shoulders of the broken mother. "Help us help this brave woman and her husband. Help us find this girl. You don't need to be reminded about the grotesque murders that took the lives of the other two girls. Or about the killer that may have struck again."

All Natalie needed to hear was the reference to the killer and she began sobbing so hard her body began to shake with seizure-like fury.

Terrible to see. But for Lisa Hepburn, a perfect payoff. "This is Lisa Hepburn on the job for Channel 3. Help us find this innocent child before it's too late."

Which of course inspired even greater visible pain on Natalie's tortured face.

"Now I know what I'm going to do on my lunch hour," Kim said as Michael clipped off the TV.

"Yeah? What's that?"

"Kill that bitch."

"Be sure and get some pictures for me," he said as he walked back to his desk.

And just where was his brother this morning?

CHAPTER TWENTY-EIGHT

The house Nicole was showing was listed at 1.4 million dollars. In a small city the size of Skylar this price gave you a clear choice, one of the sedate old homes along the three blocks of Hamilton Street or a McMansion on the far west side. Four thirty-six happened to be one of the sedate ones, but with new features such as a spa and gourmet kitchen. Steve had checked it out while parked down the block waiting for Nicole to reappear with her prospective buyers. He'd found the house listed in the newspaper he bought each morning. The nine-foot ceilings and the two-story foyer had interested him most of all. Having grown up in a small ranch-style house in a popular subdivision, this kind of architecture fascinated him.

As he sat there watching dogs, butterflies and birds exult in the blue-sky day, he found his stomach burning again. Nerves. He didn't expect her to throw her arms around him and say, *Yes, let's run away tonight!* But he hoped she would listen seriously to what he had to say. To this new source of money. Enough money to facilitate a divorce and to set himself and Nicole up in California, with more than enough to live on for three or four years if they had to.

He had to be careful not to even hint where the money was coming from. And if she loved him, as he truly believed she did, then she'd be too happy with his news to question it.

The middle-aged couple who drove the new Mercedes CL-class stepped through the front door. They were smiling and talking as Nicole locked up the house again. She wore a white linen suit—one he was familiar with in many respects—and her hair was done in a chignon, a style he especially liked on her.

They continued to chat as they made their way down the steep steps to the sidewalk, the enormous lawn making the steps seem small and fragile. The man had the respectable gray hair and poise of an executive. His wife was a little more worn with her years but had a pleasant face and intelligent eyes. His binoculars revealed all these things.

Steve drove a gray unmarked Plymouth left over from a few years ago, when the mayor had made a deal with one of his golfing buddies. The cars hadn't been worth piss. But he was sure Nicole wouldn't recognize it from this distance. And before she would get in her car and pull away he'd be talking to her.

Their chitchat seemed interminable to him. Impatience was one of his curses. It had led him to ruin a few cases he'd worked on over the years. His stomach flared up again and he pressed the fingers of his right hand against his belly.

And then, finally, the prospective buyers were encasing themselves in the hermetically sealed world of the big Mercedes. Everything looked better when seen through those windows. Was bad news allowed to play on its radio? Probably not. A Disney world for the lucky owners.

Nicole stood, heartbreakingly lovely, on the curb near her own car, waving good-bye to them. He'd never loved anybody the way he loved Nicole—not even his own children, he had to admit—so that even her slight-est offhand motion held for him the power of myth.

He stepped on the accelerator then. She was going through a slender notebook when he pulled up. Only when she saw who he was did her body freeze and her eyes become wary. She glanced at her car, gauging how much time it would take for her to get into it, lock the doors and maybe even take off before he could get to her. But it was obvious that she thought it was hope-less. She sighed deeply and then simply watched him approach.

"Twenty-four-hour police protection. How lucky can I get?"

"I know you don't like this, Nicole, but—" This was one of those times when he heard himself objectively. Few things in his life had ever been able to break his will. He won because he felt dominant over virtually anyone he was up against. But with Nicole he was a supplicant and he sounded like it. She was the dominant one.

"I need to get going."

He grabbed her arm with more force than he'd in-tended. "Will you please just listen to me?"

"Take your hand off my arm. And right now."

The dominant one, for sure.

"Look, just listen to me, will you?"

"You may not have noticed, *Detective*, but there are people watching us."

And so there were. His attention was so fixed, so fo-cused that he had to be reminded that there was some reality other than his need for Nicole. He dropped his grip on her. "I'm sorry."

"You damned well should be. This is ridiculous. I need to get on with my life and you need to get on with yours."

"Things have changed."

A lawn mower erupted into action; a UPS truck pulled up down the street; a new Lincoln SUV backed out of a driveway three houses down. The world went on. But not Steve's world.

She zipped open her purse and extracted her keys.

"Did you hear me?"

"Yes," she said, zipping up her purse again but not looking at him. "Things have changed." Now her eyes were on him again. All he could think of was that he would someday see the smile, the need in those eyes he'd enjoyed for all those months when he'd been terrified of only one thing—that it would end. That she would dump him.

"I'm coming into some money." He searched her face for some kind of interest. None. "A lot of money."

"I'm sure your wife and children can use it. You've spent a lot of money on me, Steve." And now her eyes reflected something other than anger: pity. "Money you didn't need to spend. I wasn't going out with you because of money. You were fun and interesting. There are plenty of men I could go out with who have money. I could never make you understand that."

"You said you loved me."

"Oh, please, Steve. Please. I need to get to work and so do you."

"You said you loved me." Miserable; half-insane.

"Yes, I said I loved you. And I meant it. At the time I meant it. But then it got so crazy. You wanting to run away."

"You said you thought about it."

She glanced around the street, as if searching for help. "I said I thought about it. And I did. But then I decided against it. And even without having money I might have done it. But you wouldn't let me breathe. And when you started following me—"

"That was a mistake. I should never have done that."

She bolted then. She was much quicker than he would have thought. Around the front of the car. Remote bleating. He would have chased her but the UPS truck was headed this way. He couldn't try to stop her from getting in her car. All he needed was for the chief to get a report about him manhandling a woman.

She started her car. He tried the passenger door. Locked. Of course. He knocked twice but as he was about to do it a third time she swept away from the curb, leaving him isolated, more alone than he'd ever felt in his life. The UPS truck was approaching him. The driver waved and grinned. What a moron, couldn't he sense what was going on here? Wave and grin, you stupid bastard. Business as usual for you, you lucky prick. Business as usual for the entire fucking world. But not for Steven Moore Scanlon.

He walked slowly back to his car. He was thinking that this hadn't been a good idea after all. Wrong time, wrong place. Of course she wasn't going to take him seriously when he ambushed her this way. He needed to be alone with her. Tell her about all the money he was going to come into. The money he knew he could demand from Olson.

Yes, alone. Reassure her that as crazed as he'd been since she'd started to withdraw from him, he would never be that way again. That they could go back to how they'd been at the start. Only now there would be money. Serious money. And they could go away again without sneaking off or being ashamed.

The kids would forgive him someday. Even Wendy would, eventually.

And he and Nicole would be in California.
Starting over; starting over.

Leo Rice watched all this from halfway down the block.
He wore dark glasses and a blond wig. Very different
look from the one when he'd sat and talked to Steve
Scanlon in the bar yesterday. He was still sore and angry from the beatings the bouncer and then Polly Nolan had put on him. But he knew he could not afford to
get distracted.

He smiled when he saw the babe roar away from the
curb, leaving the detective standing there with useless
clenched fists and the lost look of a forlorn little boy.

Whoever this bitch was, she sure had his brother's
killer by the cajones. Useful information. He needed to
find out more about her.

He decided to follow her.

As he was pulling away from the curb, Steve Scanlon
walked slowly back to his car. The anger was gone now
from the posture of the body. He slumped, shuffled.

He didn't look up when Rice drove his rental car past
him, intent on learning more about the beautiful woman
who was tormenting the arrogant cop.

CHAPTER TWENTY-NINE

"A couple of slices wouldn't hurt me."

"I won't do it, Dad."

"You could sneak it in."

"Right. And nobody'd smell it when they came into your room."

"All right, one slice."

"Why don't I ask the doctor here and he'll settle it for us?"

"You already know what that dumb bastard'll say."

"They have pizza here."

"And it doesn't taste for shit."

This was the ongoing Pizza Argument. On the days when Jack was alert, he badgered his son for food that was not on the menu. Yes, the place had pizza but not real pizza, Jack's argument meant. Not Domino's or Godfather's. Pizza for old farts, as Jack had once described it. The Pizza Argument was not unlike the Whiskey Argument. Or the infamous Cigar Argument.

"So you're all right. It scared the hell out of me. I turn on the TV at six o'clock this morning. And there's a story about my son being shot at. Nobody tells me anything."

They'd been through the story. Twice. His old man didn't need this extra worry, stress. He almost felt guilty for being shot at.

"I'm fine, Dad. I've told you that. I'm fine."

"He's still out there."

"I'm being very careful, believe me."

"How can you be careful when you don't even know who he is?"

"I can handle it, Dad. Honest."

"And where's that brother of yours, by the way?"

When he was growing up Michael had never been fond of his father's irascibility. But now he found it endearing. Jack sure had no plans to go gentle into that good night. He would go bitching all the way.

"He's pretty busy on this case." Though that was a crock, Michael thought. He's somewhere with the woman. The woman he's throwing his family away for.

"The girl they can't find?"

"Right."

"It's that guy with the skulls."

"What is?"

"The bastard who grabbed this new kid."

"And you're basing that on what?"

"All my years as a cop. Find him and you'll find your girl."

They sat in the sunroom. Several other residents were here this late morning. There were two card games going on, bridge if he wasn't mistaken. In one lounger an elderly man slept and in another an elderly woman knitted. Michael had stopped here for a few minutes on his way to a bar where Steve sometimes hid out.

"He's working on it and so am I."

"How come he hasn't been to see me yet?"

"We talked about this yesterday. He says he'll be here for sure."

"Today?"

"If he gets the time."

His old man fixed him with a skeptical eye. "You wouldn't be bullshitting me, would you?"

"About what? I asked him just like I said I would."

"He isn't in some kind of trouble, is he? He was always like that when something went wrong. He'd avoid me."

"Everything's fine."

"Something's wrong, isn't it?"

"Nothing's wrong, Dad. For God's sake." He realized too late that he was shouting. His father seemed to shrink even smaller in his wheelchair. Stupid to be yelling. A sure signal that something was indeed wrong.

"I get scared for him, Michael," he said in a wounded voice. "That's all I meant. He takes too many chances, the way I used to. You, I can count on. Everybody can count on you, Michael. But Steve—"

Were those tears in the old man's eyes? Possibly. Probably. Michael and Jack had never had that kind of connection. But Jack and Steve—

"You got to help him, Michael. You're the only one who can do it since I'm not going to be around forever. And I know it won't be easy. But you got to see that he doesn't get into any trouble. And I mean any kind of trouble." He reached out with a skeletal, liver-spotted hand. Michael took it. "I couldn't handle it if anything happened to him, Michael."

And then it was over. He muttered something Michael couldn't understand. And then Jack just stopped. Head lolled to the side, eyes closed, sighed in a way that was much like a gasp. Energy fled.

Michael sat there and watched him. The lined face. The twitching of the eyelids. The thinning hair. His life had made wonderful sense. His impending death made no sense at all. But then death never did.

Michael leaned down and kissed his father on his freckled bald head.

* * *

As Peter Olson peered into mouths, touched glands, examined bruises, bumps, breaks, he tried to understand the panic he'd felt the past few hours. Superficially, this one was going the same as the other two. But hearing a police report on the radio had unsettled him. He had always considered himself a rational man, not given to superstitions. But maybe he secretly believed in the concept of luck running out. Of taking one too many fruits from the bowl. Of the step too many.

Maybe his affair with Kim had been one step too many. Maybe—unthinkable as it was—he'd become transparent to her. Maybe she knew that he had no interest in her. Maybe she knew that he was simply using her, as he had during the time of the second killing, for inside information from the police.

Maybe she was playing *him*. Setting him up for a possible arrest.

Just before eleven o'clock, with eight patients in the waiting room, he took a small break, sitting in his office and poppIng a Xanax.

Just after eleven o'clock, Rosie buzzed and said, "It's a Mr. Sanders for you, Doctor. He said it's personal and that it's very important."

Sanders.

Fuck.

There was no Sanders. There was only this preening arrogant bully detective named Steve Scanlon.

"Thanks, Rosie. I'll take it."

He picked up the phone and said, "I thought we agreed no more calls to my office, 'Mr. Sanders.'"

"We need to talk."

"Not on the phone."

"Gee, really? I'm such a dumbass I'm going to start

talking on the phone? But I forgot I'm dealing with a superior human being. Isn't that right, Doc?"

Steve Scanlon's class bitterness aggravated Olson almost as much as his blackmail. He was one of those people who couldn't forgive God for not making him rich. And God help the rich person he came across.

"I have eight patients waiting for me. What is it?"

"What is it? Gosh, I wonder. What could I possibly be calling about, huh? It's a complete mystery."

Olson realized now that Steve Scanlon, as usual, had been drinking. He was especially mean when he drank. "All right. We'll talk later."

"Tonight. Your place."

"I'm not sure that's a good idea."

"You're not, huh? Well, maybe I don't give a shit that you're not sure it's a good idea. You ever thought of that?"

A bellicose child. "I guess that makes sense. Better than meeting someplace else."

"Thanks for noticing that I have a good idea once in awhile."

"I'll see you then."

"I'm looking forward to it, Doc." Slamming the phone.

The headache crossed his forehead at an angle. Never had a headache with that trajectory before. Closed his eyes. Leaned back in the chair.

A few minutes later the handsome face displayed a smile. Maybe there was a way to solve all his problems at the same time. Maybe Steve Scanlon coming to his home would prove to be a good idea, after all.

The grubby bastard would want more money. But maybe by then Olson would be prepared to give him something else. Something very different, unexpected. Something that would be most pleasant to inflict.

The grubby bastard.

PART THREE

CHAPTER THIRTY

There was not as much pain this time but she knew he had been inside her. He had come on the inside of her left thigh and the stuff had dried there. She had never seen come before but she had no doubt what it was from how other girls had talked about it. And that stupid movie *There's Something About Mary*. It was fake but it still gave you a pretty good idea. She'd had to watch it at her boyfriend's house. Her father would have never allowed a DVD like that in their trailer.

She sat on the edge of the cot in her sleeping shirt, touching her nipples. They were sore again. He'd been doing something to them. She wasn't sure what. She'd let Ted touch them and kiss them as well as touch and kiss her down there but they rarely stayed sore after more than an hour or so. What was Dr. Olson doing to her?

She slowly, unsteadily rose to her feet. She didn't want to fall down. She'd been doing that since she woke up. The drugs. Her inclination was always to stay on the cot and sleep. Made things easier. She feared that sleep was the only way she could escape this place.

She walked barefoot to where a metal pitcher and washbasin sat on a small wooden table. She washed her face and arms and dried them with the lone white bath towel. She hoped the water would wash away the drugged feeling. It didn't.

She needed to force herself into real consciousness. As bleak as her prospects looked she wanted to see if there was some way out of here.

There wasn't.

She walked back to the cot, beginning to sob.

Mr. Sullivan, please come and find me.

CHAPTER THIRTY-ONE

Kim was gently suggesting that the jerk from the county attorney's office was full of beans when the middle-aged black man appeared next to her desk and smiled. He wore a gray uniform. He was holding a vase with a dozen red roses partially wrapped in the green stuff most florists used. As she continued to talk he showed her the name on the card attached to the green wrapping. She nodded, indicating that she was in fact the intended recipient. He set them gently on her desk, smiled again and disappeared.

It was difficult to explain to the jerk why he had plenty of evidence to indict a two-time loser who'd been caught stealing yet another car when her attention was fixed on the roses.

"We need more than an admitted pimp testifying that James stole the car," the jerk said. "He and James have had issues for two years since Jamal started screwing the guy's wife."

"He stole the car. Two people besides the pimp saw him do it."

"Yeah, and trying to get them to testify is hopeless. They're afraid James will kill them if they do."

And that's where all these arguments ended. You had a pimp that a jury wouldn't believe. And you had two witnesses who were understandably afraid of testifying.

Thus far James Devon had apparently limited his years to stealing cars and doing some minor drug pushing. No violence. But he had a rep as a truly bad dude, and who was to say that he wouldn't graduate to murder if he felt the need.

The county attorney's young staffer wasn't the jerk. She was.

"Are you listening to me?"

And the answer was no, she hadn't been. He'd said something but the words were lost because she was studying the card in the small envelope attached to the flowers.

> Wonderful night for me.
> Hope it was for you, too.
> Peter

"Kim? Did you hear what I said?"

"Sorry, Sean, I got distracted."

Handsome young doctor sending her flowers. She wanted to go back to high school and brag to all the popular girls who'd always smirked at her whenever she dressed up for a special occasion. Not up to their standards. Well, how about their standards now? How about a movie-star handsome doctor sending *them* flowers? Not likely. Not likely at all.

"I said that maybe what we need to do is tell his friend Nikki that if she wants us to go easy on her for that coke rap then she'd better help us with nailing her boyfriend. She's got a kid now. She won't want to be spending the next two years upstate without her kid."

"James'll kill her if she goes against him. He might even kill the kid. That's what his cousin did that time."

"Well, we'll never nail him on the word of this pimp,

I'll tell you that. So don't expect us to take this thing any further unless you come up with a better witness."

"Maybe I'll just go shoot him myself."

"Just be sure to confess and make it easy on me."

She laughed as he hung up.

"Wow," Detective Captain Myles said as he walked back into the office. "Looks like Detective Pierce has got herself an admirer."

"How was the chief this morning?"

"You're changing the subject. Who sent you the roses?"

"Nobody you'd know."

"I don't think anybody in this office has ever had anybody send them flowers, let alone long-stemmed roses. Wait'll I tell my wife about this."

"Then she'll want you to send *her* flowers."

"That's something to think about."

Myles walked to his desk, leaving her to sit there and stare at the roses.

Her phone rang. A local high school. She'd agreed to talk to a group of college-bound high school students about police work as an occupation. The school liked having a female detective instead of a male one. The girls were more intrigued. Police work was no longer just a job for males.

When she finished her conversation, she went over and got herself another cup of coffee. She had three calls to make. The first to the used CD/DVD store where Cindy worked for three months previous to her stint at the ice cream place; the second to a woman who occasionally employed Cindy as a helper for major housecleaning and who had worked with Cindy two weeks ago; and the third to the Git 'n Go where Cindy frequently hung out.

The first two calls turned out to be brief. Neither

woman could add anything to the disappearance. They liked Cindy—the second woman even said that she "loved" Cindy like a daughter—but all they could offer were their hopes and prayers that the monster who'd killed the other two girls hadn't taken Cindy.

Inez Day, the woman she was looking for at the convenience store, worked the six-to-midnight shift, which Kim already knew. What she wanted was a phone number where she could reach the woman now.

"Well, I can give you a number," the man who'd identified himself as Merle the manager said, "but it won't do you no good. She's in Chicago today seeing her sister and she'll probably come straight to work from there. In fact she said she might be a little late getting here."

"I'm told she knows Cindy Baines very well."

Merle laughed. "Peas in a pod. Inez is like her big sister. They talk all the time. Cindy'll even help her stock aisles at night just so they'll have time to talk."

"Sounds like she might be able to help me."

"If anybody could, it'd be Inez. Say, I've got about four customers lined up here."

"Thanks. I appreciate the time."

She went to the bathroom, did her business, washed her face, combed her hair and got herself ready to visit Cindy's trailer park. The canvass had come up short. Three of the residents there had been gone. Earlier she'd tried their numbers. They said they would be home most of the day.

She was five steps from her desk when the phone rang.

"I was wondering what you were doing for lunch."

No amenities. No identification. Just the presumption that there couldn't possibly be a more manly or sexy voice in Kim's life. Which was certainly true. But he sure as hell didn't need to know this.

"I'm sorry. I don't want to leave my desk. I just want to sit here and stare at these roses."

Peter laughed. "They can't be any more beautiful than you are."

"Oh, please."

"You should wear one of those roses in your hair."

She smiled at the image. "Yes, I'm sure the chief would be delighted to know that one of his detectives goes out with a flower in her hair. Crack dealers would probably take me real seriously, too."

His laugh was rich and deep. "Yes, but you could use all your seductive powers to get your information."

"Oh, yes, all my well-known seductive powers."

"I'll see you in a few minutes," he said.

CHAPTER THIRTY-TWO

"Yes, may I help you?"

"I'd like to see Nicole McKenna, please."

The brunette receptionist was as sleek as a TV model. But the entire Gargan Realty main office was sleek, too. Mauves and yellows and bold white stripes; nubby brown couches; a plasma TV; three computer stations where you could look at homes.

Kylie, or so said the name on the desk, tried to stop staring at him but couldn't. She saw the family resemblance. "Are you Steve Scanlon's brother?"

"Yes, I am."

"Oh." Guarded now. As if expecting trouble.

"Is she here?"

"Is this—official?"

He smiled. "I'd like to talk to her."

Michael had gone to one of the jewelry stores where Steve had been charging gifts. The manager reluctantly gave the address of the recipient of his brother's largesse. He used a computer in a Starbucks to look up her name. The name led him here.

"She's in her office."

"I'd appreciate it if you'd tell her I'd like to see her."

"It's just—" She straightened her shoulders. Took a deep breath. "There have been a few incidents. I'm hoping this won't be another one. I'll get in trouble if it is."

"Incidents with Steve?"

"Yes."

What the hell is going on? he wondered. Nicole McKenna was supposed to be a nice, reliable mistress. The kind of time and money his brother was lavishing on her should mean that everything was going fine.

"There was one just a while ago. Earlier this morning."

"I promise you there won't be any incident. I'd just like to talk to her. You can just buzz her and explain that I'm here."

She stared at her phone, then shook her head. "I think I'd rather go back and tell her in person."

Doesn't want to say "I don't think you should see him" right in front of me, no doubt.

"All right."

Her body was as sleek as her face, her surroundings. She moved with simple grace, real elegance in a summery white dress with red polka dots. He'd always planned to meet a woman like this—just once, to have a fling with a woman who was all perfume and midnight romance—but he knew that he would just end up embarrassing himself if he tried. He wasn't sure, but he suspected that women who looked like this were of a different and far superior species.

She wasn't gone long. She returned with relief in her eyes and a smile on her face. "She said she'd be happy to talk to you. I'll take you back."

The long hall contained three doors on each side. All closed. An unending stream of plaques and awards and citations covered the walls. The rich smell of good coffee; the knowing, slightly condescending voices of salespeople; the almost apologetic questions of prospective buyers. The firm had two other offices in town. This was where the stars worked. A top-end real-estate office cleverly disguised not to look like a real-estate office with all those bothersome photos of homes and stacks of gift cards granting free steak dinners for serious prospects. Nothing so vulgar.

She knocked with a knuckle.

"Come in."

She was another one of the other species, only she was even more thrilling to see. Somehow she was both daring and modern and yet in some way old-fashioned, too. Maybe the soft blue eyes and the gentle way she raised her head to greet him. She was vivid and appealing as hell and watching her, Michael felt sorry for Wendy and the kids. None of them belonged to this species.

"Would you like some coffee?" the receptionist said to Michael.

"No, thanks."

"Nicole?"

"I'll be fine. Thank you. And please hold my calls."

"Of course."

Nicole offered her hand. "I saw your story on TV this morning. That must have been terrifying."

"Yes, it was."

When the door was closed, Nicole sat back and said, "I'm sure you're as embarrassed about this as I am. Believe it or not I've never been the 'other woman' before, Mr. Scanlon. And I've promised myself I never will be again."

He didn't especially want to like her but he found her words believable. "I don't know all the details. I found out about it through some Visa receipts. All the gifts were delivered to you."

"And all the gifts are sitting in my closet unused. I'll be happy to give them to you if you'd like them."

"Why haven't you accepted them?"

"Because I didn't want them. They were all Steve's

idea." The rich mouth pursed. "I fell in love with your brother, Mr. Scanlon. I didn't want to, it just happened. I made the mistake of telling him about my past. I've lived on both coasts and lived well. I've never been a kept woman or anything like that but I was always with wealthy people who were happy to have me around. Steve felt he had to treat me that way, too. He never believed me that it didn't matter to me. We talked about him getting a divorce and going away together."

Michael felt his jaw muscles bunch.

"I can see I'm saying too much."

"I'd like to know everything."

A sharp sigh. "Well, everything was fine until two months ago. He started buying me things. You saw the receipts. I kept telling him to stop, that that wasn't what I wanted. That I just wanted him. But he became obsessed. He's very jealous of my employer; he's very jealous of everybody. I guess he thought that if he kept buying me things he could make himself secure with me. But he started changing. He was always possessive, but then he started questioning me every time I couldn't account for twenty minutes here or twenty minutes there. I sell real estate. I have to go out at various times of the day and night. He started following me when I was meeting prospective clients. A few times he even got into arguments with some of the men I was trying to sell. One time was especially ludicrous. The man was very handsome and very manly but he was also gay. It should have been funny but it wasn't."

Michael was listening to all this but he was also trying to fix the time of two months in his mind. What had been happening two months ago? Where was all this money coming from? He didn't believe anything Steve had told him last night. But Steve hadn't confided in Nicole McKenna, either.

"The scenes got worse. And I started feeling guilty. About his wife and kids. I probably don't strike you as the guilty type—at least your brother never seemed to believe me when I told him that—but once things started to go bad between us I was able to see how sort of low-rent it had been from the beginning. I love having fun and traveling and having good times but not at somebody else's expense. One night he got drunk and his wallet fell out. I didn't notice it until the next morning. I'd never seen a photo of his wife and kids before. I felt like hell. And not because I'm such a moral person. I'm not. But because he'd turned both of us into a cliché, that's why. The cheating husband and the home wrecker. And with his wife and children at home."

He didn't like her but once again he believed her. She was so far removed from Steve's life but of course Steve couldn't see that. The other species. And not even handsome, dashing Steve belonged in that species.

"He's going to lose his job, Mr. Scanlon. I don't want that to happen. But my employer—Steve thinks I'm sleeping with him, naturally—is an important man in this city. If the mayor or the chief of police hears about how he's been following me and making scenes—he'd at least be suspended. If not fired. He has to accept that it's over with us. And maybe you can help me there. Maybe you can convince him that I'm not going to change my mind even if he did come into some money."

"What money?"

"I don't know. But he followed me to where I was showing a home this morning and waited for me. As soon as I started to my car he came after me. He told me he was going to have all this money and that we could go away together just the way we'd always talked about. I told him it didn't matter. He started to get violent. People were watching. It's a very upscale neighborhood. I wouldn't be surprised if somebody called the police. They didn't know he was a detective, not the way he was dressed. He was pounding on my passenger door window when I finally managed to pull away. He's really starting to scare me. That's why I'm glad you're here. I think you're the only one who can talk to him."

"He wasn't any more specific about the money?"

"No—at least I don't think he was. I just wanted to get away from him. He wouldn't let me go. I probably wasn't hearing everything he said."

Michael felt sick, angry, confused. Smashing something would help. Smashing Steve would help. He and Steve hadn't had a real fight in years. Right now Michael wanted that kind of catharsis.

As he rose, he took his wallet from inside his suit coat pocket. He dropped one of his cards on her desk. "There's my number at the station, at my apartment and on my cell. If you have any more trouble with him—any kind of trouble—I want you to call me immediately. If you see him coming toward your car, lock the doors and call me. And I don't need to tell you not to let him in. And going back and forth to your car, see if you can find somebody to walk with you."

She slipped her hand in his. Firm, but silken. "I wish your brother was more like you."

"You don't know anything about me, Miss McKenna."

She leaned back, as if he'd swiped at her. "I guess you don't have to like me."

"No," he said, thinking of Wendy, "and I don't have to like my brother, either."

CHAPTER THIRTY-THREE

They both had Caesar salads and coffee. People streamed to their booth.

They were like papal visitors, the ones who came. Paying their respects to the doctor. Kim always found this amusing. She'd never seen such unabashed ass-kissing and social climbing before. In her neighborhood people didn't pay umbrage. So courtly, this—and embarrassing. Today it irritated her.

"You should teach them to bow when they come over."

He smiled that gorgeous smile. "I have to do the same thing when I go to medical conventions. Believe it or not there are doctors in this country who make me feel like a country bumpkin, so when I see them I'm very obsequious. And I don't mind it, really. I know when I'm out of my league."

She dabbed dressing from her lips. "It's hard to imagine you in that position."

"You mean because I'm so witty and intelligent and good-looking?"

"Something like that."

"I'm disappointed you aren't wearing one of the flowers."

Her turn to smile. "The other detectives are wearing them."

"Speaking of which, any news about Cindy? My whole office is worried about her. She's a real sweetie."

"The state people will be helping us sometime today. There'll be an Amber Alert, too."

"So the sense is that she hasn't just run away?"

"It's still possible but pretty unlikely, I think."

The gleaming young blonde waitress in the uniform of red shirt and black pants. She paid perfunctory attention to Kim and then marked her territory by absorbing him with her dark eyes.

"How was the salad, Dr. Olson?"

"Wonderful as usual, Tanya."

Tanya, Kim thought. She wondered if he'd ever slept with her. Certainly a possibility the way he got around.

"Is there anything else?"

Kim realized she was probably imagining it but the words seemed loaded with innuendo.

"I'm fine. How about you, Kim?"

"I'm fine, too."

"Well, if there's anything—"

Even Peter seemed embarrassed now. The words were innocent enough but Tanya knew how to fire off invisible e-mails. The X-rated kind.

After she was gone, Peter said, "Sorry."

"I'm sure it's a curse, Dr. Olson. All these women throwing themselves at you."

"Believe it or not, it is a curse. It just gets in the way. The only woman I'm interested in is you."

Now what, Kim thought, do you possibly say to that?

CHAPTER THIRTY-FOUR

By four o'clock that afternoon dark clouds had sullied the blue sky. The taste and feel of rain made everybody hurry for cars, SUVs, city buses.

Michael had spent nearly ninety minutes canvassing the stores that fronted on the section of the mall parking lot where the green car had appeared on the tape from the security camera video. A men's store, a Blockbuster, a wedding shop, a small fine-arts gallery, a travel agency. He had waited to visit these places until it was later in the day. The people who worked nights were the ones he wanted to talk to.

Without exception everybody recognized him from the news. The way they talked they had assumed he was either in a hospital or hiding somewhere in police custody.

"You're just out walking around?" the handsome middle-aged black woman in the attractive yellow dress and pince-nez glasses said. She was the owner of Vacationland Travel, Inc. She had recognized him even before he'd reached her desk.

"I just went back to work."

"You're not afraid?"

Michael hated macho. Of course he was afraid. Every time he left his car he half expected to hear a shot. But he was proud enough not to admit it. "Well, I'm a little nervous but I've got my job to do."

She smiled. "I think you're my hero."

"So you've never seen that car anywhere around here before?"

"Oh, you know, sometimes I know cars but most of the time I don't. They're just a blur. I wish I'd noticed that one. That poor girl. I've got two teenage daughters of my own. This whole thing just terrifies me."

"I appreciate your time."

"If you're ever up for a vacation, let me help you. I'll get you a very special rate."

"Thanks," he said. "That actually sounds like a good idea about now."

This was his last stop and like the others, it had produced nothing more than the surprise that he was walking around without wearing a Kevlar vest and toting an Uzi.

The rain was hot. It stabbed at him as he increased his pace and climbed into his car. All around him people were shouting at each other about not getting wet. Rushing to cars with umbrellas or newspapers or magazines over their heads.

Inside, just as he'd started the engine, his cell phone rang.

"Scanlon."

"Scanlon, this is Bob Gargan."

He didn't allow himself to think of the implication of this man calling him. "Yes, Mr. Gargan?"

"We've met a few times. I'm an old friend of your father's. One of my all-time favorite people."

"Thank you."

"So call me Bob."

"All right."

Gargan was being decent about it. At least so far. Gargan equals real estate equals Nicole equals Steve.

"Do you have any idea why I might be calling, Michael? And please don't bullshit me."

"I'm assuming this is about my brother and what happened with Nicole this morning."

"Not just this morning. The last month or so. He scares her and he scares me. She told me she didn't tell you this because she wasn't sure you'd believe it, but he's threatened to kill her twice now. There weren't any other witnesses but I believe her."

"I'm not defending him here, Mr. Gargan, but I know Steve and I'm sure he wouldn't ever hurt her."

"Look, we can debate his threats all day. The thing is I know that your father is in very bad shape. I don't want him to hear about this. And if I go to the chief or the mayor, the press will get hold of it. That's why I'm asking you to rein him in. One more incident like this and I won't have any choice. I'll nail his balls to the wall."

"I really appreciate you calling me."

"He's obsessed with the idea that I'm sleeping with Nicole. That's not true. Strictly paternal. Has to be. I went up to Mayo last year and had a prostate operation. Not a lot of people know about it. I don't tomcat around the way I used to. So when I say it's strictly personal, it's strictly personal, capice?"

"Capice."

"The other thing he's obsessed with is the idea that somehow he's going to win Nicole back. That won't happen. She should never have gotten involved with him in the first place but from a distance your brother seems like a very attractive man. I hate to say it, Michael, but he's mentally unstable. I've had a few run-ins with him and I know what I'm talking about. Now I expect you to handle this. All right?"

"You have my word on it."

Michael could feel the grin on the other end of the phone. "And tell that old man of yours that he just got lucky the night he won six hundred dollars from me in poker. I was only twenty-five then and I thought it was pretty great hanging around cops. It's a good thing I had my inheritance to fall back on because they cleaned me out every time I played."

Gargan clicked off then.

And why not. He'd said everything he'd wanted to.

CHAPTER THIRTY-FIVE

"Myles is in the chief's office and your brother's in the can," a uniformed woman said to Michael as he approached the detective bureau. Michael sat down, checked for phone messages, then e-messages. Rain slithered down the windows. He had to force himself to think past Gargan's message and threat.

The toilet flushed. He could tell that Steve had been drinking by the length of time he'd been in the john. If he was sober it was in and out. If he'd been drinking he washed up and put on aftershave. Spent some time with a comb, too. Made sure his tie was straight, his shirt tucked in, his shoulder holster in proper position. He was one of those incipient alcoholics who could perform complicated tasks after having several drinks. With Steve it wasn't a question of competence. But it was frequently a question of judgment.

"Hey, Michael. You're all anybody wants to talk about after last night." The spicy scent of his aftershave preceded him from the john. Another standard routine from Steve. Never friendlier than when he was trying to hoo-doo people into thinking he was stone sober.

Given his mood after talking with Gargan, Michael wasn't up for his brother's patter. "You have a talk with Wendy, did you?"

"Sure. Good one. Everything's fine."

Michael tried to keep on working on a report at his computer. If he didn't keep his hands busy he was afraid he'd jump up and grab his brother.

Steve went to his desk behind Michael and sat down. "Been running down some things on Cindy Baines. Got nowhere, unfortunately."

"Myles said he couldn't find you today."

Despite Michael's accusatory tone Steve tried to keep it light. "Well, if you google Myles you'll find the headline is 'Guy who can't find his own ass with his hands.'"

Michael labored to settle down and respond to a state's attorney request for information on a manslaughter conviction the state supreme court was considering taking up. Michael had been the arresting officer. It was difficult but he managed to write two paragraphs before he realized that he needed to visit the john himself.

When he turned around to see what Steve was doing he caught a familiar sight: Steve pouring whiskey from a small silver flask into his cup. He smiled up at Michael. "Nerves. You know, the stress with Wendy and all."

"I thought you said everything was fine."

"Well, there's fine and there's fine, little brother. I mean things were fine for last night. But we've got a long way to go."

"Yeah," Michael said, unable to keep the anger from his voice. "I'll bet."

"What the hell is that supposed to mean?"

"Skip it," Michael said and headed for the restroom at the far end of the room. Easy to hear Steve cursing at him.

When he was done at the urinal he went over and washed up. He then stared at himself in the mirror for a time. Unlike Steve, he wasn't looking for beauty. He was looking for some reassurance that the person inside this body could find a way to solve the problems of

Wendy, his old man and Steve. He thought of what Nicole had said earlier today, that she didn't try to help because she was such a moral person. He wasn't such a moral person, either. A lot of remorse in his Irish heart. But he had to deal with Steve. The alternative was a paralyzing guilt. Guilt either way. Guilt because he felt helpless faced with their problems. But even more guilt if he didn't at least *try* to do something about them.

He could hear Steve even before he left the restroom. Something had made him angry. He was shouting about something.

The phone; Steve was shouting into the phone. "I know she's there. Don't give me any more of your bullshit. Now put Nicole on the line and I mean right away."

Michael went over and stood by Steve's desk. He wanted to grab the receiver from his hand and slam the phone down. His anger was mitigated by his troubled love for his brother. Steve seemed to be disintegrating.

"Bitch put me on hold," Steve snapped, holding the receiver out as if to demonstrate how badly he was being treated.

"Why don't you just hang up?" Keeping his voice even, reasonable.

Steve waved him off. "This is my business."

"Not anymore it isn't. Bob Gargan called me and told me that if I didn't pull you off Nicole he'd go to the mayor."

A deep sigh. Whipped. At least momentarily. Steve set the receiver back on the hook. Sat back in his chair. "He didn't need to drag you into this. He's just jealous because he's in love with her. She and I have problems but we can work them out."

"I saw her myself, Steve."

The body tensed. The face turned hard. The familiar

clenched expression before all of Steve's assaults. "You saw her? For what?"

"To find out what the hell was going on."

"What'd she say?"

"Look, Steve, I don't want to make this any harder on you than it already is. But she said she thought it would be a good idea if you didn't come around anymore. For her sake and yours." No sense riling him up any more than he already was.

"She said that because Gargan made her say that."

"I don't think so, Steve. I think she was telling me the truth."

"So you're taking Gargan's side? You always were a kiss-ass. Big important man calls and you fold right up."

Michael's move was instinctive. His right arm swept down and he grabbed Steve by the tie. "This is serious, Steve. What if the old man hears about it?"

Steve was out of his chair, roaring curses and throwing two punches before Michael could quite recover from the first blow. But even off-balance, still a little dizzy, Michael was able to land a hard right on Steve's jaw. Then the men stood in an open area between desks and started pounding on each other. At some point Michael knew that his nose was streaming blood and that his legs were getting weak. What kept him going was the satisfaction he felt when he heard his fists crack against Steve's face. A long time coming, this, and it felt better than he wanted it to.

Steve's fist seemed to split Michael's forehead in two. But as he reeled backwards, Steve stumbled forward and fell against him. Michael then resorted to the tactics of their childhood. Steve was always better at boxing but Michael was better at wrestling. He forced himself through the pain and disorientation from the forehead shot and maneuvered Steve into a headlock, the head-lock that Steve had always had trouble getting out of.

From the noises Steve was making, Michael knew that he was hurting him. He hoped this would calm his brother down. That they could go wash up and talk this thing through.

He was thinking this when Steve reached around and leveraged a good hard crack into his stomach, one that was just hard enough to loosen his grip. And Steve took quick advantage of it, tearing his head from Michael's arms and slamming a fist into the back of his head.

Michael was so shaken by the punch that he fell side-ways over Steve's desk, sending the computer and the phone to the floor. Steve did the brotherly thing, pound-ing two quick punches into Michael's kidneys.

"What the hell is going on here?"

The voice of God. Of a god named Myles, anyway.

It took a few seconds for the brothers to understand the significance of the voice. In the sweaty pained de-lirium of battle, nothing except their rage seemed real.

But the voice was very real. As was the body that shoved Steve aside and wrenched Michael up from where he was sprawled over the desk.

"Now what the hell is this all about? This is a god-damned detective bureau in case you two assholes hadn't noticed."

Myles' anger was growing as theirs was receding. Both of the fighters were sheened with sweat, gasping, bloody. Both had torn shirts.

"I can't believe this." Myles was shouting now. "We've got several big cases including a missing girl and you're pulling this right here where you work? I should sus-pend both of you stupid bastards."

He walked away from them. "The computer's on the floor. And it damned well better still work. So is the phone. The desk chair is overturned and there's blood on the floor. Maybe one of you children would like to start trying to put things back together. You know, so you could get on my good side."

"We just had a little disagreement," Michael said, knowing how stupid he sounded.

"Gee, really. I never would've guessed. Do you know what happens if the press hears about this? This sounds like a goddamned kindergarten or something."

"It was my fault," Steve said. He sounded sober now. And embarrassed. "I've been having a little trouble at home and Michael here started asking me questions about it. I just lost my temper."

"And you were probably drinking a little, too, I imagine. He hitting the flask, Michael?"

Myles had told Steve numerous times not to carry a flask. Michael had been surprised that Steve had been packing one today up here. But then Steve was on the precipice. Rules probably didn't matter much to him at this point.

"Not that I saw."

"You know what your old man would do if he ever heard about this? The kind of record he had in this department?" He began to sound tired, the weariness that came after the seductive spurt of anger. "I'm just glad nobody else was here to see it. Now I'm going downstairs and make sure nobody else heard it, either. A lot of people are gone already. Maybe nobody caught on." A final scowl. "Because this kind of crap reflects as bad on me as it does on you. Now pick all this stuff up and go get some wet paper towels and clean up the floor. And then go clean yourselves up before anybody sees you."

Sullen, they set to work. Michael went to the john and wetted paper towels, came back and wiped up the shimmering dimes of blood on desk and floor. Steve had rearranged everything on his desk.

As Steve sat down to check on the computer, Michael went back to the bathroom and started to clean up. He took off his shirt and went to his locker, where he kept two fresh towels. He gave himself what his grandmother had always called a "sponge bath." He ran the water ice cold and it revived him as he covered face, neck, chest and underarms with it. The he took a handful of water and soaked his hair. When he was finished, he assessed his face in the mirror. A small bruise on the edge of his right eye. A slight swelling on the bridge of his nose. A crack on the upper lip. Not too bad. Presentable.

Steve came in. He went to his locker, undressed, headed for the shower. When he finished, he came back and put on fresh clothes. He always kept a complete change handy. In the old days the other detectives had always kidded him about it. He was known as an ass bandit and he loved the reputation.

He came to the mirror where Michael stood combing his hair. "The computer's all right."

"Good."

"All this shit is my fault."

"I know."

"Well, screw you. I'm trying to be nice about it."

"If you say so." And with that Michael left the locker room.

For the next five minutes he worked on two cases that he returned to whenever he had the time. Then he went back through the list of people he'd interviewed about Cindy. Any of them worth talking to again? Occasionally you wouldn't realize that somebody had been lying to you for a few days out. Then some small thing they'd said would ring false and you'd go back to them and they'd tell you something vital. Of course the work he'd done with Cindy's disappearance might be worthless. They could be dealing with a copycat killer here so that this wasn't a pattern abduction at all. Or this could be a more personal matter, the abductor somebody Cindy knew well, somebody who hated her.

"You know how much I care about you, Michael. I'm sorry I lost it."

"Yeah. I can see that."

"How about turning around and looking at me when I'm talking?"

Michael couldn't help it. He started laughing. He swung around in his chair and said, "You're trying to apologize and you're getting pissed all over again, Steve. You're some piece of work."

"A lot of stress, all right? And I'm not handling it. I admit it. But I'm going to take care of it. I'm going to get it all back together and I mean starting right now."

The old weariness was back. There was just something in Steve that wasn't right. Michael had never been able to come up with any other way of saying it. Just something not right. He loved his brother as blood, but as another human being Steve had always troubled him.

"I hope that's right, Steve."

The Steve smile. The Steve charm. "All that time you spend in the gym, little brother. You nearly knocked me on my ass back there."

"I was trying."

Steve extended his hand. Michael took it. "You're my brother, Michael. You know how much that means to me."

"Yeah."

"Really. I mean that." This wasn't the celebrity smile. This was the real Steve smile. But Michael wasn't deceived. It was just another mood swing. Five minutes from now his rage could well be back. "You tell the old man I'll be by to see him in the next few days. I'll even bring him some of the DVDs he likes. Those Western shows he watched when he was little."

The mercurial Steve. The deadly mood swings. At least this one was friendly.

"I'll check in with you later. Got some business to do."

He straightened his tie, brushed back the hair over his ears with slablike fingers, smiled again at his little brother, then turned and walked to the stairs.

Michael had no idea what Steve was so happy about. Fighting with his brother. Getting threatened by their boss. An unhappy wife and children. A cold beauty who had dumped him.

What the hell was he so happy about?

CHAPTER THIRTY-SIX

Kim sat in one of the tape-patched booths of the convenience store. A lot of people coming in and out of the front doors. Everybody talking about the rain. Men and women hurrying home. Hardscrabble men and women in this working-class neighborhood. The kind of people her folks were. Busting their humps and never seeming to get anywhere. But never relenting, never giving up.

"Ma'am."

Kim had been so involved in her thoughts that she hadn't noticed that the crowd had gone and there was now a woman behind the counter.

The young man she'd talked to before, Jason, had been replaced by a tall, skinny woman with bright red hair that looked awfully suspicious given her probable age of sixty or so. Wore a Western shirt and cracked gum loud as gunshots.

Jason now stood at Kim's booth. "I know you were waitin' for Inez to come on duty. Well, it's six and she's here now."

"Oh, thanks." She could see now that he was staring at the gap between her blouse and her suit coat. The shoulder holster.

"You mind if I ask you something?"

The inevitable question.

"You want to ask me if I've ever shot anybody?"

"Yeah."

"No. But my partner did. Michael. And it still bothers him."

"How come?"

"Well, it's not like it is on TV. There are some people who can kill somebody and just walk away. Some officers are like that but most aren't. It stays with you. Sometimes it causes problems for you. Mentally."

"Yeah, I guess I saw something like that on *60 Minutes* one time. The cop had a breakdown."

She slid out of the booth. "Thanks for telling me about Inez."

The woman was spritzing the counter with disinfectant when Kim walked up.

"Help you?" she said, not glancing up, using a clean rag on the countertop now.

Kim had her ID ready.

Inez snorted. "Seen plenty of them. All three of my husbands were always in trouble." She quit cleaning, wrapped the cleaning rag around the plastic spray bottle and made them disappear below. Then she said, "I imagine you're here about poor little Cindy."

"I'm told you're a good friend of hers."

"I'm glad you didn't say 'were' a good friend of hers. I get sick of people saying that. If that girl was dead, I'd know it. I'd feel it in here." She thumped the chest of her Western shirt. "She ain't dead but she's sure in trouble. She didn't run away or nothing. If she was gonna do that she would've done it a long time ago. Practically ever since I knew her I asked her to move in with me. She needed a parent and neither of the freaks who live in that trailer with her qualifies, if you know what I mean."

"Did you notice anything different about her the last few days before she disappeared?"

The convenience store had started to feel oppressive already. So confined. Narrow aisles of overpriced merchandise. Glass-fronted refrigerated cases for milk and other items that needed to be kept cool. And bad food treats of every variety jammed onto every conceivable inch on the four counter surfaces surrounding Inez.

"Started about a month ago. And we had an argument about it."

"What started about a month ago?"

"Her secret. And it pissed me off. Here I've been like a mother to her for three years and she won't tell me about it. But I'll tell you, I've never seen that kid as happy as she was."

"What do you think made her so happy?"

Inez smirked. "Now, honey, what do you *think* would make a young girl like that so happy? Only one thing I can think of. She fell in love with somebody."

"But you don't know who?"

All the time she talked her jaws were pulverizing her gum. "That's what pissed me off. Wouldn't tell me. She's miserable about her boyfriend Ted and I'm always trying to help her. The way young girls throw themselves around these days it was kinda sweet that she wouldn't let Ted have actual sex with her. They did everything else. She always told me everything. But him getting inside of her—"

The electronic ding of the opening door interrupted her. A middle-aged woman with a transparent plastic scarf over her head came rushing in. "I'm an hour late. The kids are hungry and my husband's probably mad." She was talking to herself. "Do you have frozen dinners and things like that?"

"Right straight back down that aisle you're standing in front of. Get the Stouffer's if you want something that tastes like food. The rest of it isn't so hot."

"Why, thank you," the woman said. Stress had hardened what was probably an attractive face. This was a woman who didn't do a lot of shopping in convenience stores. "I really appreciate it."

"I try to sample everything we sell here. Between you and me, a lot of it's crap." She said this confidentially to Kim as the woman headed to the rear of the place. "Stouffer's is pretty good."

"Yes. I eat quite a bit of it myself. But you were saying that Cindy was happy lately."

"I'd never seen her like that."

"But she didn't say who she was seeing?"

"No. It was a secret. Which was what struck me as so strange. Here she was always telling me everything about herself—and I mean everything; I was like a shrink sometimes and that was fine with me—but this new one she was with . . . She wouldn't tell me anything."

"Did you ever see him?"

"No. The boys she went out with before, they hung out here with some of the regular kids. But not this one. Never saw him, never heard his name mentioned, never got any sense of him at all."

"She didn't give you any hints at all?"

"Not on purpose. I mean the way she talked I got the impression he was older."

"How much older, do you think?"

"At least in his twenties."

"Well if that's the case he could be in trouble. She's fifteen."

"Statutory rape, you mean? This asshole sheriff where I grew up tried to pull that on my first husband. That's how old I was when we ran off. Fifteen and he was twenty-eight. But my folks convinced him not to press charges so we came back and got married. Everything was fine till he stuck up that gas station."

Kim almost laughed. Some things could be funny and sad at the same time. And this was one of them. Inez said all this with no hint of irony or dismay. Just reporting the facts. Fifteen and twenty-eight. Asshole sheriff. Parental approval. Sticking up a gas station.

The woman rushed up to the counter with five frozen dinners. She stacked them up and whipped out a red leather wallet and dug out a credit card. "My boss forgot to do something, so naturally I had to stay over and help him. I usually try and get home early enough to make dinner for everybody. My husband works on the railroad and he gets very hungry."

Inez rang up the order. "My third husband had an appetite like that. Probably what killed him. That man could eat twelve pancakes at a time. And then six or seven sausages. Big ones. We used to get a good laugh out of it. Of course he got hooked on smack, too. That probably had something to do with him dying the way he did, though personally I think the cops made too much of it."

What was there to say? Pancakes and heroin?

After the woman left, Inez said, "Where were we?"

"I wanted to know if you could tell me more about this new friend of Cindy's."

Inez shrugged. "I wish I could, hon. But that's all I know."

Two cars on the drive tripped the bell almost simultaneously. The external heat and the air-conditioning had created moisture on the interior windows. A fog effect.

"Honey, I'm gonna get real busy now. That's Collie just

pulled up. The one in the black truck. He's my fiancé. You can't get a word in edgewise with the guy. And he won't care if you're a detective. He'll just interrupt."

Kim held out her hand. "I appreciate your help."

"You find the bastard that took her, do me a favor. Shoot him right on the spot. Right between the eyes."

Kim smiled, nodded. She wanted to get out of here before Collie appeared. She wasn't sure she could handle the two of them together.

When she pushed through the door, just in time to escape a huge man in a Cubs ball cap charging toward her, she saw that Jason was standing near her car. If he realized it was raining and that he was getting soaked, he didn't let on.

"Any reason you like to stand in the rain, Jason?"

He wouldn't meet her gaze. "I need to tell you something but I'm afraid I'll get in trouble if I do."

"God, Jason, c'mon, let's sit in my car."

At first Jason seemed to forget why they'd slid into her vehicle. He gawked around, apparently in search of guns or gizmos. He didn't find either.

Rain thrummed on the ceiling. The huge man in the ball cap came out puffing on a stogie and tucking a six-pack of beer into his arm as if it were a football. There was mist now. The lights glowed.

"You said you were afraid."

"Yeah."

"Of what?"

"Oh, shit," he said. "You're gonna be pissed off at me and so is everybody else. And I'll probably go to prison."

Prison? Wild thoughts. Was he the killer? Much as she disdained profilers, he would fit one of the types.

"You mean you killed Cindy?"

"Oh, God no! Don't even say that!"

"Then what, Jason? Tell me right out."

"Oh, shit."

"I think you said that already."

"I followed her."

"Cindy?"

"Yeah."

"What do you mean you followed her?"

"You know—followed."

He was hinting at a truth he didn't want to fully admit.

"Go slow and tell me everything."

His head dropped and she watched as he squeezed his bony hands together. The bell on the drive kept dinging cars in and out. But she was barely aware of it all. The only reality was inside this car right now.

"I followed her a lot."

"I see." And she did suddenly realize what he was saying. "Sort of like a stalker, you mean."

"It wasn't to hurt her. I loved her. I really did. I just couldn't keep away from her. She'd come in the store and talk to me—I—" He started crying. "I know I'm nobody to her but any time I'd suggest we should go somewhere together—She couldn't see that I would've taken care of her—"

"Did you take pictures of her?"

"Yes."

"Any nude photos, peeking in her window or anything?"

"God, no. I'm not like that. I just—collected pictures of her. I've got them all on my computer. Pages of them."

"Did you ever send her threatening letters?"

He glared at her. Snuffling up tears, he said, "No. Can't you understand what I'm saying? I loved her. I wanted to be near her. That's all."

She angled around so that she faced him. "You said you were afraid of going to prison. Why would you say that?"

"You know—the—what you called stalking."

His sadness touched her. She'd never had a successful relationship, one she felt secure in. She was so used to seeing angry wasted people, some of them changed by genes or circumstances into predators, that she wasn't quite sure what to say to Jason.

"I don't think you've got anything to worry about, Jason."

Wiping his nose with the back of his hand, he said, "I don't?"

"If you've told me everything. I'll have to take it up with my captain but I doubt he'll do anything about it."

He sat up straight and looked at her. "But there's one more thing."

Without quite knowing why, her stomach knotted and she prepared herself for the jolt she sensed was coming.

"I saw who she was seeing at night. I get my parents' car sometimes and a couple of nights I followed her. At first I didn't know who he was but then I saw his picture in the paper one day. I saw her get into his car the night she disappeared."

"Who're we talking about here, Jason?"

"You know that Dr. Olson? That's who she's been seeing." Then: "He's too old for her. Way too old."

CHAPTER THIRTY-SEVEN

"It's not a real big one."

"You don't need a real big one."

"Wish I could have a couple of those biscuits."

"Yeah. And some mashed potatoes."

His old man grinned. "Damn right some of those mashed potatoes." He leaned out of his wheelchair and tapped Michael on the arm. "Thanks, Michael."

"My pleasure."

"The doc know about this?"

"I called ahead and asked him if I could stop by a KFC and bring you one small drumstick. No potatoes, no biscuits."

"So you didn't have to sneak it in?"

"Sorry to spoil your fun."

"It tastes better when you have to sneak it in."

They were in the old man's room. *Wheel of Fortune* flickered across the TV screen. No sound.

After he and Steve had fought he had felt guilty and confused. Two quick drinks hadn't helped. He'd decided he needed to make his old man smile. Good for the soul. Both their souls.

Michael sat up straight, trying to look his best. He was compensating for the fact that he'd been in a fight. His dad couldn't see well enough to discern any evidence of the fight on Michael's face.

"So how's it going with that missing girl?" Jack said, starting to nibble at his drumstick. He obviously wanted to make it last.

"No big break. We're all talking to everybody we can."

"How's Steve doing?"

"Fine. Working his butt off on it." An easy lie; he'd told his old man so many lies about Steve over the years.

Jack's fingers glistened with grease from the chicken. "Be nice if one of you boys could crack this."

"You never give up, do you?"

"I never got the one case that really stood out."

"You got a lot of good cases, though. You were the best of your time."

"But never a case like this. Same with your granddad. He never got the one big case, either."

"I guess I'm thinking more about the girl, Dad."

"So am I, Michael. They go hand in hand. You find her and save her life and you've got your one big case. The one people will always remember, you know? Every time your name comes up they'll say, 'Oh, that was that Michael Scanlon. Saved the girl after everybody gave up.'" Now his lips glistened, too. He'd nibble and talk, nibble and talk. "I know I'm full of shit, Michael. But I don't have much else to do in this place but daydream. The other night I was thinking what a great governor you'd make."

"Why not president?"

"Now we're getting somewhere."

"How's the chicken?"

"I'm gonna pick this thing clean."

"I almost feel sorry for the chicken."

The old man said, "So what's going on?"

"Going on where?"

"Here. You. You're wound pretty tight."

"I am?"

"C'mon, Michael. I may be in a wheelchair but my brain still works. Most of the time, anyway. And you're my kid. I know your moods. And you're wound pretty tight."

No way he'd tell the old man about what had happened with Steve. "Just tired, I guess. Feeling sort of alone sometimes."

"You could always move in here. You'd like it. We have a lot of fun. People don't know this but we have orgies every night."

Michael smiled.

"I worry about both of you, Michael. There's somebody out there shooting at you and you won't talk about it. And there's something wrong with your brother and you won't talk about that, either."

Michael heard whispering in the hall. He and his father both looked up to see three residents standing there gawking at Michael and obviously talking about him.

Jack raised his voice. "Maybe you can talk some sense into him. Somebody tries to kill him and he tells me it's nothing to worry about."

Michael laughed. "You know who I'm really afraid of?" he said to the old folks in the hall. "This guy right here. And I've been afraid of him all my life."

They looked confused but they laughed.

CHAPTER THIRTY-EIGHT

Olson's Tudor was set on two acres, hidden from the road by a span of pine trees. The rear fell away to the deserted farm and the creek below. The west side of the house was lined with a heavy forest of juniper, rock elm and dogwood.

Protected by her hooded rain jacket, crouched between a pair of rock elms, Kim watched the side windows of the elegant home through a pair of Nikon binoculars that Myles had once used for hunting until his daughter convinced him that killing things for pleasure was not a good thing. He'd donated them to the department. She had used them on a stakeout two weeks ago and had never managed to return them.

The mullioned windows of the second floor were dark. The only light she could see was in the den and living room. No sight of Olson himself.

She hadn't decided which hurt more, the fact that she'd been betrayed in love or that she'd been so stupid not to know that he'd just been using her for information. She had to give him his cleverness. He knew what the department knew on killing number two because she'd shared everything with him. And she'd told him the few things she'd known about the department's investigation into Cindy's disappearance, too.

Humiliated on both counts. The depression would come later. Right now there was just the anger.

The rain was chilly now, slashing through the trees like a liquid scythe. She could feel the earth beginning to puddle at her feet. Smell the musk of loam and the spicy aroma of the wet green leaves.

She thought of all the nights she'd been in that house. In his arms. In his bed. And him the killer of two girls. Probably more, actually. Doubtful these had been his first victims. He was the type of killer who'd likely been at this for years. The Ted Bundy template applied here. The handsome, charming, deadly mass murderer.

His words came back to her. His sweet, sleek words. How drawn to her he was. All those hints of a future together. Plans for a pleasant weekend for them in Chicago at this gallery opening or that play or this concert.

And interspersed with these words were the questions about the dead girls. Casual words they'd seemed. Words that most citizens had about police work. Nothing more. And with Cindy the questions were even more legitimate. After all, she'd been his patient. How much he'd cared about her. How tragic it would be if anything happened to her.

Would she go in there and shoot him? That was her fantasy. Go in there and demand that he lead her to Cindy—alive or dead—and then shoot him right there. Vengeance of the law. Vengeance of the lover fooled.

But she knew better. She was a police officer and she was here to arrest a man who had killed at least two girls. Simple as that.

She wondered where he was. Why he hadn't appeared in any of the windows her binoculars scanned.

She had thought of going to the door, knocking and putting a gun in his face when he greeted her. But maybe that would only delay her finding Cindy. She had spent the past few minutes in this wooded area, her car hidden behind a stand of pines, because she knew she could sneak from here to the back door of the house.

She tried not to imagine what he might be doing to Cindy at this very moment. Images of the dead girls' skulls came to her. She felt sickened, afraid. She had loved him . . . he had been inside her . . . she had dreamed of bearing his children . . .

She pulled the binoculars from her eyes, slid them back into their case and stood up. The dampness from the stinging rain had made her stiff. Arthritis ran in the family, even in the young ones.

Moments later she saw a silhouette against the curtain of the den. His silhouette, she was sure of it. If he stayed there and if the back door was unlocked, she would have no trouble getting inside. But she needed to hurry.

She reached behind her back and pulled her service revolver free. She had no idea how he would respond to her confronting him but it was unlikely he'd just stand there and let her call for backup. But she didn't want to call for backup. This was something she needed to do herself.

A wind whipped a spray of cold rain across her face as she began to emerge from the trees. But she was forced to duck back behind them almost immediately. Headlights slit the fabric of bitter night.

Once again in a crouch, she quickly lifted the Nikon case from the large flap pocket of her jacket. She wanted to get a look at the visitor.

She hadn't needed to hurry. The driver sat in his car for a minute or two before emerging. She wondered what he was waiting for. Then she recognized the car.

What was Steve Scanlon doing here?

* * *

Steve Scanlon had taken the long way. The really long way. The totally unnecessary long way.

Following the fight with his brother he'd gone to a bar where he wasn't known. He knew he needed to stay sober so he ordered a cheeseburger, fries and coffee. The food was surprisingly tasty. There was a Cubs game on—they were playing on the West Coast—so he forced himself to watch it. It got close enough that he actually got interested.

He wanted to feel good, confident when he confronted Olson. The man wouldn't have any choice. He would arrange for half a million dollars in two payments within the next fourteen days or Steve would threaten to turn him in. Olson would be amused at first in his prick way. *Turning me in is turning yourself in*, he'd say. But Steve was sure that eventually the man would cave. Would understand the simple truth. His life was at stake. A doctor who was a serial killer? He would be on death row within a year. Olson was arrogant but he was realistic. He'd paid the freight so far and he'd pay this, too.

Steve had a single shot of Dewar's scotch before leaving the bar. Then he powered up his Trans Am and started to head for the mansion. But then stopped.

He'd first drive past Nicole's condo complex. He wouldn't try to see her. But he needed the proximity. Pitiful as a junkie. Never been like this before in his life. He'd never cried over a woman before, never thrown up when one told him that she no longer wanted to see him. It made him sick but he was helpless.

All he could think of was the excitement he'd feel when he told her about the half million dollars he was about to come into. The half million that would free them from this town. The half million that would start them fresh in California. He swung the Trans Am around and drove through the neon rain. He turned the radio on. A station that played nineties music. Growing-up music. He lucked out. Nirvana. "Smells Like Teen Spirit." He was putting it to Mary Kay Neely that year. Cheerleader. And the best-looking one. And man had she liked sex. Sex everywhere. Everywhere.

It was going to be all right. He knew it. Nineties music stoning him all the way to Nicole's place, he felt younger, stronger, better focused. Olson would go along. And Nicole would go along.

Lightning silvered the condo complex as he reached it. None of the young professionals hanging around the pool tonight bragging on themselves and hustling all the young wives who wanted to be hustled. Hey, why not, when their husbands were doing the same thing?

But with Nicole it would be different. He would be faithful and she would be faithful.

He floored the Trans Am and soared toward the river road that would take him to Olson's.

He slipped his hand down to his holster. He set the gun next to him on the seat. He wouldn't even get out of the car without it in his hand. He had pushed Olson hard. He had seen men crack before, suicide by cop. Maybe Olson was at that point.

The winding road that led to the sprawling Tudor was usually a scenic route but now, in the silver slanting rain and the brooding shadows of the trees on either side of the asphalt, the headlights revealed an area that looked tunnellike and unknowable. Dangerous, somehow.

He knew it was nerves. Liquor stabilized him. He slipped into anxiety without it. He had learned to use alcohol the way other people used medicine. To treat symptoms. The trouble being that he couldn't stop most of the time. He rarely got to be falling-down drunk. But he had learned to function at a level that would make most people incoherent.

But not now. Not even one drink from the flask he had in the glove compartment. Needed to be grimly sober, a state of being he not only hated but was afraid of.

He slowed down. Olson's place was hard enough to find in good weather. It was effectively hidden by enormous trees. At night and in a downpour it was easy to miss entirely.

There. A smudge of yellow light in the trees ahead. Olson's Tudor.

He cut the radio. Took several deep breaths as he wheeled the powerful car on to the narrow drive that led to the house. Olson should be the one who was nervous. He thought again of the flask in the glove compartment. But no. Afterward, after he was driving away from here with a half-million-dollar commitment from Olson absolutely secure . . . then he'd have his drink. He'd have several drinks.

He eased the car up to the wide parking area north of the house itself. Apparently the original owners of the place had liked to have parties. Big ones. You could probably park fifteen cars here comfortably.

He killed the engine. He wished he had the same energy he'd felt back when those songs from the nineties had wired him fifteen minutes ago. But now that he was here he felt suspicious, cautious. Could it really be that easy? Just walk in and get somebody to give you half a million dollars? Olson was a brilliant man. And a clever one. Would he really just go along?

The car became too confining. Coffinlike. His shirt was damp from sweat. He grabbed the black fedora he used on rainy nights. He zipped up his rain jacket.

For all its ferocity he appreciated the rain. The

coldness of it, the rhythm of it revived him, laced him
with that clarity and purpose he'd felt just awhile ago.

Oh no. There wouldn't be any problem with Olson. He
felt sure of it now. He'd go in there and make his de-
mands and Olson would go along. He wouldn't have any
choice.

He stared at the house. He wondered if Olson was
watching him from one of the darkened windows on the
second floor. Standing in the shadows waiting to shoot
him. But no, that wouldn't happen. How would a nice,
genteel doctor explain a dead cop in his driveway?

His gun was in his hand and his hand was stuffed inside the pocket of his rain jacket. He was ready to walk
up to the front door and ring the bell.

But somewhere inside the din of the rain he heard a
sound that startled him, troubled him. Image from last
night: the shooter on the hill above the riverboat casino. His brother almost being killed. His brother arguing that maybe the shooter had been after Steve instead
of Michael Scanlon. Now as he stood here, was he
about to be ambushed the way Michael had been last
night?

All these thoughts bursting in less than a few seconds
as he went instinctively into a crouch, his gun ripped
out of his jacket pocket, his eyes scanning the gloom to
the south of the Tudor.

He had heard somebody. He was sure of it. But his
eyes recorded nothing useful. A wide, empty stretch of
grass. A few ghosts of fog that were transparent, unable to hide anything. Sound of a distant lonely dog
momentarily louder than the rain. A train whistle in the
hills beyond.

And his own sweat. And pounding heart.

And then, behind him, "So you figured it out, too?"

And him swiveling, gun ready to fire. And seeing half-hidden inside the hood of her own rain jacket the kid-sister face of Detective Kim Pierce.

She had her own gun at the ready.

She came three steps closer. "He killed those other two girls. I just hope Cindy's alive. Let's go in there and get him."

"Dr. Olson. This is Molly. I'm on the surgery desk to-night. Mr. Fitzpatrick is complaining again. He says he needs more morphine. I wonder if we could increase the dosage."

Darren Fitzpatrick was a local semipro baseball player who'd broken his leg while sliding into second base. After successful surgery he was discharged but later the young man returned to the ER with a 104 degree temperature and redness and swelling at the surgical site. He was re-admitted and was being treated for an infection.

"Increase his morphine dose by two mg's every four hours as needed for pain."

"Thanks, Doctor. He'll be glad to hear it."

He had just hung up when he heard the sound of a motor on the drive. Steve Scanlon, of course. The eternal adolescent. The Trans Am. The cliché macho attitude and behavior. He wished it was Scanlon he would be rip-ping apart in that bathtub tonight. The man's coarseness was almost more infuriating than his animal greed.

He walked over to the wing chair where he'd been sit-ting earlier. A half-drunk glass of sherry waited there for him. He tried to relax. He sipped at the wine. The scent and the taste usually pleased him. Now they were sour. He wondered what was keeping Scanlon. He thought of going to the window, checking to see. But why give the bastard the pleasure of seeing how nervous he was?

* * *

"How did you find out it was Olson?"

Self-pity burned through Steve Scanlon. So damned close to the money, to Nicole. And then from nowhere Kim shows up. What the hell was he going to do now?

"I was at the office. Alone. This guy called in. He said he lives about a quarter mile from here. He suddenly remembered seeing Olson with a teenage girl in his car one night. Probably was the second one."

"And he just remembered now?"

"You know how it is. They just remember things for some reason."

Mumbling, sounding stupid. Did she believe him? Trying to read her face framed by the hood of her jacket.

And the rain. As if he had just now realized how relentless it was. Cutting, slashing, soaking everything in this cloying bleak night.

He'd been so damned close . . .

"I wasn't going to call for backup but now that I think about it, maybe we should."

"No!" he snapped.

There in the half-light from the front windows he had no trouble reading her expression this time. She first looked puzzled, then irritated. "Why shouldn't I call for backup?"

"We don't need it." Backup? Then it would be all gone. Not only the money. Not only Nicole. But also his life. Prison was no place for a cop. "We can handle this."

"Are you all right?"

"Sure. Why?"

She seemed to be assessing him. Was his panic that obvious?

"I wouldn't mind the publicity, Kim, that's all." The humble voice. He didn't use it often. It needed work. But it was his only chance. "All the trouble I get in, I worry about my job." The humble smile as well as the humble voice. "I've got a wife and kids to worry about. I need the credit."

He could hear her saying to herself, Oh, yes, right, the great family man worrying about his wife and kids. He said, "How'd you cop to it?"

"I'll explain later."

The look of embarrassment and misery on that girlish face pleased him. Bitch. Screwing him up this way.

"C'mon," she said.

They started angling their way through the windswept rain. He was glad they weren't moving any faster. He was trying to formulate some kind of plan here. What was he going to say once they got inside? What the hell was he going to do with her?

By the time he had the first semblance of a plan they were at the imposing vertical plank door. To him the medieval appearance of it fit exactly the pretentious personality of Olson. The entire house did, in fact. In and out.

Kim positioned herself to the side of the door. Flattened herself against the patterned brick of the archway. Gun ready. The way they'd busted many a drug dealer.

Waiting. Shush of rain, tossing of leaf-heavy limbs. Faint footsteps. Closer, closer. And then the door opening.

"Dr. Peter Olson?" Steve said.

But before Olson could speak, Kim stepped next to Steve and said, "This is official business, Peter. We think you know where Cindy is."

CHAPTER THIRTY-NINE

Michael was eating Chinese takeout when the phone rang. He was still at his desk in the detective bureau even though his official shift had ended several hours ago. If asked he would have said that he was still here because he didn't want to let go of the Cindy Baines case. Partially true. He had made two calls to people he'd interviewed previously. Follow-ups to clarify a few things. But he was also here because he hoped to clear his desk of paperwork tonight. Wrap up several things and send them into the happy mist of oblivion.

He wondered about two people. His brother's strange, blissful smile still bothered him. Steve never smiled that way. As if that long-awaited ship had come carrying jewels and gold from lands unknown.

He also wondered about Kim. Which wasn't exactly unusual. Blame the rain, blame the nighttime, but hell, he wondered about Kim many times during the day as well. He would have to give it up, he knew. And maybe it was nothing but laziness, he thought in one of those little bursts of hopefulness. Maybe all he needed to do was make a real effort to go out and find a woman for himself and he'd be over Kim. Once and for all.

But he knew better.

Just as he stabbed a fork into a plump piece of shrimp the second line on his phone rang. He dropped the savaged shrimp back into its container and lifted the receiver.

"Are you having a good time?" Myles. Sarcastic. The city council meeting.

"I take it you're not."

"They just opened the doors. And everybody just now rushed inside. I made the mistake of getting here a little early and standing around in the lobby. Now I know what it's like to be lynched. There are about a hundred people here tonight. And they were all drawing down on me. I'm supposed to go in there and speak to them formally. But they've already ripped the shit out of me. You going to tell me if there's been any kind of break at all?"

"Nothing from Kim or Steve."

"That's another thing. You and I are going to have a sit-down about that brother of yours. I love your old man but I can't handle your brother anymore. Not unless he goes to AA and not unless he really makes an effort to get with the program. I can't do it anymore, Michael. I really can't."

And he was saying all this without knowing anything about Nicole or Gargan's call.

"We'll talk, Bob. We'll get it right. I promise you."

"I'm thinking he's a lost cause, Michael. I mean to be honest."

"He's not. That I promise you."

The cell phone Myles was using didn't amplify surrounding sound very well. But Michael did hear Myles' name called.

"I have to go inside. I'm not good at this stuff. I didn't sign on to do a public relations job." Then, just before clicking off, "I'm serious about your brother, Michael. Remember that."

CHAPTER FORTY

Steve Scanlon said, "Let's go inside, Dr. Olson."

"What the hell's going on here?"

"Detective Pierce has information that we need to talk with you about."

"But you—"

"My name's Detective Scanlon. I know you're familiar with Detective Pierce. Now please cooperate with us. Make it easy all around."

Olson's glance of confusion had shifted to one of fear. His dark eyes reflected the turmoil and surprise of the moment. "I—I guess you may as well come in. But I don't know anything about Cindy. I don't know how you can even think such a thing, Kim."

"Let's go inside now, Doctor." Steve knew that this would be his one chance to take Kim's weapon.

As Olson turned and started to walk back inside, Steve moved to his right, allowing Kim to enter the house before him. That was all he needed to do. She was eager to confront Olson.

When she was only three steps across the threshold, Steve came up from behind her and jammed his gun in her back. "I need your gun, Kim."

He could feel her body tense as she angled her head to see what he was doing. "What the hell's going on here, Steve?"

"I wondered what the hell you were doing," Olson snapped.

"Your gun," Steve said.

"You're part of this, Steve? You kill young girls?"

Steve's free hand gripped her arm, twisted it with such force that she gasped and cursed. He had no trouble wrenching the gun from her hand. He shoved it into the pocket of his rain jacket. "Now go over on the couch and sit down."

She lunged at him and then she swung, her fist glancing off his left temple. Before she could set herself for another punch, he used his free hand to knock the wind out of her. She doubled over and he pushed her in the direction of the couch. She cursed at him but he paid no attention.

"I can't believe this," Olson said.

"You need to stay calm, Doc. We have to figure this thing out."

Kim was perched on the edge of the mahogany-colored leather couch that sat in front of a small display of objects d'art. She still looked gray from being hit so hard in the stomach.

Steve said, "Empty your pockets, Kim."

"The hell I will."

"Stand up and empty them. I don't want to break that cute little nose of yours but I will. Now empty them."

"I don't have any kind of throw gun if that's what you mean. I make my arrests clean. Not the way you do."

Hard to say who she resented more, Steve for forcing her to go along or herself for giving into him. But she knew it was no use.

She jammed her hands into the pockets of her jacket, withdrew her cell phone and her billfold.

"Set them down on the end table. Then turn the pockets of your pants inside out."

"What the hell is going on here?" Olson said.

"She'd better be alive, you son of a bitch," Kim said to him as she flipped up the empty pockets.

"Back pockets, too."

"Screw yourself, Scanlon."

"You see how controlled I am, Kim. You should be proud of me. I'm the loose cannon, remember? But you're the one who's losing it. Now let's see the back pockets."

"I want to know what the hell you think you're doing, Scanlon. You're holding a gun on both of us. Her, I understand. But why me? We're in this together."

"Shut up, Olson."

Steve watched as Kim showed him her back pockets. The gray contrasted with the blue of her slacks. She wasn't giving him the satisfaction of looking afraid. She'd never much cared for him, had always been condescending when he came on to her. But all he could get out of her now was a contemptuous glare. She went back to the couch and sat down.

"Now your turn."

"My turn for what?"

"Empty your pockets."

"My pockets?"

"You hear this shit?" he snapped at Kim. "He's got a piece stuffed down the backside of his pants that he didn't think I saw. Right under his shirt. You're pathetic, Doc. Now lay the gun on the end table next to her cell phone there. And then empty all your pockets."

"Is the girl still alive?"

But neither paid her any attention.

Kim looked around wildly. Had to be a way to get Steve's piece from him. While Olson was setting his gun down and turning his pockets inside out, she calculated her chances of rushing at Steve.

But he watched all this in glances and pointed the gun right at her forehead. "Don't take the chance, Kim."

Olson had all his pockets sticking out like tongues. He looked confused as much as frightened. What the hell kind of deal was this?

Steve crossed the room. He took Olson's gun and shoved it into his jacket pocket.

"Now we're all going to walk down the hall to your den. And you'd better listen carefully, Doc, because if you do one thing wrong, you're dead in your tracks. And that's the same for you, Kim. You're going in the den, Doc, and you're going to take out everything in that little wall safe of yours and you're going to leave it open and you're going to walk back out. Kim'll be standing next to me the whole time. Then we're all going back to the living room. You both understand that?"

"He's going to kill us," Kim said.

All confusion was gone from Olson's face now. Only a boyish fear remained.

"Why is he going to kill us?"

"She doesn't know what she's talking about. How could I kill you and get away with it?"

"I'm not sure how he's going to try to explain it but he's got something figured out. Think about it. He can't let me live and if he kills me then he has to blame it on somebody. And that's you. And if he blames you then you'll rat him out. Either way, we're both dead."

"You'd kill us just like that?" His doctorly voice hoarse now.

"You cut up young girls, Doc. And anyway, I don't know what's going to happen."

"But she's right. You won't have any choice."

Riding high. Adrenaline stoning him. "Well, there's only one way to find out. Lead the way, Doc."

He grabbed Kim by the shoulder and shoved her

toward Olson. She would be especially dangerous now. She knew what was about to happen. Olson was in shock. Useless to himself.

They crossed the great living room with its furnishings and artifacts that spoke of a time romantics around the world had long honored. A nexus of different ages met in this house. Such grace, sophistication. But now it was being violated by a lurid little drama that was vulgar and lowborn in every respect.

"There must be some kind of deal we can make." Pleading. The doc would be begging soon.

"Just shut up, Olson, and keep walking to the den."

Down the long museum-like hall with its lighted portraits. Steve recognized a Rembrandt and a Gauguin from somewhere. So much for his education in the arts.

Kim gave it a try about halfway down the hall. She hunched over and feinted to the left, ready to turn back on him, grab him around the waist. But she was reckless and she was slow and so when her turn was completed, she faced the point of the gun four inches from her face.

Breathing hard, she straightened up, got in line again. She said nothing. There was nothing to say.

"There's about a hundred and fifty thousand in my safe, Scanlon. Listen to me. It's all yours. And there'll be more after we can get rid of Kim's body."

"Say, that's an idea, Doc. I forgot. You can slice and dice her."

"And that won't be all the money, either. I can get up to half a million if you can give me three or four months."

They had come to the door of the den.

"Are you listening to me, Scanlon? Did you hear what I said?"

"Step inside there and flip on the light. And then just stand there for a minute so I can see you."

"There's no reason we can't work this out." On the verge of tears.

"Do what I said. Step inside and get the light on and just stand there."

"You're not listening to me, Scanlon—"

But he went. He faded to black in the unlighted doorway. Then a soft light illuminated the den. Burnished light for a man of medicine.

"Now walk back to the safe."

"Please, Scanlon; please. I—I can't even get my breath."

"The safe, Doc. Now."

He had probably shit himself by now, Steve thought. He saw that a lot with homicides of course, but it was usually the body responding to death. But what about right before death, out of sheer fear? He'd always wondered how he would react. He'd always thought of himself as tough but you never knew how you'd be when the big moment came. You just never knew.

"Move, Doc."

The guy was so scared his knees started to give out twice before he managed to reach the safe.

"I don't want to die but it's almost worth it to see him die," Kim said. "And then you'll die, Scanlon. You won't get away with this."

"Maybe not. But I'll sure give it a good try." Then: "Open the safe, Doc."

"I'm not sure I can remember the combination."

He probably wasn't lying. Panic had skewered his concentration.

"You want me to tell you what happens if you don't remember it, Doc?"

"You just need to sit down with me and talk about everything, Scanlon. We can work this out."

"Shut up. I'm really getting sick of your bullshit."

"Oh, God," Olson said. "Oh God." And now he really was crying.

"You enjoying this, Kim? Seeing him suffer? I'm doing you a favor."

But she said nothing.

The hand that tugged the portrait back to reveal the safe was shaking so much Steve could see it from where he stood.

"I don't know if I can do this." Sobbing. A ten-year-old boy now. The boogeyman had come out of the closet and was scaring the shit out of him.

"You'd better be able to do it."

"She said you're going to kill us anyway."

"I haven't decided yet."

"He's lying. Don't believe him."

"Open it, Doc. Right now."

"You're a piece of shit, Steve. Your brother will kill you if he ever finds out about this."

"If you liked my brother so much, why'd you dump him?"

The expression on her face was to be savored. That shut the bitch up for good.

As they'd been talking, he'd kept an unerring eye on Olson. The doc was now on his second shaky try on the safe. All the times he'd opened it. He was really melting down. Between tries he'd wiped his hands over and over on his trouser legs. They were probably raw by now.

And then the lovely sound of the safe door opening.

"I knew you could do it, Doc. Now step away and walk back here."

"You've got what you want. There's no reason to kill me now."

"But it's all right if I kill her?"

"Well—she's a threat to us. I'm not."

"So much for love, huh, Kim? Now get your ass back here, Doc."

Olson babbled all the way. His hands were palms-up in plaintive submission. He put panhandlers to shame.

Steve stepped back. "You lead us back to the living room, Doc. Kim, you walk right behind him."

"Is he really going to do it, Kim?" Starting to cry again.

She said nothing. Steve wondered if she was still chewing on the comment he'd made about Michael.

"Is he really going to do it, Kim?"

"Just shut up. Just walk. Don't give him the pleasure of coming apart."

"Oh, God. Oh, my God."

"Walk, you two. Now." He jammed the pistol into Kim's back.

Olson's legs started to give out on the short journey. He slumped against the wall. By now you could smell his feces. Kim righted him, then shoved him ahead.

When they reached the living room, Steve said, "You stand over there, Kim. By the door."

She'd lasted right up to this moment. All the tough bullshit. But she paled now and kept gulping. Her hands were bloodless fists. Her eyes gleamed with tears.

She was having trouble with her own legs now. The knees buckling twice before she reached the area in front of the door.

He did her the favor of making quick work of it. Out came Olson's gun from his pocket. He brought it up, aimed. She squeezed her eyes shut. He put a bullet in the center of her forehead.

Olson's scream was so shrill he sounded as if he'd suddenly changed genders. So shrill that even though Steve was holding the gun, his arms were pebbled with goose bumps.

"Listen. You have to listen to me, Scanlon. You could have so much money by keeping me alive. Think of five years down the line. I make a lot of money and I've got a good inheritance. Please listen to me. Please."

But Steve was sick of listening to him. Sick of him entirely. Fucking creep killing young girls. Doing the world a favor.

"Oh, shit, oh, shit," Olson said.

His very last words because Steve had Kim's gun in his hand now and by the time the doc could utter even one more "shit," he was starting to tilt right and then tilt left. The two bullets in his chest then did their work. The doc fell face-first dead on his expensive Persian rug.

CHAPTER FORTY-ONE

The wet elm leaves gleamed with the red and blue of emergency lights. The fresh night air following the rain was stabbed by the staccato words of six different squad car radios and two crime lab vans. Four uniformed police stood at the base of the wide front steps leading into the Olson mansion. The wail of two ambulances had scattered all the animals in the nearby woods. And the convoy of press cars and vans just now turning into the drive would keep them scattered for some time.

In the vestibule of the mansion Mayor Tom Elmore stood talking to Police Chief Bill Hoover. Elmore wore a red polyester golf shirt and black trousers. Hoover looked heavier than usual in a yellow Ban-Lon shirt and green golf pants. Both of them were flushed of face and startled of eye. They'd been playing poker with two of the assistant DA's and a retired monsignor. They weren't much at poker. They did much better at drinking. Rather than drive and risk an accident, the mayor had ordered his driver to pick them up and bring them to the crime scene. Elmore suggested that they have their driver rush into Wendy's and get them coffee on the way out. Hoover suggested that they keep the windows rolled down. The breeze would sober them up.

But the breeze didn't do half the job the sight of the two bodies did. As soon as Chief Hoover began to talk to the stunned Steve Scanlon, he learned of the carriage house and what they'd found there. They had only five minutes of trouble with the electronic lock and then the door was swung wide and the drugged, half-naked girl was helped to her feet. She fell dazed and sobbing into the arms of an officer.

All this had taken place in less than fifteen minutes. Elmore was waiting for his assistant Horan to get there. There was an election coming up. Elmore did not want to face the press when he had been drinking this much.

They stopped talking when Michael Scanlon appeared in the doorway.

"What a hell of a night, Michael," Chief Hoover said, walking over to his detective. "But the girl is alive. There's a doctor with her now. They'll be bringing her out soon."

"Where's my brother?"

"Myles is in with him, Michael. They're in the den. Steve's pretty shaken up. Imagine walking in on all this."

Michael had caught an armed robbery an hour and a half ago. A neighborhood liquor store. The owner had been on duty and had shot one of the robbers before they'd shot him in the chest. Michael and a uniformed man had combed the nearby streets. The wounded one had been deserted by his companion. He lay badly bleeding behind a Dumpster. Easy to pack him into an ambulance. As he was finishing up everything he got the call about the killings at the Olson mansion.

"I'd like to see him."

"Of course. The door's closed but just knock. I'm sure Myles won't mind you coming in."

Mayor Elmore placed a doughy hand on Michael's

shoulder. "That's quite a family you've got, Michael. First your father and now his two sons. We're proud of all of you. It's just too bad Detective Pierce was killed tonight. She was a fine officer, too."

Even Hoover winced at a few of the clichés. Elmore was in dire need of his assistant Horan.

The living room had been invaded by the crime lab. The steely stench of blood was mixed with the stark smell of various chemicals needed for crime scene work.

Michael nodded at a few of the familiar faces as he stepped around the outlines where the bodies had been. His impression of the place was that it was piss elegant but that had been his impression of Olson, too. Voices reached him as soon as he started down the hallway.

Myles would be comforting Steve. He would also be nailing down every single pertinent detail about the past few hours.

He had to knock twice before the rumbling male voices ceased.

"Who is it?" Myles snapped.

"Me. Michael."

"Oh, Michael. C'mon in."

The crime lab team had preceded them in here. The two men sat in facing wine-colored leather chairs.

Steve looked up at him and said, "Man, I'm glad you got here finally."

"So am I," Myles said. "Come over and sit down."

Michael walked over. Steve rose from his chair and grabbed Michael's hand like a supplicant. Not hard to understand, finding Kim dead like this. Kim, dead. He kept trying to make it real to himself. For once he wouldn't be the comforter to some victim's loved one.

He needed comforting himself. He tried to focus on Cindy Baines. She was alive. She was alive.

This room was everything he expected he'd find in a mansion. The bookcase-lined walls, the fireplace, the massive globe, the expensive leather chairs, the antique desk. The kind of set you saw in adventure movies, homes to the sinister and powerful.

"I'm still not sure what happened," Michael said to Myles. Steve had slumped in his chair. Cops lost it all the time and not only in rage. Every once in awhile, luck of the draw, a cop saw something that undid him. Michael had lost it one day when he'd seen a small child pulled from a river where he'd waded while his folks played Frisbee. He had wanted to kill the parents, kill himself. Howling anger, howling impotence.

"Steve ran into her earlier tonight. He said she sounded upset about something."

"She was crying," Steve said, glancing up. "I was over near the Wal-Mart. I saw her car and blinked her over. She was really upset about something. Pretty bad, in fact. I tried to find out what but all she said was that it had something to do with Olson. But she didn't say what. You know Kim and I had our problems from time to time but I was standing by her door in the rain—even with my rain jacket I was getting wet—and she reached out and grabbed my hand. Really squeezed it hard. Surprised the hell out of me. But we were good friends for a long time before we started getting on each other's nerves. I even bent down and kissed her on the forehead. I kept asking her to tell me what was wrong. But she wouldn't. Then she just said good-bye and took off."

Steve slumped back into his shock and depression. Long sighs. "I kept thinking about running into her. And how upset she was. I figured maybe it wouldn't hurt to take a run out to Olson's place. I saw lights on and decided to walk up to the door. And then as I was walking toward the house I glanced over at this line of pine trees and I saw a car parked behind them. I checked it out. It was Kim's car so I knew something was wrong. I took my gun out and ran to the house. I tried the door. It was unlocked and I went inside." Michael had never heard his brother sob before. The sound chilled him. "If I had followed her out there right away like I thought about doing, she'd be alive right now."

"It's a hell of a thing walking in on something like that," Myles said. He looked at Michael. "Your brother's going to need all the help he can get."

"He's my brother. I'll take care of him."

"But the young girl's all right. That's the big thing. Kim saved her life. She didn't die in vain, anyway. She figured out that Olson was the killer and she confronted him. They both had guns and they killed each other."

Steve said, "I should've come sooner. I could've saved her."

Anger. Remorse. Sense of failure. Michael recognized all the feelings. He'd experienced them many times himself.

Myles scowled but said nothing. Just looked at Michael and shook his head. This one was going to be a bitch. Counseling for sure. Time off, probably. "Leave you two alone for a few minutes. Then I know the chief wants to talk to you some more."

Listless nod from Steve. Myles stood up and left quietly.

"I still can't bend my mind around this, Michael."

"I know."

"Goddamnit, I should have followed her out here right away."

"You did what you could, Steve."

"I know how you felt about her."

"Yeah."

"So how're *you* doing?"

"I don't know. I'm glad the girl's alive. I'm glad Olson's dead. But beyond that I don't know."

Steve leaned back in his tall leather chair. For the first time he seemed to really see his brother. "All that bullshit we've been through lately, you and me."

"No point in talking about it now."

"I'm going to see the old man tomorrow."

"He'll appreciate that."

"I should've been seeing him all along. And I'm going to get the other things straightened out, too."

"Wendy?"

"The marriage is over, Michael. My fault. She's a good woman and she should have unloaded me a long time ago. I'm going to make things right for when we get a divorce."

"What about Nicole?"

"I don't know. It's probably over but after tonight—" He touched his hand to his forehead. "Coming in here tonight, after what I saw—Things are going to change."

Michael wanted to believe it but Steve said the same things over and over whenever his drinking got out of hand. A lot of resolutions that lasted for a few days, a week at the outside.

"I'm sorry about Kim, Michael."

"It hasn't hit me yet. But when I get home it will. When I try to sleep."

"We'll have to face her folks. Poor goddamned Irene. She's sick enough. This might just kill her."

Michael stood up. "I'll handle it. You've been through enough."

"I really appreciate that, Michael."

He went over and clenched Steve's shoulder. "You had the worst part of it, Steve. That's the least I can do."

Steve patted his hand. "It's like we're brothers again, Michael."

"Yeah," Michael said. "That's exactly what it's like."

CHAPTER FORTY-TWO

With all the press cars, vans, even news choppers over-head, the police station parking lot resembled another crime scene. These were not just local people, either. The Chicago press was here, as well, reporting not only for their own city but filing stories for the networks. A young girl had been found alive; a monster had been slain; an attractive young police officer had been killed; and the local detective who'd discovered the scene was now being sought as the only true expert on this story. Yes, there'd be various official forensic, psychological and legal statements. But Steve Scanlon had actually been there and seen the bloody ending to it all.

Mayor Elmore and Chief Hoover were being feted with admiring questions that allowed each of them to pontificate on how well the police in this city did their work and how teenage girls could now walk the streets in safety. They were crisp in white shirts and vivid ties and best suits. Only their red eyes indicated what a long night they'd had.

Before letting Steve come to the microphone, the mayor read an e-mail that the governor had sent earlier this morning.

"I want to congratulate you and your police force, Mayor Elmore, for demonstrating how important it is when the community joins forces with law enforcement to bring a terrible killer to justice."

In the fervor and fever of the heady press conference, nobody seemed to mind that what the governor said didn't make a whole hell of a lot of sense. The community didn't have anything to do with it. A detective had investigated the case, figured out who had been snatching and killing the girls, and had confronted him. And had died for her trouble.

Then it was Steve's turn.

"I know you have questions for me. But I think the mayor and the chief did a good job of telling you basically what happened."

Lisa Hepburn was in the front row of the surging pack. Royal blue was her fashion color of the day. A well-cut suit, starchy white blouse, matching necklace and earrings. "Have you talked with Kim Pierce's loved ones yet?"

"I called them about eight o'clock this morning. My brother Michael called them last night."

"How're they doing?"

Of all the irritating, dumb-ass press questions, this had to be the dumbest and most irritating. How do you *think* her parents would be doing? Depressed, angry, inconsolable. But he had a role to play here and he had to play it carefully. "They're doing the best they can. This is a great loss. Not just to them but to all of us, to everybody who knew her and worked with her." He'd been polishing those words for the last half hour. Now for a little John Wayne stuff. "She was one of the best damned cops I've ever worked with on the force. She was smart and tough."

A Chicago woman said, "But hadn't she been dating Dr. Olson for some time? You said she was smart. But didn't it take a long time for her to figure out what he was really doing?"

A Chicago male said, "That's right. Maybe she was inadvertently giving him information that helped him."

Now was the time for anger. "You're going to question the integrity of a woman who gave her life to save a young girl? Kim Pierce was one of the finest people I've ever known. Anybody can be deceived. And as soon as she realized what he was she went straight to him. And got herself killed for the trouble."

Nobly defending a dead colleague. Would look damned good on the six o'clock news.

And then something going on behind him. The press straining to identify the source of the excitement.

Steve glanced over his shoulder. The Baines mother and young Cindy herself being led to the microphone by the mayor's assistant Horan. Horan was grinning his ass off. This was a PR person's wet dream.

The mayor and the chief rushed to greet them. The mayor gave Natalie Baines a hug so enthusiastic it lifted her off her feet. Cindy looked lost and nervous. Steve noted that they'd been dressed in proper middle-class clothes, Natalie in a belted wine-colored jacket dress and Cindy in a layered-look top of contrasting greens and a denim skirt. Horan wouldn't have allowed them to look like trailer park folks.

After the mayor and the chief had taken their photo ops with the Baineses, Horan hustled the females up to the microphone. He shoved Natalie at Steve for another photo op embrace, the press orgasmic. Then the star herself, the real star, the stunned and terrified-looking Cindy. The docs at the hospital had been against her leaving the hospital but Horan had said that if he took a doc along, everything would be fine. Between Horan and the hospital PR flack the docs finally gave in.

Steve was just as awkward with the Baineses as they were with him. When they were done with the hugs, the three of them stepped up to face the reporters, Steve in the middle.

"I just thank God," Natalie Baines said, her lower lip quivering.

"I'll bet you thank God, too, don't you, Cindy?" a reporter asked.

Horan beamed.

Cindy, dazed, squinted in the direction of the questioner and said, barely whispering, "I just keep thinking about those other two girls he killed. Now I know what they went through."

Horan scowled. Who wanted a reminder of the two dead girls on a morning when the mayor's autumn election chances were suddenly looking a whole lot better?

But then Cindy came through for him. She slumped against Steve, who took her to him, and began crying. "I'm just happy to be alive."

Steve hugged her tighter and kissed her on the forehead.

Hard to know which one to kill first.

Leo Rice was sitting in a Starbucks at lunchtime surrounded by the kind of people he had always hated. The pretty ones, the sleek ones, the ones who always looked right through him.

He'd rape the women before he killed them and he would humiliate the men before he snuffed their lights out. He had to struggle against losing it when he was surrounded by these kinds of people. The only reason he came in here was because he saw this woman's ass and he was mesmerized by it. Following it right in like a homing pigeon. He thought he'd get to stare at her if nothing else but it turned out she just got something to go.

He'd caught Steve Scanlon's act on TV this morning and he played it back now as he finished his coffee. Guy was a good actor, had to give him credit. He'd lucked out with the girl showing up. One of those "aw" moments the civilians always went for. Had to be riding high now. But that would be ending soon. Very soon.

Same for the black bastard who'd kicked him around at the club the other night. He had a surprise coming, too.

He was just about to stand up when two pretty boys walked past him carrying their lunches on trays. Expensive clothes, expensive haircuts, expensive smiles. Cell phones and iPods and laptops and BlackBerrys. Had the world by the balls. The men were probably getting blowjobs from their secretaries every day and the women were probably humping every male in the office. The old rage seized him. He had to consciously stop himself from grabbing their trays from their manicured fingers and throwing them across the room. And then beating them to death the way he'd taken care of this smartass in Joliet. Did it careful, though. They could not quite prove it wasn't an accident.

He forced himself to rush past the tables, weaving in and out as if it were a game of some kind.

By the time he reached the street the craziness was on him full force. Everything looked distorted for thirty seconds or so. He blinked. Needed to calm down. Had work to do.

He fell to walking. He wasn't sure where, he wasn't sure why, just walking the streets of this Midwestern city on this very hot day, the noise of cars and trucks, the chatter of people and finally the face of a dog bringing him back to the safety of self-control.

The dog was a black Lab tied to a parking meter in

front of a health food store. Jake was who it reminded him of. Jake was the Lab he and his brother had owned until the night they both got drunk and were shooting a couple of the old man's handguns and one of them somehow put a bullet right into Jake's sweet sad Lab face. They were digging a hole to bury Jake when the old man came home and found them. The old man beat them bad and then started crying. They'd had no idea how much he'd liked that dog. And it was the only time they would ever see him cry.

He found a hotel lobby and walked over to a stand of wall phones. He chose one at the end. This was an upscale hotel so the phone book was intact. He found the number he was looking for and punched the numbers in.

"Golden Cage." Male voice.

"Is Bob in yet by any chance?"

"Bob? Afraid we don't have any Bobs here. Sorry."

"Oh. Well I was a little drunk the other night and was sort of a wiseass with one of your bouncers. A black man. I'm kind of embarrassed about it. I wondered if it'd be all right to come back tonight."

Laughter. "You mean Cale Edmonds. People get smart-ass with him all the time. Goes with the territory. Don't worry about it. If you'd really gotten to him he would've picked you up and crushed you with one hand."

Rice laughed, too. "I see what you mean."

"Everybody gets a little gnarly now and then. Just when you see him tonight tell him you're sorry you gave him grief. He won't give you any trouble. He's a nice guy."

A nice guy, Rice thought, remembering the beating Cale Edmonds had given him. "I'll do that. And thank you very much."

As soon as he hung up, he raised the phone book from its mooring and started searching for one Cale Edmonds. He didn't have any trouble finding him at all. Phone number. And address.

The nurse wheeled Jack Scanlon into the sunroom and then signaled for his sons to take their places next to him, Michael on the left, Steve on the right.

"Jack said he wanted a good picture of you all together," the stout, older nurse said. "My oldest son bought me this digital camera last Christmas so I guess I'm elected. Now everybody look happy."

"I *am* happy," Jack said from his chair. "I finally got both my boys here."

Michael and Steve had been here for half an hour. They'd walked into Jack's room together. Jack had been dozing in bed. When he woke up and saw them he teared up instantly, as if he was experiencing a miraculous vision.

He reached his bony arms out to them and they came to him, one on either side of the bed, and they heard the pure, joyous laugh of their old man in his younger years.

"Everybody was watching you on TV this morning, Steve," Jack had said. "You really handled yourself just right. I was really proud of you, Steve."

"So was I," Michael said.

"I'm just sorry you had to walk in and see Kim dead."

"Myles thinks I should probably see the police shrink."

"I know you're not much for that kind of thing, Steve, and I wasn't either. But they help. After your mom died I saw old Doc Ryan. He was kind of a crusty old bastard, for a shrink I mean, but he really helped me. That's nothing to be ashamed of these days."

"That's what I've been telling him, Dad."

"Well, that's two against one, Steve." Sly smile. "Looks like you'll go see whoever's there these days."

Steve said, "Maybe."

He held out his hands for them to take. "I asked one of the nurses to get some photos of the three of us. She said she knows how to get them framed pretty cheap so I can put a couple of them up in this room."

So here they were.

"Look pretty now, you three."

"Now that's a hell of a thing to say to us." Jack grinned.

The one thing about digital cameras. They sure took a lot of pictures quickly. The nurse angled them this way, that way, took shots of Jack and Steve, Jack and Michael, all three of them together, Jack alone.

When she finished, she said, "One of you is on your way to Hollywood."

"I'll bet it's Dad," Steve said.

"That's right," the nurse said as she started toward the wheelchair. "And he'll be a big hit."

Michael had assumed that they'd go back to the old man's room but he could see now that his father was starting to fade. The glaze on the eyes. The head lolling rightward. The breath coming fast and shallow.

The nurse saw the same thing and said to the brothers, "Jack's going to need some rest before he goes to Hollywood. Maybe now's a good time for a nap."

Jack tried to raise a hand in protest but he only managed to lift it a few inches off the arm of his wheelchair. He was exhausted.

Michael watched as Steve bent down and kissed the old man on top of the head and then hugged him. He hadn't seen Steve this affectionate toward old Jack since they were young teenagers. He felt the love and admiration for his brother he once had. Hard to believe that angry, self-absorbed Steve could find this kind of tenderness within himself. But maybe the sight of Kim lying on that floor had changed him by brute force.

Jack was asleep by the time the nurse pushed him out of the sunroom.

"I should've been seeing him a lot more than I have, Michael."

"There's still time."

"Not much. At least that's what I'm afraid of."

"Well, both of his docs say that he's hanging in there."

"I hope so."

They started walking back toward the front doors and the parking lot. Both of them had had their faces on TV over the past few days so a number of residents waved at them. It didn't matter why they were momentarily famous in this small city. All that mattered was that they were celebrities of a sort.

The early afternoon sunlight was blinding. Michael leaned against the trunk of his unmarked police car and said, "I know you've got the inquest and then you get your week off."

"Yeah. But I still don't know what I'll do with it."

"Spend some time with the kids."

"Oh, right. Sure. I'll be doing that. But I mean in general."

"That doesn't mean you have to spend time with Wendy."

"Hey, Michael, back off, all right? We're getting along for the first time in a long time. Don't start lecturing me about my family life, all right?"

"Guess you're right. I'm sorry."

"Just so much shit in my head right now. Can't think straight. I just keep thinking about Kim lying there on the floor." Deep sigh. "I guess I need to be alone and figure out how to come down from last night."

Michael tapped his brother's arm. "You're right. You need to do what'll help you through this."

"I really may see the shrink."

"Couldn't hurt."

Another surprise hug. "Sorry I'm such a bastard sometimes, Michael."

"You're not a bastard today, Steve. You made Dad happier than I've seen him in a long time."

"He's the best, man. And so are you."

Then he was gone.

All the way over to Cale Edmonds' house Leo Rice was still pissed about the price of the baseball bats he'd seen. He hadn't bought a bat since he was in seventh grade and back then they'd cost a couple of bucks. He'd gone to Wal-Mart expecting to pay eight, nine bucks, maybe ten or eleven at the outside. But standing in front of the ball bat selection he couldn't believe what he saw. What did they call that? Oh, yeah, right, sticker shock. He had sticker shock of the century. While he found a bat that would do what he wanted for thirty bucks he was stunned to find prices that went up to two hundred and fifty dollars. You got one of those plastic helmets with it, yes. But who would pay two hundred and fifty dollars for a ball bat?

He walked up the side of Cale Edmonds' small brick house. He stood in front of his sporty red car and shouted, "Hey, Edmonds!"

Then he got to work. He hefted the bat over his shoulder and drove it deep into the center of the windshield.

He did the headlights next. He was going to move to the driver's window but that was when he heard the back door flung hard against the house and the word "Motherfucker!" screamed several times.

Leo Rice had gambled and won. The big black steroid monster came roaring out of the side door dressed in an aqua muscle shirt and red boxing trunks. He didn't seem to have a gun with him. Cale Edmonds believed his physical strength made him invincible.

He came screaming up to Rice, ready to jump him. But that was when Rice turned and jammed a gun in his face.

"Hi there, coon. Remember me?"

He brought the gun up in an arc and broke Edmonds' nose with the barrel of it. Even facing a gun, Edmonds lunged for Rice but he was off-balance and Rice had no difficulty bringing his knee straight up between the man's legs. With a broken nose and a crippled body, Edmonds sank to the driveway.

"You won't be sticking that thing in no white girls for awhile," Rice said. "And you won't be showin' off for your boss for awhile, either. That's what you were doing the other night, showin' her what a big tough man you were. Well she's gonna laugh when she sees you tonight, way you look now. And don't bother about the cops. You call the cops you'll be getting her in a whole lot of trouble. She gave me a rifle the other night that the cops have been lookin' for. And if they come for me, the first thing I do is mention her name."

"You motherfucker, you motherfucker." Over and over.

The pain from the broken nose must be kicking in, Rice figured.

He'd laid the ball bat across the hood. He picked it up and carried it to the rear of the flashy car. He creamed the window even better than he'd creamed the wind-shield.

Then he jammed the Ruger into his belt and walked away, the bat over his shoulder as if he were heading out to play some ball.

CHAPTER FORTY-THREE

WELCOME HOME
CINDY

Jason Lewis had started to work on the sign as soon as he'd started his shift this morning at the convenience store. He took a piece of cardboard from a Cheetos display that had been left in the back room of the place and started carefully designing the sign with red and black Magic Markers.

He'd developed a pretty good eye for rudimentary design from all the comic books he'd read since age five. The layout artists really knew how to make things dramatic. At the bottom of the letters he would carefully put tape on the backside of a photo of Cindy. Then he would set it in the front window for all to see.

His sign work was hampered by the usual crowd of customers in for gas, smokes, junk food and all the other overpriced items the store stocked. Most people didn't stay long on the average day. They were in a hurry, frantic about pleasing bosses or finding prospects to call on next. Today was different. Today they lingered and today they talked about the infamous Dr. Olson.

"You could see just by looking at him there was something wrong with him," a beautician told Jason. "I tried to get in to see him once for my neuralgia. But he was too booked up so I went someplace else. It gives me the creeps even thinking of him putting his hands on me."

"That lady cop saved the state a lot of trouble and money," a trucker said. "They put him in prison, somebody would've killed him right off anyway. Even prisoners hate guys like that."

"I saw his picture on TV this morning," a mailman said. "When you look close at him he looks gay."

"I just feel so sorry for the family of that woman detective," a schoolteacher said. "She was in a history class of mine. Very smart and very sweet."

By midafternoon, Jason had the sign up in the window. The frustrating thing was that nobody said anything about it. Were all these people blind? How could they miss it right by the door?

But then they were starting to talk about Olson and Cindy less, too. Jason had noticed that most news stories had a shelf life of about four to five hours. And these were the major news stories. Because after four or five hours another major news story had replaced it.

So now Jason stood behind the counter in his Robert Plant T-shirt, spritzing the area with Windex where coffee had recently sloshed over the paper cup. Windex not only picked up the stain, it took away the stickiness, too. The wonders of modern science, as a comic book hero in one of the alternate comics always said sardonically.

When the door opened and the bell rang, Jason glanced up, expecting to see a customer. Instead it was Inez. Her shift wasn't due to start for four more hours. He wondered why she was here.

"Fix me a couple slices of pepperoni pizza and grab me some coffee, will ya, Jason?"

Today was her red cowgirl outfit. Red spangly shirt, red spangly slacks, cute little red cowboy hat perched at an angle on her head. She looked like an aged cow-girl doll that'd get wrapped up as a Christmas gift.

She was almost always polite when she asked Jason to do something for her. Everything was please this and please that. But not this time. She'd given her order and then went over and slid in one of the patched-up booths and lighted up a cigarette.

What the hell was wrong with her? Jason wondered as he slid two humongo slices of pizza into the micro-wave. She was treating him the way she treated irritating customers. Smoking inside was against the law. And what the hell was she going to use for an ashtray? That was one of the problems with Inez. She certainly had her moods.

When the microwave beeped he shoved the two pieces on a paper plate, used the silver metal teat for black regular coffee and carried her meal over to her.

The drive was empty for the moment, so he perched himself on the edge of the booth seat across from her.

"You really shouldn't be smoking in here, Inez."

She had already jammed the V end of the pizza in her mouth. As he watched her lick her lips after each bite it struck him as obscene. Maybe because it suggested that Inez still had sex and the thought of old people having sex made him uncomfortable.

She took another big bite, a spiderweb of cheese clinging to the corner of her mouth. "You going to call the law on me?"

"You know better than that. But if Kelly showed up he'd fire us both."

"Kelly's an asshole."

"I agree, but he's the one who inspects all these places. You know how he likes to surprise us."

After another bite, she said, "You know who I keep thinking about?"

"Who?"

"That lady detective. We had some nice talks. She was real patient with me. Let me rattle on and on. I liked her."

"Yeah, I think about her, too." He had never told anybody except Detective Pierce about seeing Cindy with Olson. If he'd told her the day Cindy disappeared, Detective Pierce would probably still be alive. He was wondering if the police knew about what he'd told her. People would hate him if they knew that he'd held back information. They'd blame him for the detective's death.

"They still don't know how she figured it out. About that bastard doctor, I mean." Then she went back to her pizza.

"Well, you know how detectives work. They just figure things out all of a sudden."

Around a mouthful of pizza, her cigarette burning like pagan smoke on the edge of the table, she said, "That's on TV. I don't know if that's how it works in real life."

The bell from the drive dinged twice. Jason slid out of the booth, glad for the respite from talking about the lady detective.

He should have called the police right away. Even if it meant he'd be in trouble himself.

He should have; he really should have.

CHAPTER FORTY-FOUR

This time the eyes were gentler on Steve and no smirks lurked in the smiles. He walked along the swimming pool in the dying day, tense at first but relaxed by the time he reached the stairs leading to Nicole's condo.

Not too difficult to understand why the yuppies in their bikinis and swim shorts were kinder to him today. He wasn't a hero but he was a man who had experienced something unimaginable to most civilians. Hell, to most cops. And they'd likely seen at least sound bites of him with Cindy and her mother. And heard his version of what had gone down last night. So no sneers. Not today. He'd gone from this angry cop they all feared and hated to this marginally sympathetic man they wouldn't feel comfortable hating. At least for the moment.

A few of the women, including a very sexy one in a knitted yellow number with her tanned plastic breasts spilling out of their cups, even gave him encouraging glances.

His eyes traced the rise of the steps leading to the corridor, where three condos lay. Any confidence he'd felt just now vanished as he thought that she just might refuse to see him. All the way over here he'd argued with himself about it, how everything that had happened to him last night might change her mind about him. Make her realize that she loved him after all. Make her want to go away with him when it was appropriate. Make her start that new life that they'd always talked about.

But now he realized that it was just movie bullshit, thinking like that. She probably wouldn't even let him in the door, let alone take him in her arms and tell him everything was all right.

He took his time going up the stairs and when he reached the corridor, he stopped to straighten his shirt and tie, tug the jacket down over his shoulder holster. Sometimes she'd been bothered by the sight of his gun. She wasn't a cop groupie like the chicks who slept with you because they found weapons to be erotic.

Hers was the last door down what seemed like an endless carpeted corridor. Before he knocked he went through his nervous routine of tie-and-shirt straightening again. Then he raised his hand and let it fall half-force against the door. Wanted to be heard, didn't want to spook her, remind her that he had often pounded on her door these last two months.

The door opened immediately and there she stood in a blue and white vertically striped top and white shorts. She had a cell phone to her ear and said, "Yes, thanks. He's here now." Then she collapsed her phone and said, "Somebody down at the pool."

He felt foolish. So much for all the confidence he'd felt walking along the pool. One of them had warned her.

"Spies."

"Friends, Steve. They care about me."

What a hell of a way to start this, he thought, standing miserable and uncertain in her doorway.

Then she shocked him. She crossed the threshold and took him in her arms and held him tight. He felt a rush of elation he hadn't known since she'd first started hinting that they should break up. He was afraid he would cry. All he could do was cling to her, lover to lover, sister to brother, child to mother.

"I'm so sorry, Steve. It must have been awful."

And then she eased her arms away and turned back inside. "I was just going to have one of those 'sissy drinks' as you call them. Come in and I'll give you a little scotch."

Two things here. Realizing now that her embrace had not led to a kiss of any kind. Realizing the emphasis she'd put on the word "little" in her offer of scotch.

Her condo had always intimidated him. Severe in all its glass and metal majesty, even the chairs and twin couches designed with brutal modernity. And framed pieces of original art that made no sense to him whatsoever. Fortunately she had a fine view of the river off her rear balcony and her bedroom was comfortably traditional.

She brought his drink to him and sat down about two spaces away on the couch closest to the river view.

"I didn't really know Kim, of course. I'd met her at a couple of social functions. She seemed so smart and decent. I really liked her."

She set her heels on the glass coffee table with its stacks of *Vogue* and *Marie Claire*. Those magazines had always intimidated him, too. Trying to be fashionable meant Nicole was trying to attract men. Men other than Steve. That was how he'd interpreted the presence of the magazines in the living room, anyway. Some kind of betrayal of their relationship. He wanted to lock her away, his exclusively.

He looked with aggrieved longing at her gleaming tanned legs. They broke his heart, just the sight of them. They'd been his once. It was all a kind of desperate insanity, how much he loved her.

"It was rough talking to her folks."

She said, "I can't imagine what they must feel like." Then she leaned over and touched his shoulder. "Or you. How you feel."

"I just keep thinking that the little girl is all right. That way I don't have to think about Kim."

"I suppose a lot of people are handling it that way." She kept her soft hand on his shoulder. "And my God, Peter Olson. I had dinner with him a few times before I met you. He was Prince Charming. He and Bob Gargan were good friends at the country club."

Her hand told him a lot. Told him that she would listen to what he had to say. Told him that she would at least give it serious consideration.

He reached up and took her hand and said, "This is going to change me, Nicole. Change me for good."

She gave a little jerk in reaction to his words, a little drawing back that told him he'd made a mistake. He'd known he'd have to be patient in presenting himself anew. But he'd moved too fast, made it too obvious.

She eased her hand out of his, leaned back toward her end of the couch.

"Please, Steve. Please don't start again. I was going to call you. In fact, I started to two or three times. See how you were doing. I know how hard this has been for you—with us, I mean—and then to walk in on what you did last night—But I decided that if I *did* call you, you might take it the wrong way. You know, misinterpret it and—"

He turned himself around so that he was facing her. He was a salesman now—selling Bibles, housewares, satellite dishes, it didn't matter, the pitch was the same, convince the little lady of the house that she really needed this product, him being the product, of course—leaning forward, eager and quick.

"It really has changed me, Nicole. Listen—"

A soft smile. "People don't change that quickly, Steve. And even if they did—"

"And that's not all."

"Steve, listen, this is exactly why I hesitated to call. I want to be your friend. I like you—I probably even love you in some way. But it just won't work for us. For me it's over. I just hope we can be friends."

But a good salesman would never let himself be dissuaded so easily. "You didn't let me finish, Nicole."

"Can't we just be friends, Steve? That's what I'd really like. Take a break for awhile, not have any contact. And then we can be friends again. That's how it was in the beginning. We were just friends."

"That's how it was for you. It was never like that for me."

Slim hands in lap. Eyes downcast. Long sigh. "Please, Steve. Please, let's not talk about it anymore. In fact, I need to take a shower and get dressed."

Now came the closer, the clincher, the sales point that no little lady of the house could ever resist. "I have money now."

And what he saw—or didn't see—startled him. Because she didn't look up from the hands on her lap. Didn't shift position in any way. Didn't say a word or even make one of those little sounds that meant she'd heard him.

"I have money now. Real money. Serious money."

Still she didn't look up: "Oh, Steve. I'm sorry this is so hard for you." Now she faced him. "I really have to get ready."

"It's Gargan, isn't it?"

"Please, Steve. God, we're just friends. The company is having an awards ceremony tonight. That's all."

"You're sleeping with him—I don't care what you say."

He knew it was gone now, all his planning, all his self-control. And when she stood up and began walking toward the door—escorting him out, obviously—the old rage was there and then he was on his feet, too. And grabbing her and twisting her around and backhanding her hard, very hard.

She fell backwards against a chair, then bounced forward to the floor on her hands and knees. Blood in the right corner of her mouth; crazed sobs, near hysterical.

He had never hurt her before. But his rage was such that he wanted to go on hurting her. Gargan would have his hands all over her tonight. Gargan would be in their bed tonight.

He knew vaguely that he was in trouble. She would tell Gargan and Gargan would call the mayor and the mayor would call the police chief. But he was blind pissed and right now he didn't give one shit about consequences.

She had rolled into a fetal position, hands between her knees, still sobbing, blood snaking down her chin.

He walked over to the door. "You're a slut and that's all you'll ever be. You put out for anybody who's got enough money. You're lucky I didn't do a lot more to you, bitch. A lot more."

He slammed the door on her moans. He heard a door open somewhere behind him down the corridor. He started walking faster. Certainly didn't want to see anybody. Then he saw the smear of blood on his hand. Bitch. Lucky she was alive.

He took a deep breath before descending the steps and entering the pool area. Put on a face. A mask. Like Olson's mask. Walk past the people around the pool looking cool, composed. Then he remembered that somebody had used a cell to warn her he was coming. What if she used hers to tell them what he'd done to her?

The number of people along both sides of the pool had doubled. Two barbeque grills were at work, the smell of starter tart on the air. Somebody had music going and a few couples were dancing, showing off their perfect bodies. The kind of people he saw in clubs. Lawyers, probably.

One woman smiled at him. He smiled back. So Nicole hadn't called anybody down here. Or if she had, the news hadn't made the rounds of the poolside yet. The smile relaxed him just enough for him to study her breasts momentarily. They looked like hers. Then a bitter moment of remembering Nicole's breasts and how he would never know them again. Bitch. He'd done so much for her.

He had to squeeze through a small crowd of people at the entrance to the center court. New arrivals home. Hadn't had time to get into swim gear yet. Just standing here, probably telling each other how important they were. A few recognized him. Even a few hellos. But he just kept walking.

He glanced down the steep front lawn to the street below where he'd left his car. He felt better already. Away from all that defeat, all that humiliation. A few drinks at the riverboat and he'd be all right again. Have to put up with a lot of questions about walking in on Kim and Olson but he might get lucky with one of the dining-room waitresses he'd had his eye on.

The sun was streaking the sky, dying red, dyeing clouds pinks and yellows and dusky blues. A restful time. Sit at the window in the casino and watch the sunset over the river, the darkening day reminding him of high school keggers that always started just about this time, young and strong and able to talk just about any girl he wanted into bed. And with none of the mental baggage that came later. It was the mental baggage, it started so early, before he was one year a cop, insomnia and even nights when he couldn't get it up, everything getting so crazy, including him and—

Who the hell was that leaning on the passenger side of his car? Standing there with an insolent smile on his brutal face. White short-sleeved sports shirt, pack of smokes riding in the pocket, a big tat on each arm. Who the hell was he and why did he look familiar?

"Hey, friend. Heard you had a rough night."

The Chicago cop in the bar. That's who it was. What the hell was he doing leaning against Steve's car and smirking like that?

"Something I can do for you?"

"Thought I'd say hello. Remember me?"

"Yeah. But you didn't answer my question."

"Like I said. Thought I'd just say hello."

"Right. You just happen to show up where I'm visiting somebody."

The man pushed off from Steve's car and said, "By somebody you mean Nicole McKenna, right?"

Something was wrong here. Steve had been about to move closer to the man so he could swing on him but something held him back now. "How do you know about Nicole?"

"Oh, it's not just Nicole I know about, Steve. I know about everything."

"Is that right?"

"You set that shit up pretty nice last night. Got to hand it to you, Steve. I knew guys in Joliet who come up with stuff like that all the time. The difference is you pulled it off."

"I should've spotted you yesterday. An ex-con."

The smirk was back. "I didn't see all this on TV, Steve. I was peeking in the window out at Olson's place. I saw everything you did."

"Bullshit."

The air that had seemed so fresh, so clean moments ago as he'd left the condo complex was now clammy, rank with the stink of heat and exhaust fumes and hot asphalt.

"Maybe I should run you in."

"Be my guest."

"Who the hell are you?"

"Last name's Rice."

Two kids went skateboarding by on the sidewalk. Their laughter made Steve jealous. To be that young, free.

"Oh, shit."

"Yeah. That's sort of what I said when I found out you killed him."

"He didn't give me any choice."

"Right. He didn't give you any choice, Scanlon." He stepped forward, cutting the distance between them in half. "And I'm not giving you any choice, either."

"What the hell's that supposed to mean?"

Rice put his hand out, palm up, as if expecting a gift. "I want half the money you took out of Olson's safe last night."

CHAPTER FORTY-FIVE

The usual mix. Hot dusk, hotter night. A stabbing, a mugging, an attempted carjacking. The three detectives on the night shift were gone handling these cases, leaving Michael alone in the office.

He was finishing up two reports on his computer when the phone rang.

"Michael?"

The voice. Heard it twice today. Kim's father. Drinking. Not really drunk, just mournful, adrift in grief. Took inexplicable comfort in hearing Michael. Probably others, too. Probably several others getting these calls.

"Hi, John."

"I'm sorry to be calling again."

"It's fine."

"My wife, she's not doing very well. But we were talking awhile ago and she wanted me to tell you something."

Michael hesitated, assuming John would speak.

"We wish she'd married you, Michael."

"So do I, John."

"You know we talked to her about it. Did you know that?"

"No, I didn't."

"She was a grown woman and free to do what she

wanted but when she stopped seeing you, we told her she was making a mistake. And when she didn't start seeing anybody else for awhile we thought she might go back to you. My wife and I were really hopeful. But then she met Olson—"

Irene Pierce must have been sitting nearby because at the mention of Olson's name, she started crying.

"If she hadn't met him maybe she'd have gone back to you and this never would've happened."

They'd be doing this the rest of their lives. Maybe Michael would, too. Going back over everything until it became an obsession. What if. If only. Endlessly.

"We just wanted you to know how much we care about you, Michael."

"I appreciate it."

"And we were wondering if you'd say a few words at her funeral."

"Well, I'm not much of a speaker, John."

"Just a few words. From somebody there who knew her and cared about her."

"Well—"

"If the chief does it or the mayor, it won't be the same."

"I guess I could say something. I'll give it some thought."

"It doesn't have to be long. We'd appreciate it, Michael. We really would."

"It'll be my pleasure, John."

"Well, I'll let you get back to work. Thanks again."

Funerals were gravesides too hot, too cold, too windy. Funerals were hams, beef roasts, cakes, pies, cookies. Because he was Irish, funerals were also liquor, beer and old men laughing loud. When the younger ones laughed they tried to be discreet. But the old ones with their wild tales of the living and the dead sounded almost triumphant. It would be them someday being mourned but for now they'd slipped by again.

This funeral would be different because the circumstances were different. So dirty, sleazy. Two dead girls, a freak doctor and a wonderful young woman who just happened to be a detective. There wouldn't be much laughter at this one.

After hanging up, he sat at his desk, numbed. Less than twenty-four hours ago she'd been alive.

He forced himself to his feet and walked over to her desk. Her perfume was faint on the air. She had small framed photos of her niece and nephew to the right of her phone. The surface was well ordered. He remembered kidding her about her neat-freak tendencies. She'd once shown him a second-grade report card with a gold star on it. For neatness.

This was his third visit to her desk today. He was turning it into a shrine. And each time he'd come here he'd looked at the to-do list she'd made. Another thing they'd once laughed about. She'd written in her perfect grade-school penmanship the various places she needed to go yesterday.

He ran his finger down the narrow lined page once again. But this time he focused on the last line. "Git 'n Go—see Inez at six o'clock. Cindy."

There was a phone number next to "Git 'n Go." He dialed it. Female. "Inez, please."

"Hold on a minute."

Same voice saying, "I like that blouse, Janie. The color matches your eyes." Then the sounds of a cash register.

"Hello."

"Is this Inez?"

"Yes."

"My name's Detective Michael Scanlon."

"Oh. You're that cop's brother."

"Yes."

"That whole thing's so terrible. But we're all happy that at least Cindy is alive."

"Did you talk with Detective Pierce last night?"

"Sure. Hold on a sec." Then: "Thank you" to somebody. Then: "Yes. She was a mighty fine lady."

"I'd like to know what you talked about."

"Well, Cindy, of course."

"Did you have any idea that Dr. Olson was involved in Cindy's disappearance?"

"No. Hell, no. If I did I would've called you right away."

"So she just asked you questions about Cindy in general?"

"Pretty much. Just kind of rehashed what she'd asked me the first time."

"So then she left?"

"Right—well, she left the store but she ran into Jason outside."

"Who's Jason?"

"He works days here. But he hangs out here at night sometimes. He had this big crush on Cindy and he got to see her that way."

"When you say she ran into Jason, did she stop and talk?"

"Yes. I could see them through the window. Talking. And then she took off real fast. Sort of surprised me."

"Did Jason tell you what they were talking about?"

"No. I got pretty busy. He sat over in one of the booths. And then he just got up and left."

"Do you have a phone number and street address for him?"

"He lives with his folks."

"That's fine. Just please give me the number and the address."

"Is something wrong?"

"Just following up on some things."

"Jason's one of the good guys, Detective Scanlon."

Taking off fast after a talk with this young guy Jason. He had to force himself to concentrate as he wrote down the number and address.

CHAPTER FORTY-SIX

After she put the kids to bed, Wendy went downstairs to watch a TV movie on Lifetime. The male star was a hunk she'd had her first sexual crush on at age twelve. She'd followed his career haphazardly since then. His days of fame as a prime-time star were gone but he'd turned into a decent actor and still looked pretty good. Plus she liked his costar, a one-time sexy ingénue who'd also turned out after her first fame to have some real talent.

The day had been hell. She'd finally stopped answering calls about two in the afternoon. She had kept the kids home from daycare. The press and friends who wanted to commiserate about Steve's news conference had laid siege for most of the day.

Steve had appeared about four. They'd had a civil enough half hour together with the kids sharing the large pizza he'd brought. Then, saying he was busy, he went outside. She'd watched him, expecting him to go straight to his car in the drive. Instead he'd gone into the closed garage, making her curious. He'd spent some time in there. Then he'd reappeared, climbed into his car and driven away.

But now she didn't want to think about any of it. He was alive. She still loved him in some terrible way and so she was happy that he was all right. But it was done now. There would be the divorce and there would be a new life.

She was thinking all this as she used the programmer to click the set, consciously willing herself to relax.

Her show came on, the hunk's name appearing before the title.

And that was when she heard the car come up the drive.

An hour before, Leo Rice and Steve Scanlon had sat in a booth across from each other in the bar where they'd first met. "Doesn't sound to me like you have much choice, Mr. Detective."

"Knock off the Mr. Detective bullshit."

"Sure thing, Mr. Detective."

All the trash he'd had to deal with as a cop, none had ever been as grating as Rice. Steve had always been in control before. Now it was Rice who was in control.

The bar was half-full. Country music on the jukebox, a Cubs game on the big-screen TV.

"You know the deal."

"There is no deal."

"Fine, Mr. Detective. Then I call your brother and I call your wife. At first they won't believe me. But I'll plant the seed. You know how that works, Mr. Detective, when you plant a seed? It starts growing a little bit at a time but the thing is it never stops growing. It's always there."

"Shut up."

Rice leaned back and looked at his bottle of beer. "You know you'll have to split that money with me; why make it hard on yourself? One phone call to the chief of police and your ass is in the slammer for the rest of your life. That doesn't leave you a whole lot of room here. So you lead me to where it is and you give me my half and I'm out of your life."

A dozen different plans had raced through Steve's mind since he'd come over here from Nicole's condo complex. Rice had followed in his own car. A dozen different plans and none of them felt right. He needed to keep the money and kill Rice. There was no way Rice would take half the money. He would take it all.

He saw Rice's gaze lift and fix curiously on him.

"You thinking hard, Mr. Detective?"

As a matter of fact, he had been. He had been so concerned with keeping Rice from knowing where the money was that he hadn't realized he could trap the man by leading him to it.

The money was in a leather bag in a storage barrel in the garage. He'd stuffed the bag down there last night, covering it with blankets he put on the floor when he was working on his car.

Rice planned to get all the money. Then he'd no doubt do what he'd come to Skylar to do, kill the man who'd killed his brother. But what if Steve honked when they pulled into the drive, bringing Wendy to the window so that she could clearly see Rice and him? And see Rice's car.

She could identify Rice. And to get the money Rice would have to leave his fingerprints in several places in the garage. Nobody knew about Rice as yet except Steve. Would Rice risk killing a cop in his own garage?

But Steve didn't have a hell of a lot of choice.

"Maybe you're not as smart as you think you are," Steve said, not really able to say anything else. Feeling drained now.

"Maybe I'm not," Rice said. "But I guess we'll soon find out, won't we?"

CHAPTER FORTY-SEVEN

Jason Lewis came to the door in a Fantastic Four T-shirt and a guilty look on his face. Sometimes they made it easy for you, Michael thought. Their faces answered your question. Yes, they had done something and they knew they were in trouble. Your job was to find out what they had done.

The Lewis home was an old-fashioned two-story clapboard house with a one-stall garage in back. Working class, comfortable. Michael had called here fifteen minutes ago. Jason had answered, said that his parents were out bowling.

"I'd like to come in."

"Like I said on the phone, Mr. Scanlon, I don't really know anything. I mean I didn't say more than a couple of words to her."

This was the third time he'd called Michael "Mister." Apparently he thought all authority figures were high school teachers.

Michael opened the screen door and began walking in, forcing the young man to backtrack. The living room was modest-sized and filled with inexpensive Early American furniture. A glowing Jesus stared at Michael from a framed painting above the couch. A stairway to the right led to the second floor. A kung fu video colored the screen of the TV set. The sound was muted.

"Why don't you sit down over there, Jason?"

"I guess. I mean, I have to, don't I? I mean, if you say so?"

Michael didn't answer. He sat in an armchair and looked over at Jason on the couch. "You spoke to Detective Pierce last night."

"Not for very long."

"You spoke to her the day before and then last night you went out and talked to her on the drive."

"I guess so."

"You mean you don't remember?"

"No, I guess that's right."

"You talked to her on the drive and then she took off in her car at a high rate of speed."

"Did Inez tell you that?"

"Yes."

He shrugged bony shoulders. "Yeah, I guess that's about right, too."

"I knew Detective Pierce for a long time. She wasn't the type of person who drove that way. You must've said something to her that got to her somehow."

"Nothing special."

"You're lying."

"You heard me."

The pause control slipped off. Kung fu cries and violent music ripped the air.

"Oh, shit." Jason made a stab for the channel control device. He turned the set off. "Sorry."

"You're not telling me the truth, Jason."

A second interruption. A car pulling up on the driveway.

"My folks. They bowl early. My dad has to get up early."

"We're getting off the subject. I want you to tell me what you told Detective Pierce."

"Hi, honey." Female voice accompanying the opening of a side door. Footsteps on stairs. "Hi, honey." This time a question, curious about not getting a response.

"In here, Mom."

Attractive fortyish woman in a gold bowling shirt and black jeans. Mama lion, taking instant dislike to the sight of a man in her living room with her son.

"Hello," she said tentatively when she saw Michael.

"He's a detective, Mom."

"A detective?"

The father appeared behind his wife. A large, square man with intelligent eyes and a ready frown. His bowling shirt matched his wife's.

"This man is a detective, honey," she said, explaining Michael's presence.

"A detective?" He glanced at his son. "Jason never gets in trouble. Why's a detective here?"

Michael stood up. "My name's Michael Scanlon."

As he flipped his ID open to show his badge, the father said, "You're the one who got shot at the other night."

"Yes."

"Well, you sure as hell don't think my boy had anything to do with that, do you?"

"No."

The couple came into the room carefully, as if this were Michael's house, not theirs. The man came over to Michael and put out a hefty hand. They shook. "I'm Dave Lewis. This is my wife Nancy."

"Nice to meet you folks. I was just about to ask your son a few questions about Cindy Baines. He knows her from the Git 'n Go."

"Cindy?" Nancy Lewis said. "Well, she's still all right, isn't she?"

"Yes. She's fine. It's just that I have questions about a conversation he had last night with Detective Pierce."

"The one that doctor killed?" Dave Lewis said.

"Yes. We're just doing follow-up work on the case."

The couple looked relieved. "Well, that shouldn't be any trouble," the father said. "Just tell the detective what you talked to her about, Jason."

"Why don't I put some coffee on?" Mrs. Lewis said brightly.

"Wait a minute, Nancy." Her husband grabbed her arm, holding her still. His face was grim.

He obviously saw the fear in his son's eyes. "You're not cooperating. What's going on here, Jason?"

"Nothing. We just talked a little bit is all, Dad. Me and Kim."

"Well then if it's nothing, tell the detective," Nancy Lewis said. "He already said that you're not in any trouble."

Jason huddled into himself. His brown eyes glistened with tears. He was a small child again. He wanted his parents to protect him, Michael knew. But they had betrayed him just now. They were forcing him to share a truth he didn't want to.

"Jason, now you damned well better start talking to this man."

"But Dad, if I do—"

"If you do—what? You won't get in trouble for telling the truth."

"Yes, I will, Dad. Yes, I will."

Michael said, "I'd like to talk to Jason alone."

"What's going on here?" Nancy Lewis said, dread in her voice.

"What the hell did you do, Jason?"

"Nothing, Dad, I—"

"Why don't you go in the kitchen, folks? I just need to talk to Jason for a few minutes. Then we can all get together again."

"C'mon, honey," Dave Lewis said, taking his wife's arm.

"Are you lying to us? Is he in trouble?" she snapped at Michael.

"I just need to talk to him, Mrs. Lewis. It won't take long. I promise."

"I'll fix you a drink," Dave Lewis said his wife. "I could use one myself."

"You walk into your own home and you find a detective sitting in your front room," Nancy Lewis said, tears in her own voice now.

After he heard them in the kitchen, Michael seated himself across from Jason again and said, "Now I want the truth, Jason."

CHAPTER FORTY-EIGHT

When Wendy heard a second car pulling up on the drive she was surprised. She hurried into their bedroom to see what was happening. The west window overlooked the drive and the garage and half the backyard.

The phone rang, interrupting her. She grabbed the receiver so the kids wouldn't wake up. They were tired tonight and were asleep before she'd left their rooms.

"You busy?"

Her sister.

"Kind of."

"You all right?"

"Steve just pulled in. And another car behind him."

She'd talked to her sister three times today. She'd been fully updated. "I thought he was gone for good."

"So did I."

"Well, if you need me—"

"Thanks. I just want to find out what's going on."

She went to the sheer white curtains and peeked down on to the dark drive. She recognized her husband, of course, but not the man just now stepping from his car. He didn't look familiar at all.

The man paused to light a cigarette and then started to walk over to Steve. He had the same kind of powerful body the Scanlon boys did. But there was an insolence in the way he walked that surprised her. He walked right up to Steve, crowding him. Steve stepped back. Steve didn't usually step back from anybody. What was going on here, anyway?

By now, her eyes adjusted to the gloom, she could see their faces well enough to confirm her sense that these two men were wary of each other.

Then the man jabbed his finger into Steve's chest and Steve, responding the way she would have expected him to, lunged for the man, slamming him back against the car.

She was out of the bedroom, racing down the stairs to the first floor. Then through the house to the kitchen and the back door.

The security light came on as soon as she set foot on the back stoop.

"Wendy?" Steve shouted.

She hurried to the gate that opened on the drive.

The two of them stood a few feet apart, staring at her. Now that she could see the man better she saw that he was the kind of thug Steve had spent his years on the force arresting. There was a brutality about him that he could not hide even now as he smiled.

"Nice to meet you, Mrs. Scanlon. Steve was just going to show me something in the garage."

"What's going on, Steve?" she said, disregarding the other man's words. One of the man's hands was behind his back. All she could think of was a gun.

"Just what he said, Wendy." Steve was usually a smooth liar. Not now. He couldn't keep the anger from his voice. "He's interested in those old weights of mine. I thought I might as well get rid of them."

"I'm sorry if we woke you up or anything, Mrs. Scanlon. I probably should have waited until tomorrow."

Again, she refused to respond to him. Those kind of unctuous words coming from a thug like him were sickening.

"The weights are in the basement, Steve. Not in the garage. You know that."

Panic on Steve's face. Rage on the other man's.

"Oh," Steve said. "Well, he wanted to look at the mountain bike, too." He tried for a joke. "You know, the one I paid all that money for but then never used?"

She wondered if Steve knew how ridiculous he sounded. Usually if she'd questioned him about what was going on out here, he would have told her to go back in the house and he'd explain later. He would have tried to sound pleasant but there would have been irritation in his voice. He certainly wouldn't have sounded like a simpering sitcom husband.

What was going on?

She knew he was in trouble but she didn't know what kind. She wanted to go back inside and call the station and have somebody rush out here. But even though she was through with him she had to think of the kids. What if he'd made some kind of a deal with this man? She'd always known that Steve took his share of graft. Skylar was a satellite for various mob interests in Chicago. Maybe this man was from one of those interests.

"Honey, just go back inside. Everything's fine."

The word "honey" was ludicrous on Steve's lips at this point in their relationship.

"I'm sorry again about disturbing you, Mrs. Scanlon."

"Who the hell are you?"

"Honey, don't—"

"I'm a friend of your husband's. I used to be a detective myself. We have a few old friends in common. I was just passing through town and then we got to talking about his weights and his bicycle. I need to get in shape, so—"

"You're lying."

"Wendy!"

"What's going on here, Steve? This is where your children live, in case you forgot. I saw you take a swing at him after he pushed you. This isn't some old friend."

Now Steve was Steve. "You go in the house, Wendy. Now. I'll be in soon and I'll explain everything. I care about the kids and you do, too. So right now we need to cool it. You need to let me handle this."

The man didn't say anything. He just smirked.

She knew there was nothing left to say. Despite the heat she felt chilled now, chilled and alone under the vast starry sky.

She turned then and went back inside. She went straight to the dry bar in the living room and poured herself two fingers of bourbon and drank them quickly. The whiskey burned but she hardly noticed. All she could think about was Steve and the thug. And the mysterious trouble Steve was most certainly in.

But the whiskey offered no help and neither did her irrational closing of the front room curtains. As if she could close off reality.

She could think of only one thing to do and she did it.

"I didn't hurt her or anything. I just followed her."

"And that was when you saw Cindy get into Dr. Olson's car."

"Yes. Am I in trouble?"

"*Is* he in trouble?" Jason Lewis' father had been listening to the last part of the interview from the hallway. Michael had heard him there but since he already had the information he needed, there was no reason to order the man back to the kitchen.

"Not if he's telling me everything," Michael said, watching as the wife now appeared in the doorway, too.

"You shouldn't have followed her, Jason."

"I know, Mom. It was stupid."

"Do you think we should get a lawyer, anyway?"

"No, I don't think so. Stalking is a crime but I doubt the county attorney would push this." He looked at Jason. "But if you had called the police right away, Jason, there's a chance that Detective Pierce would still be alive."

"Oh, Lord," the mother said. "Oh, Jason. You should have let them know."

Michael saw the tears glisten in Jason's eyes.

"I know my son," the father said. "I know he's sorry. You might have done the same thing yourself in those circumstances."

"No," Michael said. "No, I wouldn't have. I would have called the police right away." He knew he was ruining their lives. At the moment it felt good.

Michael's cell phone toned before any of the Lewises could respond to what he'd just said. "Hello."

"There's something going on here, Michael." Wendy. Rushed. Scared.

"You're at home?"

"Yes. Steve and some man pulled into the driveway about twenty minutes ago. I watched them from the bedroom window. The man shoved Steve and Steve tried to hit him. I ran out there. They just wanted me to go back into the house. They didn't want me to know what was going on. He claims he was a detective but he's a very creepy guy, Michael. Very creepy."

"Are they still in the driveway?"

"They just went into the garage about five minutes ago."

"I'm on my way." He flipped the cell phone closed and stood up. "I need to be going."

Dave Lewis stared at his son and shook his head. "You should have called the police, Jason."

"He didn't know that woman detective would be killed, Dave. Leave him alone." The tone of her voice suggested that the family would have many arguments to come.

"As I said, there's a chance she would be alive if he'd called," Michael said, not backing away from his previous words. To Jason, "That's the way it is, Jason. And I think you know it."

"Yeah," Jason said. "Yeah, I know it."

Michael extracted a card from the jacket of his suit coat and laid it on the arm of the couch. "If you want to talk about anything, call me at one of these numbers."

Nancy Lewis was sobbing by the time Michael reached the front door.

CHAPTER FORTY-NINE

The interior of the two-car garage smelled of gasoline, oil, the remnants of grass trapped in the blades of the power mower. In one corner, hung neatly on the wall, was a collection of power tools, dated and dusty now. There had been a time, those early years of marriage, when Steve had at least tried to make a show of being a faithful husband, when he'd started to build himself a small workshop.

As Steve and Rice came in the side door, Steve glanced at Wendy's four-year-old green Chevy SUV in the far stall. In front of the vehicle was a line of four hard rubber barrels where Wendy and Steve kept various items that they couldn't quite bring themselves to throw away. The barrels represented exile for sweaters, books, odds and ends of dishes and knickknacks and clothes the kids had outgrown. Once every year and a half or so the Goodwill truck backed up the drive and emptied the barrels inside.

"Your wife's good-looking."

"I'll tell her you said that. She'll be glad to hear it."

"You're lucky I don't make her part of the deal. Nice clean snatch like hers."

"Shut the hell up."

"You gonna tell me you care, Mr. Detective? The way you run around on her?"

The gun lay between two ski sweaters, which in turn lay on top of the leather bag. Would he be able to slide the gun into his waistband quickly enough?

"I'll go get the barrel."

"Oh, no," Leo Rice said. "You drag those barrels out here to me one at a time so I can see them for myself. Then you tell me when you hit the right one. I'm gonna go through it myself. And that money better be in there."

Steve could argue but with a man like Rice, an argument now would be transparent. Rice would know that Steve had had some kind of plan with the barrel.

"Get your ass in gear, Mr. Detective. I want out of this town as soon as we're finished here. So hop to it."

There was no easy shortcut to Steve's house. Reaching the interstate that skirted Steve's neighborhood would take just as long as taking the city streets. The problem was the AA baseball game that was just now ending. Skylar was a baseball town and even though the league the Skylar Skylarks played in was one step up from a mediocre high school league, the ancient stadium was at least half-filled every night the team was home.

As he rushed along Fourth Avenue, the fastest way to get to the east side, Michael kept trying to make sense out of the past twenty-four hours. All day he'd been fighting back certain thoughts. Nobody else seemed to have problems with Steve's claim that Kim had suggested she was upset with Olson. But Kim had come to despise Steve. She saw him as everything she hated about bad cops. So even if she was upset, would she really tell Steve anything? It made no sense to Michael. And if he doubted that part of Steve's version—what about the rest of his story?

What a hell of a thing it was, doubting your own brother in something like this.

He hit a red light and pulled up to a BMW convertible full of college-age boys and girls. He envied the hell out of them.

Then he hit the gas with enough force to lay rubber for at least ten feet. He heard the kids laughing behind him. Some middle-aged fart showing off. Hilarious.

He still had twenty blocks to go.

The barrel with the money was the closest to the far wall. With so little space to work in, reaching it before dragging the others into the empty space would be impossible. Steve's only chance would be to wait until he reached the last barrel and then move fast enough to grab the gun and duck behind the SUV.

He walked over to the first barrel, gripped the handles and tugged it out into the open space.

"That isn't the one?"

"No."

"Get the next one then."

For the first time Steve detected a hint of fear in Rice's voice. Maybe he was thinking of Wendy in the house, thinking maybe she'd call the station, thinking maybe he wouldn't be able to get away before the cops showed up.

"Move, Scanlon. This is taking too long."

Watching perps melt down was one of Steve's real pleasures. Even now, even in this circumstance, the look and sound of Rice's anxiety was good to hear and see.

Steve walked over and reached down for the second barrel. This one was much heavier. It made a harsh scraping sound as it bumped over the concrete floor.

"Not that one, either?"

"You can look for yourself."

"Get going. I'm tired of waiting."

When you came right down to it, Steve thought, Leo Rice was just another con. Tougher, craftier, but still and all part of the breed. And his increasing apprehension was proving it.

Barrel number three. He took his time reaching it.

"Don't be stupid, Scanlon. Just bring that thing out here without any bullshit."

"Sounds like you don't trust me, Rice." Happy to be sarcastic again, as if he were in control and not Rice.

"Slow and easy when you bring it out here."

"Have to be slow and easy, Rice. Not enough room to do anything else."

"Shut the hell up and get to it."

Steve reached down. This close there was only room for one hand on one handle. He gave the barrel a jerk and pulled it between vehicle and wall.

But what he was thinking of, as he reached the clear section of garage again, was barrel number four.

The money, the gun and his last chance for keeping everything secret. It was all there in barrel number four.

When he was seven blocks away, Michael used his cell phone to speed-dial Wendy. "I should be there in a few minutes. I'm going to park down the block so they won't hear me come up."

"Maybe I should call the station."

"No. Please don't, Wendy. Just stay inside with the kids and let me handle this."

"What's going on here, Michael? Be honest with me."

"I'm not sure but I know I can handle this. Okay?"

"If you say so, Michael, sure."

"Everything will be all right."

"We're splitting up—but I still care about him."

"I know you do." He saw the Catholic church three

blocks from Steve's house. "I'm almost there. But I want you to promise me that you won't leave the house no matter what happens, all right?"

"But I want to know what's going on."

"I'll come and tell you what's going on. You stay in the house. Promise me that, Wendy."

"Now you're really scaring me, Michael. But—I promise."

Chapter Fifty

Steve shoved the third barrel in line with the other two. He saw the sweat on Rice's face. "You going to take it all?"

"Of course. Don't be a dumbass."

"And here I thought we'd actually split it." A cold smile.

"I want that barrel right out here. And then I want you over there in clear sight while I open it up."

"You going to kill me?"

"Not unless you're stupid. I can take all the money and you can't do a damn thing about it. You're like a coon I took care of. He can't go to the cops, either." Rice was enjoying himself again.

A siren. Steve recognized that it was some distance away and headed in the opposite direction of his home. But the sound obviously bothered Rice. He was close now, Steve knew, close to all the money. And close to avenging his brother's death. He had no plans to let Steve live. None at all.

"Spook you a little? That siren?"

"Just go get that barrel."

"Maybe my wife called the cops. You ever think of that? Maybe my place'll be surrounded by the time you get the money."

"This kind of bullshit doesn't work on me, Mr. Detective. Just on punks that don't know better. Now get busy."

"I'd be worried if I was you, Rice. You scared the hell out of my wife. She just might have called the station. She's got a lot of friends down there."

Rice had stood in the same position for the past five minutes. Now he walked over to Steve, his gun leading the way. He brought the barrel of the gun down hard against the right side of Steve's head. Then he brought his knee up between Steve's legs. He'd done these things in less than a minute. Steve collapsed on the floor.

"I'm gonna go over there and get that barrel myself. I'll pull it out here and all the time I'm doing it I'll keep you in sight. Remember that."

Steve fought rage, tears, panic, despair.

There was no way now he would ever be able to get the gun from the barrel and kill Rice.

Wendy checked on the children quickly. Beth slept on her back and usually slept peacefully. Nick slept on his stomach and fitfully. She gave each a kiss knowing that she might be at her bedroom window for some time. She needed the touchstone of her love for them to face the confrontation between the men in the garage.

The lights were still off upstairs. Traffic on the street was light. She listened for a car to pull up near the driveway.

She said two prayers and then opened the bedroom curtains slightly and searched the darkness below. The interior garage lights seemed to glow maliciously like the eyes of monsters. She wondered what they were saying in there, doing. She wondered what this was all about. She had the woeful feeling that after all these years of living just the way he'd wanted to, somebody from the past had caught up with Steve. He'd always bragged to their friends about the brawls he'd had with some of the men he'd arrested. And laughed off the threats they'd made in court when they were being tried.

She wanted to be down there. Inside the garage. But she had promised Michael and—

There was Michael now. Moving up the far side of the drive toward the garage. With the door down, there was no way they could see him. He looked up at the bedroom window once. She wasn't sure if he saw her or not.

Not until he walked in front of the garage door was she able to see the gun in his right hand.

A man pulling a hard rubber barrel from in front of the green Chevy SUV, Wendy's car, to the empty space in the garage where three other identical barrels stood.

Michael had never seen the man before but since he was holding a gun on Steve, the man's identity didn't matter at this point.

Michael saw all this from the window next to the side door of the garage. He crouched down immediately after, listened. He had to be careful. Just by opening the door he could get Steve killed.

The man had a harsh voice. He sounded pleased with himself. "All going to hell on you, isn't it, Mr. Detective? Big, tough detective. You kill Olson and that detective and you think you're home free. Just the way you felt when you killed my brother, I bet. No reason to kill him at all." The man's voice raised in pitch. "Just had to be a cop, didn't you?"

"I didn't have any choice with your brother. I told you that."

"Sure you didn't, Mr. Detective." Then: "You're a piece of shit, you know that? You blackmailed Olson all that time and chased that fancy snatch of yours all over town and you thought you were ridin' high. But it didn't work, did it?"

"Just take the money and go."

"The money better be down here, asshole."

Michael slipped away from the window, flattened himself against the wall. He'd had two panic attacks in his life, both work related, and he felt as if another one was coming on now. He was trapped inside his body. He wanted to escape himself and the terrible burden of accepting what he had just heard.

Kim dead at Steve's hands. A serial killer protected by Steve. His own brother Steve. Crazed fragmented thoughts. *Summer at the lake with Steve and the folks. Steve babysitting him through his first heartbreak. Steve guiding him through his first year as a uniformed cop.* Wendy and the kids, his father, himself. He couldn't imagine even looking into Steve's eyes now, seeing the truth that had always been Steve.

He raised his head to glimpse the bedroom window again. This time he saw a ghostly impression of Wendy against the glass. God, when she found out—

"Hey, Mr. Detective. You planted a gun down here. Very smart. You were probably thinking I'd let you dig the bag out for yourself and then you'd shoot me with this gun. I'm real sorry it didn't work out that way for you."

Silence again.

Then: "That's a lot of money in there. I imagine Olson kept it on hand in case he had to get out of the country. Probably had a couple of bank accounts in different places, too. The kind of money you were getting from him every month, you could have done a lot better. But you're just a dumb cop, man. Just a dumb cop."

Michael remembered the day Steve called him to tell him his mother had died. He felt the same disbelief then that he did now.

And then he was reaching for the knob on the door, and then he was flinging it open and moving inside.

"Freeze right where you are. Leave the gun in the barrel and turn around and face me. Then put your gun on the hood of the Chevy. You've got Steve's gun in your belt. Put that right alongside it. And do it now."

"Aw, man, Michael. I thought I was dead for sure. This bastard was going to kill me."

"Shut up, Steve."

Steve's face—shocked. "What the hell's wrong with you?"

"I said shut up."

Rice laughed. "You're one dumb son of a bitch, Scanlon. Your brother was outside listening. He knows you killed that detective and Olson." Then: "You ever kill anybody?" Rice smirked at Michael.

"As a matter of fact I have."

Rice shrugged. "Figures. Nobody ever blames the cops."

Michael raised his Glock. "Now."

Rice took his insolent time setting the two guns down on the hood of the SUV.

"Now move over toward Steve."

"He's lying, Michael. You've got to believe me. He's lying. I didn't kill Kim. You know how much I liked her. She was part of our team, Michael. You and me and her. You know how it was."

"I don't think he's buying it. Look at his face. He looks pretty pissed off to me." Rice seemed to be enjoying himself.

Steve was coming apart. He kept lurching forward.

"It's all bullshit, Michael. Honest. He's the one who killed them. He's crazy. I don't think he even remembers doing it."

"This joker's story just gets lamer and lamer, don't it?" Rice smiled.

"Michael—"

Michael, keeping his Glock aimed right at Rice's head, moved slowly up the length of the Chevy. When he reached the hood he picked up Steve's gun and jammed it behind his belt. Then he picked up Rice's and did the same thing.

"What the hell you going to do, Michael?"

Steve sensed it, then. And moments later Rice did, too.

Rice said, "Hey man, listen, we can work this out. There's money enough for everybody here. And nobody has to know what your brother did. I'll take a third of it and leave town and you'll never hear from me again."

Michael moved back down the length of the Chevy.

"Hey—" Rice started to say.

Michael tore Steve's gun from his waist and put two bullets in Rice's forehead. He dropped Steve's gun in the pocket of his jacket and then yanked Rice's gun from his waist. He had to act quickly to make the story work. And because to hesitate would mean he wouldn't be able to do it.

"God, Michael—Michael, listen—I'm your brother!"

"Not anymore you're not."

He shot Steve three times in the chest.

PART FOUR

CHAPTER FIFTY-ONE

At ten o'clock the next morning, Michael Scanlon, looking tired from the long, sad night before, entered the First National Bank of Skylar. He was dressed in a conservative blue pinstriped suit, a white shirt and a blue club tie. He walked to one of the service desks. The attractive blonde in the summery yellow dress and the shining chignon was on the phone but when she saw him, she smiled and pointed to one of the chairs in front of her desk.

The bank was crowded. Lines at the teller windows. Most of the service desks occupied. Clusters of businessmen speaking in quiet voices as if they were in a church, though a few of the more lurid laughs would not have been proper in the house of the Lord.

The blonde's name was Gwen Spinelli. They'd dated a few times a long time ago. They'd had a good enough time but somehow had never made it into bed. She'd gotten herself married two years ago. The ring dazzled on her finger. They'd never been close enough for business transactions to be uncomfortable. So when he had banking issues he always came to her.

She hung up, leaned forward on her elbows and folded her hands on her desk. She had green green eyes and a lopsided smile that was erotic as hell. Except for this morning. He was a corpse inside.

"First of all, Michael, I'm really sorry about your brother. Getting killed by that convict. It isn't fair. It makes me sick."

Some but not all of the story had been on the morning news and in the newspaper.

"I wish I could have saved him."

"I can't imagine what you're going through. Everybody's praying for you and your family, Michael. His poor wife and kids."

Yes, Michael thought. And that was why he was here. There was only one thing he could do for them and he had figured out how to do it.

"I appreciate it, Gwen." He managed a smile. "Last time I saw you, you were still pregnant." He nodded to the plastic cube filled with photographs of a sweet-faced infant.

"And Tom already wants another one." She shrugged. He liked her. She was clean and shiny and fun and honest. "I guess I do, too. Though I want a little break from morning sickness." Then: "I'm sorry. This isn't the right time for mom stuff."

"It's fine, Gwen. It's a relief hearing about something else. We didn't wrap things up at Steve's house until just before dawn. I've had two hours' sleep."

"Peter Olson. God. I dated him a few times. I couldn't get past his ego. And then he turns out—" She made a face. "Now that I've got a little one of my own, people like him are all the scarier. God, when I think of what he did in that carriage house—" She unclasped her hands, brought one of them to her beautifully crafted chignon.

Her phone again. She checked caller ID and said, "It can wait. Now, what can I help you with, Michael?"

He held up the briefcase. "This. I'd like to rent a safety deposit box."

"Of course. We have different sizes. Let me run through them for you and tell you about rates and everything."

He took the middle size. That would be sufficient.

"Mandy Roget is in charge of the safety deposit boxes. I'll ask her to handle it from here on."

"Thanks, Gwen."

She swiveled to her phone but before picking up the receiver, paused. "I know everybody says this but if there's anything I can do—"

"I appreciate it. The big concern now is Wendy and the kids."

"I met her a few times. She's a sweetie."

"She sure is."

"The poor woman. And those kids—"

Michael was starting to suffocate from all the somber good wishes. He guessed this was because he still felt no remorse for what he'd done. He worried about Wendy and the children but not about killing his brother. The rage that had pulled the trigger had been hot last night. Now it was cool but more lasting in this form. He still had to force himself away from thoughts of what Kim's last hour of life had been like. He could not afford to deal with those images now.

Gwen punched in three numbers and then spoke with somebody briefly. "Mandy will be right here, Michael."

The tomblike room was walled in with safety deposit boxes of various sizes. Michael felt as if he were in some surrealistic church. Mandy had offered polite smiles and more words of pity. He felt trapped in the celebrity all of it had created for him.

She gave him forms to sign and the box he was to use and then left. She had good legs. He was grateful for the distraction and doted on them as she walked away. Then he set the briefcase on the table and set to work.

The money was in neat stacks. He had counted it three times to make sure how much was there. He had also contrived the lie he would tell Wendy. That Steve had indeed won a good deal of money at the tables. But that Michael had developed his own gambling habit without Steve's luck. He'd ended up owing Steve a lot of money. He would tell her that he would pay her back over the years and that he had already saved the first installment. A big one. He would pay her out to help with the kids and the house and he would tell her not to report it to taxes. This was gambling money, after all.

She had been wild in her grief last night and finally the doc from the medical examiner's office had given her a sedative. Michael had driven the kids to her sister's place, where they'd stay for a few days.

He'd talked to her on the telephone this morning, explaining that Rice had probably forced Steve into the garage to kill him. It was clear that Rice was out to avenge his brother's death at Steve's hands, even though Steve had acted properly in the matter.

Already two different bartenders from The Illini Inn had called in to say they'd seen the two men together. The first bartender said that he'd overheard Rice introduce himself by a different name and claim that he was a former police detective himself. The second one said that he'd seen them together earlier last night. Apparently, Michael said, Steve had believed the man's story to the extent that he'd had a few beers with him.

Then he said that he'd pick her up at one and go with her to the funeral home.

"Oh, Michael, I don't know what I'd do without you. Thank you so much."

"I'll be there at one."

He had one stop to make before going to Wendy's.

* * *

The old man was sitting alone in the sunroom reading the newspaper, his wheelchair turned to the east so that he could see the timbered hills where he'd grown up. Michael had talked to his father this morning as well but this was the first time he'd seen him.

When he took a chair across from him Michael studied the old man's face. His father still wore his cop face, the mask that hid real feelings. Michael wondered if he knew his son was here. Then the old man put the paper down in his lap and looked at Michael.

Sounds of the nursing home drifted on the noontime air. Clamor from the dining room; the squeak squeak squeak of nurses' shoes in the corridors nearby; a doctor being paged.

The old man sat back in his chair. His eyes hadn't left Michael's face. "I cried like a baby last night. They hooked me up to an EKG, thought I was having a heart attack."

"I'm sorry, Dad. Are you all right?"

"I lost my oldest son, Michael. How all right can I be?"

The old man's gaze made him uncomfortable. He would have expected sorrow but now there was a kind of suspicion in those faded blue eyes.

"I wish I could have saved him, Dad. The same way I wish I could have saved Kim."

The old man lowered his head. He wore a short-sleeved blue shirt. His arms were thin as sticks. Everything had the smell of medicine. Michael felt sick to his stomach. Then, abruptly, the old man was watching him again. "He was in some kind of trouble, wasn't he, your brother?"

"Not that I know of."

"You're not talking to some goddamned reporter,

Michael. You're talking to your old man. Do me the favor
of not treating me like a child just because I won't be
around much longer. At least tell me the fucking truth."

Michael sighed. "He's dead, Dad. I don't see where it
matters anymore."

"It matters to me."

"Yeah, he was gambling again. Probably had to do
some people some favors to make up for it."

"Peddle his badge, you mean."

"Right. Peddle his badge."

"I figured. That's why he wouldn't come around. I
could always read him. He was a lot like me except
I stayed honest."

He wasn't like you at all, Michael thought. But of
course didn't say it.

"So when you got in the garage they were already
dead?"

"Uh-huh. That's right."

The old man sat up straight in his wheelchair. Used
an uncertain hand to pick up his glass of water. He
smacked his lips while he drank.

The eyes of judgment were once again on Michael.
"Back when I first got out of the academy there was a
situation like this. One cop said he found another cop
and a perp dead. Claimed they'd killed each other."

Michael thought about the word "claimed." It had a
lot of implications.

"Then come to find out the cop who found them had
a grudge against the cop he said he found dead. Seems
the dead one might have been sleeping with the other
cop's wife."

"Why're you telling me this, Dad?"

But the old man kept right on with his story. "Most of
the people on the force knew what had happened. Or at
least suspected. But you know how cops are. Just like

priests and heads of companies and presidents of the United States. They keep everything covered up as long as they can. I'm told that the DA in those days wanted to go after the cop but the chief back then convinced him it would be bad for the community. They found an excuse to let the cop go and he moved away a few months later. And that was that."

The old man tilted his bald freckled head forward and nodded. Michael was uncomfortable seeing the skull this way. He didn't want the old man to die.

Both men were silent for a time. Then Michael said, "What're you trying to tell me, Dad?"

"What do you think I'm trying to tell you, Michael?"

"Goddamnit, Dad. I don't like this. Not at all."

"I don't, either. But I'm pretty sure you killed your brother. Soon as I heard about it I started wondering about it. And I've been mulling it over ever since."

Michael ran a hand through his hair and sighed. He didn't know what to say. His father watched him like a hanging judge about to pronounce sentence.

"I needed to say that, Michael. I was a cop too long to bullshit myself."

"Well, you said it."

Another silence. "I think you did the right thing."

"What the hell're you talking about, Dad?"

The old man touched frail fingers to his throat, as if it hurt him to speak. "I don't know what happens when you die, Michael. I wish I had your mother's faith. I could really use it about now. But if there's a hell I'm going to it for sure—for saying what I'm about to."

What was he going to say now? Michael wondered. He'd already accused Michael of murdering his brother. What else was left?

"He was a bad cop and a bad man, Michael. Took me a long time to admit that to myself, but after watching him over the years I didn't have any choice. I love Wendy and I love those grandkids of mine. He didn't deserve them. Now they'll be able to go on and have a better life. You did them a favor."

"I still don't know what the hell you're talking about."

"You don't have to worry about the department. They'll want to wrap this up fast and get it over with. They'll want to move on to giving Kim a big funeral. Kim and Steve will get their plaques down at the station and you'll get a raise and become captain when Myles retires. And that'll be that."

"Maybe I'll quit the force. Do something else. I've thought about that."

"You won't quit the force. You're too much of a cop for that. A good cop."

And then all his energy was gone. The old man had rallied to tell Michael what had been on his mind. But once again he was a nursing home resident, ashen, weak, slumping in his wheelchair.

"Come here, Michael." He held out a knobby hand for Michael to take.

Michael stood up and walked over to his father. The cold hand with the thin flesh the texture of butterfly wings. "I'm sorry you weren't my favorite, Michael. You should have been. You were always the good one but I couldn't see that. I'm sorry, Michael. You did the right thing last night."

The old man had started to cry.

"Just promise me you'll take care of Wendy and the kids. That's all I care about now, Michael. Just promise me that."

Michael felt his own eyes sting. He bent down and kissed the old man on the freckled head. His father wouldn't be with him much longer and the thought of it smothered him with dread.

"Promise me, Michael. Promise me."

Michael leaned back and looked at his father. "You're one hell of a good father, you know that, Dad?"

A weary smile. "And you're one hell of a good son. I guess we're even."

"Yeah," Michael said, "I guess we are." Then: "You need anything?"

"Sleep. I need some sleep, Michael. Send my nurse in here, will you?" He swallowed hard. "You just worry about Wendy and the kids, Michael. I can take care of myself." Another weary smile. "I always was tougher than either you or your brother."

Michael found a nurse for his father and then left the Gentle Hands nursing home to pick up Wendy. He thought of her pretty face and soft brown eyes, of her radiance when she sat reading to the kids on the couch at night. He thought of her so that he didn't have to think about anything else, about anything else at all.

"Explosive movie potential." —*Publishers Weekly*

PETER TONKIN

Author of *The Coffin Ship*

The freighter came like a ghost off the hazy horizon, strafed by gunfire, abandoned by her crew…and laden with explosives. Richard Mariner is aboard a new high-tech sailing vessel when he encounters the fire ship, never realizing it's only the beginning of a deadly adventure…

As Mariner sails through the Indian Ocean, he learns the prize tanker in his family's fleet, Prometheus II, has been seized by terrorists in the Persian Gulf, and his father-in-law has been kidnapped in Bahrain. To wrest back what's rightfully his—and to protect his loved ones—he'll have to race through treacherous waters and take on a group of terrorist pirates that even the world intelligence agencies can't locate—a trial by fire Mariner can't afford to fail.

THE FIRE SHIP

A Richard Mariner Novel

ISBN 13: 978-0-8439-6222-2

☐ **YES!**

Sign me up for the Leisure Thriller Book Club and send my FREE BOOKS! If I choose to stay in the club, I will pay only $4.25* each month, a savings of $3.74!

NAME: _____

ADDRESS: _____

TELEPHONE: _____

EMAIL: _____

☐ I want to pay by credit card.

☐ **VISA**   ☐ **MasterCard**   ☐ **DISCOVER**

ACCOUNT #: _____

EXPIRATION DATE: _____

SIGNATURE: _____

Mail this page along with $2.00 shipping and handling to:
Leisure Thriller Book Club
PO Box 6640
Wayne, PA 19087
Or fax (must include credit card information) to:
610-995-9274

You can also sign up online at **www.dorchesterpub.com**.
*Plus $2.00 for shipping. Offer open to residents of the U.S. and Canada only.
Canadian residents please call 1-800-481-9191 for pricing information.
If under 18, a parent or guardian must sign. Terms, prices and conditions subject to
change. Subscription subject to acceptance. Dorchester Publishing reserves the right
to reject any order or cancel any subscription.

GET FREE BOOKS!

You can have the best fiction delivered to your door for less than what you'd pay in a bookstore or online. Sign up for one of our book clubs today, and we'll send you *FREE* BOOKS* just for trying it out...**with no obligation to buy, ever!**

If you love fast-paced page turners, you won't want to miss any of the books in Leisure's thriller line. Filled with gripping tension and edge-of-your-seat excitement, these titles feature everything from psychological suspense to legal thrillers to police procedurals and more!

As a book club member you also receive the following special benefits:
- **30% off all orders!**
- **Exclusive access to special discounts!**
- **Convenient home delivery and 10 days to return any books you don't want to keep.**

Visit **www.dorchesterpub.com**
or call **1-800-481-9191**